Sinning Man's Heaven

The Hypocrite Runs to Mexico

Roy Milner

INKWATER PRESS

PORTLAND • OREGON
INKWATERPRESS.COM

Copyright © 2010 by Roy Milner

Cover and interior design by Masha Shubin

Marijuana ©2010 Andre Blais. BigStockPhoto.com
Desert Road ©2010 Mark Pullen. BigStockPhoto.com

This story, while fictional, is based on actual events. In certain cases incidents, characters, names, and timelines have been changed for dramatic purposes. Certain characters may be composites, or entirely fictitious. This story is created for entertainment purposes. Opinions, acts, and statements attributed to any entity, individual or individuals may have been fabricated or exaggerated for effect. The opinions and fictionalized depictions of individuals, groups and entities, and any statements contained herein, are not to be relied upon in any way.

All rights reserved. No part of this book may be reproduced or transmitted in any form or by any means whatsoever, including photocopying, recording or by any information storage and retrieval system, without written permission from the publisher and/or author. Contact Inkwater Press at 6750 SW Franklin Street, Suite A, Portland, OR 97223-2542. 503.968.6777

www.inkwaterpress.com

ISBN-13 978-1-59299-467-0
ISBN-10 1-59299-467-9

Publisher: Inkwater Press

Printed in the U.S.A.
All paper is acid free and meets all ANSI standards for archival quality paper.

1 3 5 7 9 10 8 6 4 2

For the *"Cascadians"*
I love each of you more than you'll ever know
Special thanks to U.R., G.B., and all my family

Contents

Foreword vii
Chapter 1: Lost 1
Chapter 2: Droned 4
Chapter 3: The Doctor 11
Chapter 4: The Diagnosis 17
Chapter 5: The Cure 21
Chapter 6: Go 23
Chapter 7: You Got a Gun? 35
Chapter 8: Stoned At last 41
Chapter 9: You're Not My Mother 50
Chapter 10: Four Twenty 56
Chapter 11: So Close, Yet So Far Away 66
Chapter 12: You Gotta' Be Real Careful 69
Chapter 13: The Entrance 76
Chapter 14: Mexican Chiba and Ms.
    Lorenzo's Little Sister 85
Chapter 15: Cockroaches and Machine Guns 96
Chapter 16: Independence! 100
Chapter 17: The Love Of Mexico 107
Chapter 18: Coke 119
Chapter 19: Gilbert 130

Chapter 20: The Ghosts of Guadalajara............. 136
Chapter 21: Hooky 146
Chapter 22: More 150
Chapter 23: A Day And Night On The Town 152
Chapter 24: Celebrate The Great Divide 159
Chapter 25: Swearing In Spanish 164
Chapter 26: B.S. 168
Chapter 27: The Great Escape 174
Chapter 28: Pigs And Pyramids 192
Chapter 29: The Famous Adele 198
Chapter 30: Rags To Riches 202
Chapter 31: My Country Is Better Than Yours .. 206
Chapter 32: Do You Believe In God? 213
Chapter 33: Back To The Real World 220
Chapter 34: Please Bang Our Daughter 226
Chapter 35: The Climax 239
Chapter 36: Hell 250
Chapter 37: Get The Hell Out Of Dodge! 256
Chapter 38: What Sunday School Teachers Say. 263
Chapter 39: Music, Memories And Nicotine 274
Chapter 40: Ground Hog's Day 277
Chapter 41: Hot And Cold 282
Chapter 42: Radiohead (Not The Band) 289
Chapter 43: Oh Canada! 293
Chapter 44: Home 298
Chapter 45: My Next Trip 306
Chapter 46: Was Shaw Right? 313

Foreword

I wasn't going to write a foreword, but just as I am about to go to print I find myself haunted by one looming notion. You see I intentionally regressed my mind by ten years in order to write this book from the point of view of the twenty-one year old male, but being thirty-one I feel I should put in a quick word before you journey back with me. I realized there are two or three incidents in this otherwise terrestrial tale which some of my more, shall we say, skeptical readers might struggle with; the kind of folk who consider themselves "Naturalists" or "Realists." So I turn to one of my favorite authors on the subject of what is "Real":

> (Humans) tell each other, of some great spiritual experience, "All that *really* happened

was that you heard some music in a lighted building"; here "Real" means the bare physical facts, separated from the other elements in the experience they actually had. On the other hand, they will also say "It's all very well discussing that high dive as you sit here in an armchair, but wait till you get up there and see what it's *really* like": here "real" is being used in the opposite sense to mean, not the physical facts (which they know already while discussing the matter in armchairs) but the emotional effect those facts will have on a human consciousness.
–C.S. Lewis; *The Screwtape Letters*

So, while some names have been changed, and some conversations moved for chronological effect (though much less than you'd think), I maintain that the situations and events described in this book, both physical and spiritual, are indeed factual. In short, you had to be there.

Oh, and sorry about all the drugs and swearing.
–Royboy.

Sinning Man's Heaven

CHAPTER 1
Lost

Thursday, September 30, 1999

Let me assure you there is a Hell. Not the corny fire and brimstone crap you see in the movies, but the real thing. I got just a taste of it on that day in southern Mexico—the worst day of my life.

I awoke in agony after the craziest bender you could ever imagine. My best friend, Graham, lay beside me in the car when it struck him: "Shit! It's nine thirty! I gotta' go pay these people off— oh man, I feel like death." He barely managed to pull himself out of the driver's seat and groaned, "They're taking me to a bank in town. Should be back in an hour, then we can get the hell out of here."

Everything about our last month on the road had been completely insane, and it all came to a crashing halt the night before: Graham had smashed up these people's brand new car and owed them everything we had before we could leave town—we were screwed. We spent the rest of the night aimlessly drowning our sorrows in tequila and cocaine.

So I lay there alone that morning in our battered Tercel, almost oblivious as to where I was, suffering from the hangover of hangovers. That's when it happened. At first I thought I was having a seizure from all the chemicals in my system, but as my head was thrown back I saw the huge concrete building on my right cracking up the middle! Chunks of concrete fell and hit the car on my side; I scrambled over the shifter and rolled out of the driver's side door. The quake knocked me on my ass and sent muddy puddles into the air that splashed down on top of me. My eyes were so swollen I could hardly see much else. When the shaking stopped I climbed back into the car in confusion. My brain was so fried that the reality of the situation didn't fully sink in until I noticed the smoke in the distance. There was fire on the horizon—then I realized that the shape of the horizon had changed. I couldn't see anyone around who might need help, and even if I had, my head was throbbing with pain and dizziness. I lay in nauseating anguish waiting for Graham to return—only he didn't.

A horrible fear began to creep up on me. I didn't have any money or gas left, and I barely spoke a word of Spanish. What the hell was I supposed to do? Hour by hour crept endlessly by as the fear grew into a terror which far outweighed any hangover. I lay in torment staring at the clock, trying not to panic as nightmarish thoughts carved themselves into reality.

He never came. I begged God for mercy, but an infinity of hellish speculation gave way to despair as my spirit plummeted into the abyss with the realization that my best friend was buried somewhere underneath the rubble. I was lost and alone…

CHAPTER 2
Droned

Six Weeks Earlier

I spent most of that summer getting *droned* (drunk and stoned) with the boys on our island in British Columbia, Canada; just like the summer before that, and the summer before that, and— okay; fall, winter and spring too. Aw man, we had some good times though: trekking all over the peninsula, drinking and smoking dope; having bonfires on the beach every night, drinking and smoking dope; lying on the couch at Craig's and Spidey's house while watching movies, playing Nintendo, and drinking and smoking dope. But there was a lot going on this particular summer. I'd head down the road to my uncle's bakery at 9:00 p.m. to roll buns and bake bread until 3:00 a.m., only to return home to pickle myself with whatever I could afford: mushrooms, acid, preferably ecstasy.

I gave drum lessons in the daytime. My folks had

a pretty big house and we had converted the basement into a music studio, which was both soundproof and totally sweet. Nobody knew it, but honestly, that was the only time I was sober. I was teaching some great kids, and even at the young age of twenty, I took that responsibility very seriously.

On Friday and Saturday nights I had this great gig at the Sunny Bay Café, a charming little restaurant on the water. Our quartet would set up right there on the dock amidst the dinner tables and play jazz standards all night; it was real cozy. My old pal Jimmy played a mean trumpet, while this brilliant cat named Gil came and played stand up bass, and he could *frickin'* wail. I loved *swingin'* alongside those kids while the waiter snuck me pints.

Then there was Lori; beautiful, talented, mysterious Lori. This weird little girl was only seventeen and she could already make you feel something from the piano. I spent a lot of time moping around the peninsula, smoking cigarettes with *Led Zeppelin* on my headphones, just stewing over the thought of her. At first I ignored it, but it became inevitable as I fell deeper in love with her with every passing month. Her young age, my growing addictions, and something I couldn't quite put my finger on had me scared to death to tell her, and it was slowly driving me insane.

One night she came to one of my parties in the studio and I asked if she wanted to walk up to the park where I prattled on in a drunken stupor about—I don't even know what. I wanted to express my undying love so bad I thought I was going to puke, but instead I beat around the bush with this stupid rhetoric crap that completely eluded my consciousness, leaving me certain I had proven myself nothing if completely retarded.

Now bare with me a moment while I relate this little soap opera, which needs explaining to get into the real story. I did finally work up the courage to tell Lori my feelings days later; but somehow, even being the romantic that I was, I blew it. It was my nerves. I get real nervous. I'll spare you the embarrassing details; the point is, after I spat it out she pretended not to have had any idea—even though I knew better—and she acted all confused as I drove her home in awkward silence. That's why what happened the next night completely floored me.

After our gig she got stoned with me for the first time. We were supposed to watch my favorite eighties flick, *Goonies*, but ended up listening to one of my favorite albums: *You* by *Gong*—total psychedelic brilliance from 1974. I told her we had to go up to the park and get baked to fully experience it, which she wholly agreed to. We dangled on the swings and passed a joint back and forth. She admitted having gotten stoned only once before with a couple of her friends two weeks earlier and said, "But this weed must be a lot better 'cause I already feel it," to which I replied, "Only the best for the girl of my dreams!" She giggled and snatched the joint back, which finally made me feel comfortable with her. We had a lovely time wandering back down the street staring dreamily up at the clear night sky. My insecurities were swept away as we began mumbling stoned nonsense—how marvelous to have her in my world. We stumbled into my bedroom and left the lights off so as to not disrupt the glittering starlight pouring in through my large windows. I put *Gong* on and we sat next to each other on the side of my bed that was pushed up against the window so we could trip-out on the glossy neighborhood. My street had transformed into a delicious sci-fi movie.

"Everything looks so magical!" she exclaimed. "Look at *ET*'s family over there!" She pointed at my neighbor's shrubbery as the music swelled with perfect weirdness. We continued chatting like maniacs, taking turns pointing out bizarre discoveries until she said, "I wish I could just sit here with you looking out your window forever."

Wow. That felt so amazing to hear. I slowly reached over and took her hand. She fell silent... Not knowing whether that was good or bad I sat for a moment with her hand still in mine, giving her every bit of assurance I would stop if she wanted me to. Then I slowly brushed my fingers up her arm and over the back of her neck. She quivered but still sat motionless. I grazed her cheeks, ran my fingers through her hair, and still she was a statue without expression. It was strange, but she didn't stop me, so I pulled her close and caressed her chin, and then ever so gently pressed my lips to hers. I kissed her again, then again, until slowly she lay back on the bed and kissed back in the sweetest way, much to my relief and excitement. She blossomed like a spring flower, kissing first softly, then tenderly, and then to my ecstatic surprise, passionately. The moment I had yearned for half a year for had come! Oh the joy! The bliss! After an unquenchable summer she finally lay in my arms actually biting my bottom lip! We made out for three marvelous hours and I didn't let it go beyond that; no fondling and no clothes coming off, just sucking face like teenagers. She *was* a teenager, and I was a young man swimming in delight.

Around four in the morning we finally sat up and she said the strangest thing:

"Mark, ask me some questions."

"Um, alright... Did you like what we just did?"

"Yes," she blinked.

"Do you know I'm in love with you?"

"Yes."

"Is that okay?"

"It shouldn't be..."

"What?"

She pressed her face into her hands with a loaded breath then barely whispered, "You're asking the wrong questions."

Then it dawned on me: "Are you seeing somebody?"

"...I'm kind of going out with Tim..."

...*WHAT IN THE HELL*??? Tim was one of my students! She went to high school with him—he was only sixteen! I sat completely stunned, the impossible notion of being in a love triangle with a couple of kids flooding over me, turning my skin red with embarrassment and anger, unable to breathe a word.

She continued mournfully; "I told you we tried

weed for the first time two weeks ago, but we were lying in that field by the ferries tripping out, and I kissed him just for fun and, next thing I knew—"

The loves of my short life, incredibly romantic tales of a much more profound nature, always with girls older than me, rushed through my mind as I cried inside, *how could it have come to this?* Taking a few seconds to pick my brain up off the floor I wheezed, "Why didn't you say something? Why didn't you stop me before I kissed you?"

"I don't know," she said beginning to cry softly, "We were having such a good time and—"

"Why didn't you tell me yesterday before I was stupid enough to say I love you? What are you trying to do to me?"

"I'm so sorry... God, I'm out of control; I don't know what I'm doing!"

This sounded like baby talk to me. I stammered, "W-well what now? Who do you like better?"

"I don't know; I didn't know you loved me! You took such a long time to make a move I thought you had lost interest, so I made a move on Tim."

I held my hand up to my chest and said, "Why Tim? He's one of my students!"

"I know, but he's had a crush on me since grade 10."

Grade 10?! Come on! I thought I was going to be sick! How could I fall into petty drama like this?! She was right; she had no idea what she was doing. That's newfound power in the hands of youth. I gulped,

Roy Milner

"He's got a little crush, but I'm completely in love with you!"

"There's so much to sort out in my head," she quietly sobbed. "I'm so sorry Mark. I have to go." And then I was alone.

CHAPTER 3

The Doctor

That morning after Lori dropped the bomb on me I drove to Graham's house to seek encouragement and weed.
   We sprawled out on the front lawn, drank some of his you-brew, and smoked a *fatty* while I shared my ordeal. His advice was assuredly cynical as always: "Just play it cool and wait it out. If she chooses you, fine. If not, better yet, 'cause then you'll be free to do whatever you want when we hit the road."
   It was nice to laugh. For two years we'd been talking about running away to see how far south we could get. Graham was working at a gas station with our buds Shaw and Jordan—we were both saving to try and disappear one day. I couldn't stop thinking about having Graham all to myself. I moaned, "I can't wait to get out there man; the road's calling like a

Zeppelin tune. If only I didn't have to worry about Tim."

Graham chuckled, "You're 6'5" dude. Go put the fear in him."

So that's what I did. I drove to his house and freaked the crap out of him, but only for a few minutes—I actually loved the kid. Besides, it broke his heart when I told him. In the end it brought us closer because now we had to suffer the grueling wait for her decision together.

The days crawled by without a word from Lori. It was torture, so I made a lot of visits to *Doctor Octopus*. Now *The Doctor* is a legend of pot-smoking lore. It lived at Craig's and Spidey's place in a walk-in-closet designed specifically for getting four people as high as humanly possible in the shortest period of time. This closet was home to all sorts of drug paraphernalia, complete with every traffic sign we had ever swiped (don't ask me why young guys do this) and a black light for that perfect stoner ambiance. And right there in the middle of it stood *Doc Ock*. See, about a year earlier the hospital had been renovating and they sold off all this old medical junk from the seventies. Craig was always into weird gadgets and the like, so he and Joey went down and found this massive artificial lung. It had a plastic chamber about one and a half feet in diameter and height, which fit snuggly into a metal compartment equipped with a pump, rubber tubing, knobs and doohickeys. This remarkable contraption sat on a sturdy three-foot stand with wheels so you could push it around with ease. Needless to say, they jumped at the opportunity to take it home and do some alterations. When the boys were finished it looked like something out of a David Cronenberg film. I mean this thing was the ultimate four-person death-bong, standing at about four and a half feet, with a huge bowl that could hold about a gram at a time, and four long tubes to suck on (which gave it the *Doc Ock* look). Man it was loud with four guys huffing on it. You'd have a couple gallons of water bubbling away while everyone fought for their hit. If you paused for even a moment you'd get the air sucked out of your lungs so that you'd choke like a little girl.

Anyways, *The Doctor* and I got along famously that week while my boys took good care of me. I would have done anything for those guys—save sparing them my pity-party. Shawbuck (the only one of us who had quit smoking pot) put it bluntly, "If you love her so much then why don't you get your shit together? Quit *smokin' up* and do something about it."

"I know, I will, I'm just not ready yet—"

"Oh come on. How long have you been a pot-head? What's it gonna' take for you to be *ready*? Does your faith condone getting loaded?"

"I don't pretend it does Shaw! Look, I wish I could be as perfect as my little brother; I'm just not ready yet."

"*'Just not ready'* doesn't make any sense! Maybe you should read your bible more, even if it is loaded with faults."

"When have you ever picked up a Bible to know?" I protested.

"I don't need to," he smirked, "all the Christians I've met are proof enough there's better books to spend my time with."

Shaw and I would play chess twice a week and inevitably start up like this until it turned into a full-blown theological debate; one it seemed I always lost. But he still loved me.

After that particular episode I ended up back at the studio with Spidey and Joey. We spent the rest of the night getting good and crocked. Around 1:00 a.m.—just before they left—I sorely discovered that I had polished off my treats. Spidey had some beers left, so I asked him for one. He replied, "Nah, it's just enough to get me drunk tomorrow."

I begged, "C'mon Spidey, I'm all out. Just one?"

"Dude, you drank a liter of wine *and* a six-pack! You don't need anymore."

I turned to Joey and coaxed, "You wanna' spark another one of your *doobs*?"

"I'm cooked man, and he's right."

"If you're cooked fine," I said, "but I want a nightcap. C'mon, sell me a joint."

"Dude, look at yourself! You don't need anymore."

I got really annoyed and blurted, "Fine! If neither of you guys is going to help me out, I'll just drive downtown and buy another dime bag."

Joey cautioned, "You'd better not, Mark! Man, I've been worrying about you."

Sinning Man's Heaven

"Yeah," Spidey agreed, "you've been going pretty hard lately."

"Look who's talking!" I said. "C'mon you guys, we all party a little hard sometimes! I just want a nightcap."

Joey went wide-eyed, "Not like this man, just take it easy all right? Promise us you're not going to drive anywhere tonight!"

The anger I'd learned to hide began to surface. Checking myself, I lowered my voice and replied, "Yeah, sorry you guys; you're right. I won't drive anywhere."

"Promise?"

"I promise."

I said it so they'd leave, then I got in my mom's van and drove downtown. It was the first time I'd broken a promise to a bud. But you see nobody, not even my best buds knew just how bad my habits had become. I'd regularly put the van in neutral on a late night bender and roll down the driveway without waking my folks; then I'd speed back home, kill the engine, and coast back up the driveway undetected. I had lots of secrets. These late night adventures began as a teenager, when I rarely slept and earned my stealth. I'd crawl out my window and walk the four kilometers to Vanessa's bedroom to read her poetry or climb in and fool around. That may sound cheesy now, but when your sixteen it's the most magical thing in the world. She was my first love and it killed me when she moved away; then my sleepless nights lost their romance, taking on a much fouler nature to

15

fill the void: the drugs, the alcohol, and when I got too lonely, pornography.

When I got home with more weed I locked myself in the studio where I strummed eerie chords on my guitar and sang bitter, starving lamentations to an invisible audience of millions. After exhausting myself I fell into bed, but this old uneasy feeling returned and kept my tired brain from shutting off. I felt compelled to open my Bible and turned to Galatians:

> *You were running a good race. Who cut in on you and kept you from obeying the truth? That kind of persuasion does not come from the one who calls you. A little yeast works through the whole batch of dough...*

CHAPTER 4

The Diagnosis

The following Friday I was back at the Sunny Bay Café. It was my twenty-first birthday, so my mom turned our gig into my party. All my friends and family were there, and it was *fixin'* to be a grand ole' night, except that I was entirely depressed that the only thing Lori had said to me in a week was a civil, "Happy birthday". Tim showed up and I asked him if she'd said anything yet. He whispered, "No man, it's really weird! I've seen her a couple times but it's like none of this ever happened!"

We began our set. It was torture trying to make music with her; my playing grew worse by the minute. Then, as I clenched my jaw and dragged along behind the band, I noticed this handsome Asian kid with spiked hair and glasses sitting close to us and digging the tunes. He watched me pretty intently, even though I was giving about five percent.

When the noise finally came to an end and the rest of the band was packing up their gear, I let my broken thoughts spew out onto my brother: "Yuck bro, I feel sick. She won't even talk to me! Who is this chick? One second she's biting my lip, the next I'm invisible!" I was so disheveled that the words came out loud enough for this bizarrely interested Asian kid to hear, and as my boys helped me carry my drums up the dock he smiled and said, "Nice playing man." I thought, *yeah-right buddy*, but politely said, "Thanks."

We got my drums up to the van, Shawbuck, Joey, Craig, my brother, and I, when I lost it: "The hell with this! I can't take it! When is she going to tell me what's going on?" Shaw looked me straight in the eye and said, "Just go back down there and ask her."

"But I'm so scared of what she's gonna' say."

"If you don't find out now you won't be able to enjoy your night, right? At least you'll know." I took a long, deep breath. He was right.

"I'm going for it," I said, my voice wavering. I could tell they were all surprised. Joey stuck his thumbs in the air excitedly, "Good luck man!" They held their breath in anticipation as I walked the plank back down to the restaurant with my heart pounding. I was so aware of life at that moment that everything became unbearably beautiful. The half moon set the waters ablaze with a transcendent glow and the stars shone clear as the twinkle lights on the railings. A cool ocean breeze blew through the summer flowers, which swirled around the trees with a sweet fragrance that promised never-ending summer nights of reverie and delight. There was Lori, looking lovely as ever, sitting under a deck-umbrella with Tim and— and that Asian kid? He smiled again as I turned to Lori and spoke softly, "Lori, could I talk to you for a second?"

"Why?" she asked.

What the hell why? Why do you think? I thought. Tim looked at me wide eyed and shrugged. Calmly I motioned, "Please, just come here." She rose and made the long walk back up the ramp quietly behind me. We stepped down a small path in the shadows beside the garden. Her perfume, blending with the summer wind and flowers smelled intoxicating. My chest throbbed and my tongue went dry as I began. "Lori, I'm sorry things went the way they did, I would have done it all differently, but you left me totally in the dark and..."

She just stood there starring blankly like she always did as I continued, "And I'm dying here Lori, just dying. I'm totally in love with you and you haven't said a word since that night. Please just tell me how you feel; I can't wait any more."

Still, with that same blank, emotionless expression, she shook her head ever so slightly and said matter-of-factly, "I don't love you." Then, with one last cry for mercy I asked faintly, "I can't ever kiss you again?"

She shook her head, then turned and walked away. Silence. Horrible, death beckoning silence. I stood alone in the shadows just outside the mélange of late night summer colors emanating from the restaurant's deck-lights like some awful Tom Hanks and Meg Ryan movie. It dawned on me who the Asian kid was: a twenty-five year old percussion major from the university whom I'd been hearing mention of. I could almost taste the blood in my face from the humiliation. No doubt Lori had fallen for her third drummer in a row. Her dad was a drummer, so it figured.

"Fuck I hate musicians," I proclaimed in marvelous contempt. It was done.

CHAPTER 5

The Cure

The day after my birthday, Shaw and I were early at it in his room *sluggin'* tall-cans and digging hard on *Led Zeppelin One* to keep my misery at bay. The two of us had been deeply fixated on the last track *How Many More Times* all year, and it drove us both near orgasm. We stared at each other wide-eyed, haunted to our very cores by Jimmy Page's guitar, when suddenly Graham walked in, plunked himself in front of the chessboard, and said, "Markman, it's crucial that you sit and talk with me at this very moment over a bowl." I half-chuckled and fell onto the adjacent beanbag chair as he filled his pipe and continued, "How much do you have saved?"

"Um, around thirteen hundred."

"Thirteen? You're supposed to be saving up! Where did it all go?"

I muttered, "I dunno', summer expenses."

"Your summer cost twice as much as the rest of us!"

"Yeah?" I challenged. "If my drug dealer bartered for blackberry pies then I'd have more cash too!"

It was true! Graham was a brilliant entrepreneur. He'd walk all over the peninsula picking blackberries, then bake these delicious pies and trade them for weed. Shaw and I laughed heartily as Graham blew a smoke ring and said, "Either way, I've gotta' get you out of here. Remember that van we looked at? I bought it. We leave in a week!"

"Are you serious?!"

"Yeah dude. I'll cover you if you run out of bank—you can pay me back some day." What a dude! Old Graham, boy. Suddenly my life had meaning again! I called our buddy Dave first thing to ask if he'd cover for me at the bakery and he instantly agreed, saying that his job at Dairy Queen was driving him nuts. I was as excited as a guy with a broken heart could be.

Graham's van broke down just before we were going to leave, but before I could get disheartened he proclaimed, "Screw it man, we've gotta' go now or it'll never happen! Let's find a cheap old beater; I don't care what it is or if it makes it home, just as long as it gets us to Tijuana."

He bought a beat up old '86 Toyota Tercel and we left the next day.

CHAPTER 6
Go

Tuesday, August 31, 1999

My friend Jocelyn was once in Vancouver playing a gig with her band, and she later told me that when they arrived at the club, Graham was sitting outside on the street curb holding up a big sign that read, "MAYBE I'M GOD."

Graham was like the secret attic in your childhood home where you experienced déjà vu for the first time, a home away from home, and yet a complete mystery. He traveled in broader circles than the rest of us, always elusive, always picking up with new groups of friends. It made me crave his company even more. That's why I was so honored to have him taking me away. But we'd always been there for each other, like earlier that year in March: I was on my way out the door to meet Lori for lunch when Graham phoned from a pub. It was the first time I'd heard him crying and he pleaded for me to come. I ditched Lori and found him sitting on a bench overlooking the ocean, anxiously sucking on a cigarette and wiping tears from his swollen eyes.

"Read this," he choked, handing me a crumpled letter. "It's from my dad."

"But your dad's dead," I said.

"Exactly. He wrote it from his deathbed and my mom just gave it to me."

Graham was only two years old when the cancer took his father's life—the exact same age I was when my father tragically died breathing gas fumes in a damaged well. This pivotal event in our lives sent us on paths that were frighteningly similar. We were both raised in the church by very devout Christian mothers (where I also acquired a very strict stepdad), we both had to wear glasses (Graham still wore his), we were both straight-A nerds more interested in reading books in the library at recess than making friends, and we both became incredibly pious young followers of our parent's religion in our teens; which brings me to our spookiest likeness. In middle school I began suffering brutally for my eccentricity and faith at the hands of various schoolmates. By grade seven it was even worse, and I endured a complete nervous breakdown. For two weeks I was at home with diarrhea, constipation, and painful stomach-cramps. I put on such a show that my mom had to take me to the emergency room twice. On the second visit, after sticking a stool softener up my butt, the doctor said the symptoms were all in my head.

Well, at the same exact age again, Graham put on an even better show than I did! His classmates gave him such a hard time that he decided he couldn't walk anymore and lay around his mom's house like an invalid, paralyzed with the fear of returning to school, and somehow managed to keep this up for the entire school year! His uncle even had to come over from the mainland for those nine months to help out, pushing him around in a wheelchair and carrying him up the stairs. Of course, when summer came he was miraculously healed and playing street-hockey again by August. The kid was incredible. When we met in my senior year of high school and discovered all this about each other it was almost incomprehensible! That's why Graham called *me* on the day he received his father's untimely message from beyond the grave.

In short, the letter told a now decidedly atheist Graham that life without Jesus is meaningless, and that if he didn't follow God's Word he'd lead a fruitless life on the road to hell. When I was done reading he asked, "What do you think?"

"Whoa, that's loaded man," I answered with a deep breath. "I wish for your sake he hadn't worded it quite like that, but you already know what I think."

"So that's it? There's no room for anything else? You believe that unflinchingly, even though you live the same lifestyle as me?"

I squirmed on the bench, "My faults aside, yeah."

"Wow. So you *still* consider yourself a 'born-again-Christian'... Aw man, but this is so messed! Wouldn't you be pissed if your mom gave you a letter like this from *your* dad at the wrong time?"

"The wrong time?"

He sat up and explained: "My dad told her to give it to me on my *nineteenth* birthday, but she waited until now, now after I just finished explaining to her why I don't believe in God anymore. It's like she was keeping it in her arsenal to use against me when the time came! I mean, what if she'd given it to me a year ago like she was supposed to, before I'd resolved this whole one-universal-being thing in my head? Maybe it would have even convinced me to believe again. Probably not, but who knows? She shouldn't have taken that away. It's the only piece I have of him now; why did it have to be like *this*?"

That was Graham—sort of. More like a vague snapshot of one of the many sides nobody ever saw of him.

"Dude," he said the day we were packing to leave, "I told you to bring as little as possible; do you really *need* all that?" That's closer to what he was usually like.

"What? Five things is nothing! My sports bag for clothes, my backpack for trekking; a sleeping bag for *sleeping*; there's no tape deck or radio in the car so we *have* to have a ghetto blaster and a box of tapes! Yes, I *need* it all."

"Fine, whatever."

I was a little annoyed because he had the same things as me minus the music—you have to have music on a road trip. After I put my stuff in the car

I asked timidly, "Dude, hotels are pretty expensive and we could be gone a long time; don't you think we should bring a tent too?"

"Yeah," he sighed, "I guess." Graham was funny that way.

I borrowed my brother's tent then ran upstairs to give my mom and sister a hug goodbye. *"Please be smart Mark!"* mom said desperately, and then we were off.

We got on the four o'clock ferry headed for Vancouver. By the time the cars were loaded and all passengers were above deck it was 4:20 p.m. Now for those readers who don't know the significance of this I'll explain. It's an urban legend that "420" is the code number used by cops for "marijuana smoking in progress." Also, April 20th is the international day where colleges around the globe celebrate the consumption of cannabis; so everyday at *four twenty* a.m. and p.m., stoners across the globe light up. Graham and I always made every effort to observe *both* times of the day.

The car deck of the ferry was completely vacant, so we sparked our last British Columbian *doob* before hitting the states. On the upper deck we drank in the ocean winds and kicked the sack (*hackey-sack*) before an audience of giddy Japanese tourists.

Once on the mainland, Graham leaped into fifth gear and stretched his new car's legs a little. I slammed a can of Pepsi I'd bought on the ferry and we used it to smoke our remaining roach.

"Now you promise me you're not hiding any dope anywhere, right?" Graham asked.

"Yeah dude," I said, "I promised I wouldn't try it, didn't I? Don't worry."

But we were definitely stoned because before we knew it the border into Washington State was in front of us and we still hadn't ditched the stinky can. Frantically, I rolled the window down and tossed it as inconspicuously as possible into a flowerbed before any guards noticed.

"Visine!" Graham exclaimed. I plunged into my bag and quickly handed it to him. He handed it back and I used it too.

"Aw dude!" I panicked as we got in line, "I hope it kicks in before we get up there!" I swear Graham's eyes faded to white the moment the border guard said, "Destination?"

"Renton sir," Graham lied.

"Business or pleasure?" the guard asked taking one look at his messy long brown hair and near hippy attire.

"Pleasure," replied Graham.

"What's in Renton?"

"We're going to visit my aunt and uncle."

"Pull up to the yellow lines on your left and get out of the car please." *Crap*. We did as we were told and a second guard in his late forties escorted us into the small building. He motioned for us to sit on a bench out of view from our car and said we'd be in big trouble if we so much as moved. Ten long minutes crept by as we sat there, stoned and anxious.

"They're not going to let us into their country dude," said Graham.

"Feeling guilty?" the first guard said as he came back in through the door followed by the second guard who held a small white bag. "Come over to the counter and stand behind the yellow line; I need you boys to explain a few things." They walked slowly behind the partition and began emptying the bag one item at a time. We were both surprised by what they took from the car: first my teaspoon, which I had innocently left in the back pocket of my backpack. "What do you use this for?" asked guard number two. I told the truth, "My tea." (I always carried orange pekoe around in a thermos).

"Do you see this black stuff on the end of it? That's marijuana residue! How did that get there?"

Crap. I couldn't believe they found that little speck. I told the truth, "I used it a long time ago to clean a pipe."

Then guard number one held up my scissors, "And these were used to cut marijuana with." Guard number two held up my *rollies*, "And I suppose these are used to roll cigarettes?"

"Well," I said bluntly, "considering they were sitting next to my sack of Drum, yeah."

"Don't get lippy with me kid! ZT!"

Graham asked, "What's ZT?"

"Zero Tolerance! I can send you packing like that!" he proclaimed snapping his knubby fingers.

"Sorry sir," I lied, "I'm just saying I haven't smoked weed in along time."

"What do you use this for then?" he asked holding up an empty pack of Capones, "Looks pretty handy for keeping joints in doesn't it?"

"Actually, yes it does, but like I said it's been a long time."

Then guard number one pulled out Graham's Yogi Bear *Pez*-dispenser. I couldn't help but laugh, "Oh man, you guys are good!" Guard two crossed his arms real smug like while guard one asked, "Why does this have residue in it?"

Graham told the truth, "I once put an unfinished joint in there because I had nowhere to keep it."

I cut in, "Okay, so you've proven we've smoked pot before, but do you think we'd be stupid enough to try and bring anything across the border knowing how strict you guys are?" I knew they needed solid green evidence to keep us out, *ZT* or not. Guard one changed the subject before the other could yell at me, "So how long are you planning on staying for and why?"

"A week or so," said Graham, "to visit my aunt and uncle in Renton." Guard two looked at me, "Why are *you* going to Renton?"

"I've got vacation time so I'm tagging along," I said. Graham had preplanned our alibi because he was certain they'd send us home if we said we were driving to Mexico for fun. I knew they knew we were lying but it didn't matter. They gave us *all* our stuff back and let us go. What else could they do? As we got back in our car we saw a van being taken apart by three guards and a drug-sniffing dog. Graham laughed

"Markman, you sure know how to handle yourself when you're high in the face of authority. I was sure they were gonna' send us home!"

As we cruised towards Bellingham he told me about one of the most frightening moments in his life at an airport in Thailand, a scene right out of *Midnight Express*. You see, Graham was the smartest kid I ever knew and he was accepted into this big deal international program three years earlier that took one or two kids from each country and put them all together in Hong-Kong for grade twelve and their first year of university. During spring break he went to Thailand with some schoolmates to explore; needless to say there was some extensive pot-smoking going on and he kept a small matchbox to store his roaches. They were in line at the airport waiting to board their flight back to school when it dawned on him that the matchbox was still in his bag! He began to panic, realizing that if he pressed his way back through the line the guards would know something was up, so at the last second he pulled the box out of his pack and carefully slipped it between the waste band of his underwear and the small of his back. To his horror the guard at the door noticed his sweat and grabbed him by the arm, leading him into a small room with one hanging light bulb and three higher ranking military personnel. They made him strip to his underwear. He stood there trembling as one guard ran both his hands up his thighs and buttocks.

"Dude, his fingers even grazed the matchbox," Graham told me with his low wavering voice.

31

Unbelievable. They didn't find it. If they had it would have meant life in prison, or worse. I couldn't even imagine it, my little buddy with his cute chipmunk face, thick glasses and his long brown hair, dangling from a noose. That's how close it was.

"Dude, man," I said, "that's a miracle! Somebody was looking out for you!"

"Yeah, maybe..."

We stopped at this strange mini-mall just north of Everett, the likes of which you don't see in Canada. Graham ate at Taco Bell while I got a Subway sandwich and some batteries for the ghetto blaster. I thought it was so cool that you could buy beer in almost any store and scored a twelve-pack (in Canada you have to go to a liquor store or pub). We picked up our first packs of American smokes, Camel and Marlborough; then sped through Seattle and most of Washington as the sun set. When it got dark I took the wheel and we started drinking.

"Not too much," Graham said, to which I responded, "Don't worry about it."

"I know you're the pro drunk driver. Just don't let your first slip up be on this trip, okay?"

I drove us past Mount Saint Helens and into Oregon State. Portland looked like huge gleaming shards of black marble through my buzz and the starlit sky reflecting off the tall glass skyscrapers. Three hours blew by and we switched back right before Eugene. It was one in the morning when we ran out of gas just outside of the town.

"What the hell?" Graham exclaimed. "The fuel gage still says half a tank!"

"Aw shit man, and we don't have any weed!"

"Well that adds a new dimension; now we have to keep track of our miles!"

It was cold outside, so we put on our coats and slammed a beer each. We brought two more for the walk and climbed the highway's steep banks up towards a massive parking lot that seemed to be the most likely direction for a gas station. While trekking through the silent streetlight-lit suburb of Eugene, a young black dude, maybe our age and almost my height, crossed our path and asked, "Wasup' boys?" We told him our story and asked if he knew where we could score some dope.

"I might know one guy, but it's almost 2:00 a.m. and your guys' situation is all fucked up." He apologized and told us where the nearest gas station was before moving on. Graham repeated what he'd said, "Your guys' situation is all fucked up," and laughed, "That guy had us dialed man!" I thought that was so funny; Graham always said the coolest shit.

We found the station and borrowed a jerry can, then made the two-mile walk back. To our relief the car started right up and we drove back to the station for more gas. I hated Eugene. We couldn't find our way out and lost a lot of time before finally getting back on the highway. Graham drove until we got to a gas station in "Nowhere, Oregon" around 5:00 a.m. We gassed up again and stocked up on donuts and Doritos. I tried to buy more beer but the attendant

Roy Milner

said, "Sorry pal, we can't sell alcohol between two thirty and seven. Graham retorted, "So there's only *four* hours in America when you can't get drunk?"

I told you Graham always said the coolest shit.

CHAPTER 7
You Got a Gun?

Wednesday, September 1, 1999

Graham fell asleep that morning but I ate some donuts and polished off the last beer while driving through Oregon and on into California, stoked that we had cleared two states in one night. Around 8:00 a.m. Graham stirred, "Dude, find a diner or something. I need breakfast now!" We found a greasy spoon in some hick town where all the good ole' boys were coming in for their morning coffee. We ate our eggs while the working crowd eyed us two outlandish hippies suspiciously.

The guards from the Washington State border must have done a number on our car because the passenger side window wouldn't roll up anymore. They had noticeably torn off the inlay of the door while searching for contraband and damaged the lever in doing so, so we went to another gas station and borrowed some pliers. I managed to get it up but the lever was toast and had to be replaced.

We desperately wanted to get out of the U.S., which is so much more expensive than Mexico, so we threw on a mix-tape Spidey had made specifically for our trip and barreled up the rolling red and green slopes of California. Spidey made the best tapes. He entitled this one *Sex, Drugs, and the American Highway*. The music fit so well with the incredible terrain, but I started to *jonze* for some weed. Being high would have made it so much sweeter, if not as memorable.

Graham stopped at a gas station on the summit of a smooth cone shaped hill with dirt so red we both commented and agreed it must have fallen from Mars. I bought some smokes and a huge bottle of red wine. At the bottom of the Martian-hill the highway opened up wide and flat and we made great time. There was a song playing on Spidey's tape by *I Mother Earth*, their first album without Edwin—I think I liked it better. It took me back home and made me aware of just how relieved I was to be leaving all that unbearable drama behind, with no clue as to what lay ahead of us in that strange Spanish speaking country I knew hardly anything about. I starved to get there as another *I Mother Earth* song followed: *"The California waves, the California wa-a-aves..."* We didn't actually get to see the waves of *Cali*; we were in too much of a hurry, but that song made up for it.

Five sober hours of steady highway driving dragged by in the increasing heat until we finally came to a busy, dusty town to gas up and eat lunch.

The first place we saw was a little eyesore of a burger joint that looked like it was once a Saturday-night-drive-in, so we got burgers and fries and ate outside on the picnic tables. A mean looking hick pulled up in a beat up old truck, gun-rack and all, and said gruffly, "It's fuckin' hot today, hey boys?!" then sauntered inside like he'd been riding horses and roping Indians all day. He came back out with his grub and sat at the table next to us. He was big and brown with that tough leathery skin that older Californians have from years in the sun.

"You boys sure as hell ain't from 'round here!" he declared. "Yu' lost er' somethin'?"

"No sir," Graham said politely, "we're coming down from British Columbia."

"British Columbia? Where the hell is that, England?"

"Heh heh, no, just above Washington State, in Canada."

"Well hell, yu' must be burning up down here!"

"Not *too* bad yet," I said. "It gets pretty hot up there in the summer."

He looked confused and said, "I thought yu' all lived in igloos or some shit like that. Is that just in winter?"

Graham chuckled again, "No, that's *way* up north, we hardly get any snow."

"I'll be damned... So what the hell yu' doing in *Cali*? You got relatives or somethin'?"

"No, we're going down to Mexico."

"Fuckin' hell! Stupid punk kids! I'll take yu' out back and beat the shit outta' yu', take your wallets and spare yu' the trouble!" He cursed every second sentence. If I didn't think he was going to kill us I would have found him amusing.

"Why the hell yu' wanna' go down to that shit hole for?" he continued. Graham laughed nervously and winced behind his dirty glasses, "Just for vacation, and I've got some friends from school down there I wanna' see."

"Which way yu' goin' through?"

"Tijuana."

"You got a gun?"

"No."

"Stupid fuckin' kids! You gotta' get a gun! Those spics down there are some twisted fuckers, they'll rape your mama and …" He got pretty graphic, graphic enough to scare us into considering a new route. After insisting once more that we buy a gun he turned a shade friendlier and told Graham to bring him our map. He traced the highways with his gnarled finger from wherever the heck we were east to Arizona, then told us to head south for a town called Yuma saying it was "still a shit hole but a safer bet." We thanked him for his advice and asked directions to the nearest car parts place where we bought some pliers and a new window roller. On the way Graham said what I'd been thinking, "That guy was hilarious. I thought he was going to kill us! Buddy's got issues."

After one long hot hour and eight smokes we sort of fixed the window. I stripped our new handle. Neither of us knew anything about cars, but we managed to get the glass back in place. From then on we had to

Sinning Man's Heaven

use the pliers to open and close the window; at least it worked.

It was now the longest either of us had gone without a toke in a long time and we were getting edgy with each other as I circled a nearby lake in hopes of finding a place to spend the night. I was determined to take a swim but Graham grew increasingly tired and annoyed as I hunted in vain. Every square inch of beach was private property, so in the end we ditched the lake, cruised up a steep hill by a farm, and flopped down in a field next to a couple wild deer. Darkness fell as we settled in the grass. Graham reached into the bottom of his sleeping bag and said, "Look what Joey gave us as a parting gift." It was a two-six of Jack Daniels. We chased it with Pepsi and beer from the last gas station and called it dinner before passing out.

I awoke from a terrifying dream around 2:00 a.m., dreadfully hung over. Ordinarily I drank wine and beer, but when you drink hard liquor in the same fashion on an empty stomach you know there's going to be trouble. I plumb forgot. My head pounded and my stomach churned. Graham was already awake because it was freezing cold, and when he saw me sit up in agony he groaned, "Let's go." I was way too hurtin' to drive so Graham sped down the hill and bought a Redbull at a 24-hour corner-store. He slammed it to stay awake while I puked on the curb. We drove two more miles then I made him pull over in front of a vet's office so I could puke some more. Then we sped up the windiest, steepest, nastiest mountain in the state and I got out at the top to wretch, gag, and dry heave. Part way down the other side Graham pulled over next to a steep cliff and said, "Forget it, if I don't get some more sleep I'm going to drive us off the edge!" We both fell into a hazy half sleep...

Dark figures with horned silhouettes danced around the car and pressed their black faces up against the windows trying to writhe their way in. Even as I woke to the abnormal chill I saw their shadows whisk over the hood of the car. Graham woke at the *exact* same moment with a start and gasped, "Wha—"

"Dude," I choked in paralyzing fear, "did you feel that?"

"Yeah, like people were running around the car staring through the windows..."

It was so eerie, and let me tell you so real. We both felt the same presence. Graham tried to reason: "Maybe it was some kids trying to mess with us."

I checked my watch; it was literally four twenty. "At four twenty on a Thursday morning, on a mountain in the middle of nowhere? Yeah right Graham, that was something else and you know it!"

He rubbed his eyes and croaked, "That was messed up..."

I felt just awful and squirmed in discomfort as Graham sped down the dizzying roads of the haunted mountain. When it leveled out he laughed nervously and pointed out a road sign. True story, it read "Devil's Pass."

CHAPTER 8
Stoned At last

Thursday, September 2, 1999

We drove over the Golden Gate Bridge at around nine that morning, the first time either of us had seen it. Graham couldn't have cared less at this point; he had barley slept all night and now we had to find our way out of San Francisco, which was beyond frustrating in rush hour traffic. He drove straight through until the afternoon and gave up in a semi-desert town called Salinas. We ate lunch in a colorful family seafood place; or rather Graham ate a burger and some squid rings while I nursed my fading hangover with a Pepsi. I needed weed bad. Two young white kids who thought they were black left the restaurant and Graham honed In on them. We followed them out to their daddy's black mustang convertible and he asked, "Hey, can you guys help us out? We're from out of town."

"Maybe," said the short one. "Whas'up?"

"We're trying to score some weed," Graham whispered cautiously. The kid suddenly stuck his chin up an extra two inches like he was some important businessman or a pimp and said, "Yeah, I got an eighth I can sell yu'. I don't smoke myself, but my buddy always leaves some lying around my place. I can't get it right now 'cause my dad's home but he leaves for work at three, so try me then."

He gave us his phone number then drove off. Meanwhile, we gassed up at the nearest station and asked a real cool looking Hispanic kid on a *BMX* if he was holding to tide us over. To our luck he had a joint and a dime bag, both of which he sold us for fifteen bucks.

"Finally!" I cried as I drove up the main strip to find a good place to light up. On the outskirts we found a Smucker's Jam making factory!

"I love Smucker's Jam!" Graham chimed, so we parked in the open lot full of cars (great camouflage) and hid in some bushes by a tall fence and sparked the joint. We didn't have anything to smoke the roach with so I guzzled a beer and fashioned a pipe with the empty can. What a relief! That Californian bud wasn't too shabby and I felt a million times better. Just as our buzz was peaking Graham said, "Let's go in the factory and get a free tour!"

Paranoia washed over me. "I'd rather not dude, you know how when you go a couple days without any hoots then smoke one right to your head you get twice as chide? Well I'm feeling it bro."

"C'mon man, you're the one with the big *Carpe Diem* sign in your studio! Let's get some free jam!"

He had me there. "Okay, lead the way." We marched inside the giant industrial building, stoned as anything, no doubt red-eyed and perfumed, and Graham said to the fat unsightly lady at the desk, "Hi, we we're wondering if you give free tours?"

She looked at the both of us like we were right out of the loony bin and answered, "Umm, no, we don't give any kind of tours, I'm sorry."

Graham leaned closer in; she must have smelled it on his breath, "No tours? Wow. Well, can we go inside and have a look around?"

"No, I'm afraid that's against regulations."

"Okay, then can we have some free jam?"

"I'm sorry sir. Maybe it's best if you just leave."

We turned and dawdled back out the way we came staring at the walls as if we were in some great historical museum. When we got back to the car Graham cursed, "Damn, I love Smucker's Jam man!"

I laughed heartily and lied, "Yeah man, once we got in there I was stoked to check the place out!" For some reason I didn't want him to know I was completely relieved to get out.

At three we found a pay phone and tried to call that kid with the eighth. No one answered. We took turns calling for a while between rounds with the hackcy-sack, but had no luck.

"I thought that kid was talking smack," declared Graham. "I guess we'll just have to stretch this dime bag as far as we can."

With Salinas behind us we carried on down the road for a few more hours, lighting smoke after smoke, trying to keep what was left of our high as we dug on the landscape, which grew drearier with every mile. Before sunset we found ourselves at San Antonio Lake. The park official at the gate wanted twenty bucks for the night and we weren't at all interested in sleeping in another field, so we paid the outrageous toll and found a sweet little camp site right on the water. I'd never seen land like this. The ground from the water's edge all the way up to the horizon with its smooth rolling slopes was entirely petrified ruddy sand. With the exception of a few gray gnarled trees and some withered yellow grass, there was nothing to see but dirt.

As soon as we got out of the car I ran into the water. The bottom was great for tripping out on, with small red pebbles and random patches of green lake weed. The water was lukewarm and blissfully refreshing after two days without a shower. I'd been dreaming of a good swim ever since we left and Graham was real weird about it.

"You never want to swim back home; how come you're so set on it now?"

"I don't know, because that's what you do on vacation. It's great out here man, c'mon!"

"No, I'm good, I'm gonna' start a fire."

"Dude, you stink! Get in here!" I shouted.

"I said no thanks! I'm starving dude," then he set to work making a fire to roast our wieners.

Four campsites down from us there was a party

Sinning Man's Heaven

of eight yuppies playing with their speedboats and *sea-doos*. One of them had a *suped-up* truck blaring drug inspired rap, so we *mozzied* on over to ask if they were holding. The guy we asked kind of snorted like we were crazy for even thinking to ask. Rejected, we walked back to set up our tent in the dusty purple haze of dusk, and Graham scolded me for never having read *1984*. He summarized the bulk of the story with intense adoration and sent my mind spinning with wonderfully grim images; the kind of sci-fi desolation that for some mysterious reason we both reveled in beyond our means of understanding. Graham's eyes lit up when he talked about books, which was a lot. The guy had read everything. In high school he was famous for having read *Webster's Dictionary* cover to cover twice, to which he replied, "No, that's an urban legend. I only read it once." When Jimmy, our trumpet playing bud was first getting to know Graham he said, "I love talking with that kid. I learn at least two new words with every conversation!" The three of us used to sit around cups of tea and dream up the craziest notions. That was before I started partying. When I was eighteen Graham said, "You used to be the most eloquent person I knew; now you talk like a normal person." That was my first wake up call, and it went both ways: soon after that Graham started getting high in Hong Kong. When he came home I noticed the same thing.

After we got the tent up and night was in full bloom, three black dudes showed up in a big truck and staked out the site next to us. Graham walked over to say hi while I kept an eye on our *smokies*. The biggest of the three, about my height but built like a NFL defenseman, came back with him and shook my hand, "'Sup bro? I'm Charles. You got something to hold this in?" He had a big handful of *skank*-weed!

"Aw yeah dude!" I exclaimed. "We've had the hardest time finding weed out here!" Graham had a huge smile on his face. He looked like a cute little kid at Christmas in the firelight. I pulled my smokes out of the pack and stuffed the dry shake inside and said, "Sweet man, what do we owe you?"

"Don't worry about it dog; it's not very good anyways."

"Where you guys from?" Graham asked.

"Salinas. We're having a huge party this weekend so me and my homeys are setting up. I'd better go help. Hey, come have a beer after, okay?"

The guy must have been an angel. He was a total homey, the sweetest, kindest, warmest homeboy I'd ever met.

"Those guys are awesome!" said Graham. "They're setting up all those tents for their friends, plus they give two stupid white kids a bunch of free weed. We've gotta' return the favor!"

Just then the *other* big guy came over with a couple of beer cans the likes of which I'd never seen.

"'Sup *boiees*? I'm Wally, thought you might need some juice."

"Holy shit!" I said. "You guys are the nicest people we've met in the entire country!"

"Aw, no worries bro, all good people, all good

people. You can't chill by the lake without a tall Bud right?"

"Right," said Graham, and we proceeded to stare at our free beers in awe. They didn't have these in Canada back then, beer cans the size of your forearm, seven hundred and ten milliliters, or twenty-four ounces. *Brilliant.*

We slugged our beers and wolfed down our *smokies,* then rolled up a fatty with the *skank*-weed. Homeboy was right; it was awful stuff. The nastiest, stalest, most foul tasting dirt-weed I'd ever smoked. We huffed our way through the joint, which had little effect, so we uncorked the big bottle of red wine I'd bought on Mars and rolled another joint with some Drum in it to help the flavor. All vices together made for a decent buzz; that and the weary day's drive hit Graham and he passed out in the tent, so I wandered over to the other campfire to share my wine.

Wally passed me a *doob* they were burning and told me to pull up a lawn chair. I looked around at the small camping village they had created: six tents and a myriad of lawn chairs and ice coolers. I praised their efforts, "Damn man, you guys are fixing for a sweet party tomorrow, eh?"

They laughed drunkenly. "Yeah man!" Wally said to the other two. "I told you Canadians say 'eh' all the time. HA!"

I laughed back, "Yeah G!" They could have kicked my ass for that but instead they laughed even harder.

"You guys gonna' stick around tomorrow?" Charles asked. "There's gonna' be some sweet honeys,

G; would love to get some of that skinny white boy action!"

"Oh man, I wish we could! We're trying to get to Mexico as soon as possible."

"Mexico? You gotta' gun?" Charles asked.

I laughed, "No, but I'm starting to think we should." I passed the joint to the smallest of the three and he declined. Charles said, "Pooch don't smoke weed, he's a church boy."

"Your name's Pooch?" I asked.

"That's what they call me," he said distantly. He was obviously preoccupied with some nagging thought.

"Does pooch mean the same thing down here?" I asked.

"Like a stank dog? No no, just DJ Pooch," Wally said.

"Well, in B.C. when you're smoking a bowl and it burns out we say 'it's pooched!'"

Wally and Charles bellowed in drunken hilarity pointing at their forlorn buddy, "YEAH DOG! HA HA! POOCH!!! You hear that Pooch?!" Pooch just sat there indifferently and I wondered if the girl of his dreams was making out with another DJ.

Wally passed me another huge Bud-Light. We started talking about music and they were surprised by how much I knew about American rap. I started beat-boxin', something I'm actually pretty good at, and Wally laughed himself into a stupor while Charles rapped over my beat. Pooch finally smiled a little. When we were done our performance Wally said to Charles, "Pass me that blunt, *eh*!" Charles got real serious for a moment and said, "Sorry bro, it's *pooched*!" They both nearly choked to death from laughing so hard. Those guys were the real deal and I almost wished we could have stayed for their party, but Mexico was beckoning. Besides, I would have gotten way too anxious once a whole crowd arrived. My agoraphobia was getting worse all the time.

Early next morning, Graham and I took down the tent and packed up the car while truckloads of party people arrived. We didn't get to say goodbye but I said a prayer for Pooch as we rolled back onto route 101 hoping to find highway 58 on our new course to Joshua Tree.

CHAPTER 9
You're Not My Mother

Friday, September 3, 1999

We stopped to gas up when a burly Hell's Angel type with a handlebar moustache and a naked lady on his t-shirt rode up and noticed our license plate.

"Hey, where you guys from?" he asked. Graham told him we were headed down from Canada to party in Mexico. He replied in amazement, "Well you got balls man!"

As we drove off Graham half laughed, "Shit dude, maybe we should reconsider this whole thing. If *that* guy thinks we have balls then imagine what we're in for!"

I dozed off and woke sometime around noon. We had lunch at McDonald's and it was not at all like back home. It made me feel gross. To ease the nausea we had a little toke just before reaching Mojave. Then

I was pumped—one of my all time favorite bands is called *Mojave 3* and they make the sweetest road-trip music on the planet: chillin' acoustic guitar grooves drenched in sincerity and soothing, reflective vocals. Their song *All Your Tears* was playing as the afternoon sun blazed against the rocky cliffs and the windmills spread across the open hills like wild flowers spun frantically in the warm summer breezes. Graham screamed down the highway at full speed as I let my arm sway in the waves of air tearing past the open window. It was a glorious moment, one I had dreamed of ever since Graham first mentioned a trip south: *Mojave 3* in the Mojave Desert. Perfect. I took the wheel when we started to see our first Joshua trees and we smoked our Camels straight through until nightfall.

It was Friday night and Joshua Tree was humming with energy as teenagers whizzed around in jeeps and convertibles. The little grocery we stopped at was packed full of party-folk in cowboy hats stocking up for the night. We bought a two-six of whisky and a twelve-pack like we saw the locals doing. The surly clerk told us there was a camping ground up on the hill so we checked it out. The sign at the office said fifteen bucks a night and asked that you slip it in a slot in the door, but we figured we'd paid America enough to sleep on their dirt and chose a site further down the hill where it was unlikely we'd be noticed. A cute little blonde chick was standing by the pay phone and we both made eyes at her; she looked the other way indifferently. Graham asked if she was okay and she said she was waiting for a call.

"Probably her big cowboy-boot stomping boyfriend," Graham sighed. I wondered if he was as horny as I was.

I wanted to start a fire to cook up my can of beef soup. Graham got weird on me again: "You can't have a fire out here; you'll burn the whole campground down!"

"What? What are you talking about? It's me! Don't worry about it!"

"It's *stupid* dry out here man; one spark lets loose and we're screwed!"

"Dude! It's all sand here! Why are you being so paranoid right now? I'm a friggin' professional and I want to cook my soup! Look at all the space here! Quit worrying so much. I'll get right out in the open away from any brush and put nice tall rocks all around it, okay? Jeez!"

"I'm telling you, it's a stupid idea! Just eat your soup cold!"

"Look mom, I need my soup hot! Jeez Graham, look!" I said pointing up the hill, "Even the locals are having a fire!"

The tension was mounting. It was the first real argument we'd had after four years of being bros, excluding our regular debates on the existence of God. I took off up the hill to collect firewood grumbling under my breath, "The guy will drive across the country half-cut but won't let me cook my bloody soup!" I marched back silently with the wood and gathered some rocks to form a fire pit.

"Oh shit!" Graham exclaimed, and I thought he

was going to start in on me again. "Look what I found inside my floss container!"

He presented a big, gooey, beautiful British Columbian roach. I didn't know whether to punch him in the head or give him a big hug. I laughed, "What! You dick! You wonderful, glorious king of dicks! How did that happen?"

"I can't believe those guards didn't find it! I went camping with Joey and Jordan a few weeks ago and we smoked a fatty right before bed. I was too tired to find my roach box and I *completely* forgot I stashed it there!"

"Oh my gosh! Of all the shit they pulled out of the car how did they not come across that! We should be dead 'cause of you! And after all that bitchin' at me to not sneak anything over!"

"I'm soooo sorry man... I can't believe it! How?"

"It was God dude, God's looking out for us 'cause we're a couple of morons!"

"Ha ha! Yeah dude, God wants to make sure we still get a nice Canadian buzz!"

"Well I'm making a fire dude, you owe me!"

"Yeah, I do, it's still a bad idea though."

"If I burn the whole park down it's my problem not yours." The trip was getting weirder by the second, and that was nothing...

After my fire was going and my beef soup was cooked I spilled half of it on the rocks, much to my poor stomach's dismay. I polished off our hotdogs to make up for it then we got drunk. I pulled the tent out and Graham started up again: "Can't you just sleep on the ground tonight?"

"No way. I've never been in the desert before; who knows what might creep up and bite us?"

"Yeah, but I want to leave early tomorrow and packing up the tent will waste time."

"You've gotta' be kidding Graham! It's my tent; it'll take me two minutes to take it down. Just relax, okay?"

I settled down to write in the tent and Graham bundled up in his sleeping bag by the fire with his sketchpad. He was writing and drawing the strangest comic book about the male versus female condition and why it always makes us feel inept and lost, or something thereof, beyond our feeble abilities to comprehend. He always drew the most incredible stuff.

Before bed we hot-boxed the tent with the dime bag we'd gotten from the blonde Hispanic kid in Salinas, then I put my fire out. Graham passed out next to the ashes and I was glad to have the tent to myself; he smelled like hockey player rot. Then something started to happen to my brain: we'd only smoked two joints but the high was way different than any weed I'd ever smoked. The air seemed to turn into a tarry liquid and a dreadful, senseless fear swarmed over my entire being. I was having a really bad trip, like the time I lost ten pounds on a trip across Canada then ate an eighth of mushrooms, or countless other occasions with acid, only marijuana doesn't do that. I realized the buds must have been sprayed with Lysol; something punk kids do to try and "improve" the effects of their weak product. I could tell because my mouth tasted like toilet bowl cleaner. This felt completely foreign, unexplainable, and purely evil. My head swelled with poisoned blood and paranoia. I began to see visions of the withered black creatures from Devil's Pass lurking outside the tent. I prayed Graham wouldn't be eaten by demon coyotes and slipped into a long nightmare filled with treacherous peril and deep distresses. When I woke up early the next morning though, strangely enough, I felt fresh as a daisy.

CHAPTER 10
Four Twenty

Saturday, September 4, 1999

Things were back to normal that morning as if the night's arguments had never happened, but I still packed the tent up in record time just to keep Graham happy. He had fallen asleep before really feeling the deadly effects of the Salinas weed, but told me he had had feverish dreams as well and agreed the buds must have been laced. We tossed what little remained, which left us with just the British Columbian floss roach, enough for but a couple tokes each.

"Damn man!" I cursed. "Where are we going to find more weed out here?" It was always on my mind. America just wasn't cutting it, so I immediately decided to start drinking more.

Graham checked his email at a weird little internet-café and warned his pal Philippe from school back in Hong Kong that we were on our way to Guadalajara

Sinning Man's Heaven

to see him. Then, after I laid my hands on the car and prayed for God's blessing on it, we hit the desert road and slugged some beers as we headed for the heart of Joshua Tree. It was absolutely spectacular. I had never seen the desert before and this was the epicenter, with all that open space, all that nothingness, and all that bloody heat! I thought it was hot in my uncle's bakery in August but this was beyond our ability to cope! We both had sunburns within an hour and cursed and spat and laughed our asses off. This was living!

Mojave 3 in Mojave had been awesome, and now I was kicking myself for leaving *U2*'s *Joshua Tree* at home.

"Dumb ass!" Graham joked. "You drag fifty tapes across the continent and forget the most vital road trip album of all time!"

It didn't matter; we had a hoot listening to *Hawkwind* while coyotes ran up to the car and we snapped pictures and smoked our Camels. A long winding slope led us up to a touristy rest area with those twenty-five cent binocular things and the view just *slayed* us. There was nothing but dead wasteland for what felt like all eternity. It seemed we would never find Arizona in this new dimension they called Hidden Valley, and we didn't much care. We were drunk and enchanted by the extraordinary rock-towers jutting out of the scalding sands and leapt and ran around them madly, searching the crevices and archways and tunnels and shafts for some mystical gateway. But it got unbearably hot and we gave up our quest and returned to the Tercel. The thought of breaking down here scared the hell out of me and I prayed silently every ten minutes for our little engine.

Our beer was now boiling and undrinkable. Four hours of tortuous, blistering road lead us onto sheer flat plains with hardly even a Joshua tree. My beer buzz was long gone and I wanted to smoke our B.C. floss roach, but it was all we had left and we agreed it should be saved for a "real emergency." I was feeling it now man, I wanted to get high so bad. My skin was red-raw and my brain was drying up, just crying for some THC. I even drank half a hot beer to no avail.

"Man, this country sucks now dude!" I complained.

"I know," said Graham. "Imagine the crazies that live out here, a different breed; all lost, no cares, just breathing dust and waiting for the end of it all..."

"If I had to live out here I'd be completely baked all the time."

"You *are* completely baked all the time!" Graham chuckled.

"I'm gettin' the feeling we won't be gettin' high for a while man; nothing grows out here! Man! We should've stuffed a couple dime bags in your floss!"

Graham laughed at me, "Yeah dude." Everybody's got a catch phrase; Graham's was always, "Yeah dude." I loved how he said it too, with that low, hungry for life proclamation. He meant it.

After an hour of nothing, no trees, no people, no buildings, we finally saw a little burger trailer parked in front of an old rotting gas station with a huge sign missing some letters. It read "SCANCO." Graham bellowed with laughter and told me to snap a few shots with his camera. You couldn't have said it better.

After gassing up we went over to the trailer for lunch. There were three picnic tables in front, one with a family of four fat Texans slurping down fries and sodas, one with three tough biker dudes who looked over like they'd flatten our skinny white butts if we even so much as smiled at them, and one waiting for us. Graham went up to the window first and ordered a bacon burger and fries. There was an older woman cooking the burgers and another in her late twenties wearing a "COPS" t-shirt doing the short orders. The girl at the register was about twenty-three and almost cute for a fat chick. I had a hard time not giggling when she said, "Hey darlin', what can I git fer ya?" with a gaping smile that revealed two missing teeth. *Classic.* I ordered the same as Graham and she said, "Are you sure you don't wanna' make that soda a large?"

"No," I said, "I'm good."

"There ain't no more stops fer fifty miles or so, you might git thirsty. Our Pepsi's real cold!"

She convinced me. "Okay, make it a large then."

"Sure thing darlin', that'll be four twenty... Hey, four twenty, my favorite number!"

I did a double take. "W-whoa," I stammered in desperation. "You know what four twenty means?!"

"Of course! I just got an ounce two days ago!"

I COULDN'T BELIEVE IT! Nervous anticipation gripped me by the throat. "Do you have any here?"

"Sure I do! Just wait 'round a little and I'll give you some when things slow down."

"I CAN'T BELIEVE IT! IT'S A MIRACLE!" I sang.

She laughed and exclaimed, "My cousin knows the guy who brings it down from Fresno. Hell, there's nothing else to do 'round this shit hole so me and my boyfriend just git stoned and watch *Half Baked*. Ever seen it?"

"Oh yeah man! Jim Breuer is hilarious!"

"I love that movie, we watch it every night!"

Wow, I thought, *that's so wonderfully pathetic.* I told her I loved her and went to sit with Graham to wait for our food. He looked at me and said, "What are you so happy about?"

"Dude, the most amazing event in the history of *Stonerdom* has just happened! That fat chick is gonna' give us some weed!"

"WHAT?! You had the nerve to ask *her?*"

"No, that's the beauty part! I wouldn't have even dreamed to ask, but my bill came to four twenty and *she* brought it up!"

"Oh my god, that's fucking awesome! We're in the middle of nowhere dude! That's beyond coincidence— holy smoker's karma, eh?"

I was totally elated and still completely stunned. If she hadn't convinced me to order that Pepsi then the whole incident would never have happened.

We ate our burgers and sat waiting for everybody to leave. Graham went back to the station to pee and two chicks pulled up in a jeep. The one driving was a thin, attractive brunette about my age and we caught each other looking. The other was a short Asian girl all done up but not as pretty. When Graham came back I pointed them out and he said, "Na' dude, neither of them."

After the bikers rode off and the fat Texas family oozed their way back onto the road the jeep girls finished their sodas and went into the station, so my new best friend came out with two tightly rolled fatties and smoked them with us. It wasn't BC bud but it was cleaning product free and it did the trick. Sweet relief at long last!

The older girl with the "COPS" t-shirt came out and glowered at the three of us: "My boyfriend is going to be here soon and he better not catch you smoking that shit Louise!"

"Ease off Mona," Louise said. "*Sergeant Dan's* not going to be here fer fifteen more minutes."

"Your boy friend's a cop?" Graham asked.

She snickered, "Yup!"

"Okay, well we have to be going now," he said and handed the still burning joint back to Louise. She took one more monster hoot, the likes of which I've never seen a chick pull, then licked her fingers and put it out. She handed the roaches to me along with two freshly rolled joints and smiled, "Here darlin', yer gonna' need these to get to Arizona!"

"Louise, my little desert flower, I'll never forget you," I cooed.

"Don't mention it, smokers karma right?" She was a white trash angel, sent from above to keep us high and flying. Sergeant Dan pulled in to get his bacon burger almost the moment we left.

"Sweet timing!" Graham said. "This is so bizarre dude!" We just couldn't get over it. We said it over and over again: "Four twenty man!"

"Four fuckin' twenty!"

"That freakin' Pepsi!"

"Pepsi is definitely better than Coke!"

"We missed that pig by mere seconds!"

"Four twenty! I can't believe she called it!"

"I can't believe she had any!"

"I can't believe this trip!"

"This is messed dude. Mexico is going to be crazy!"

We were humming. Graham checked his watch: "Hey, it's four ten! Let's pull over in ten minutes and smoke the floss roach!"

"Sweet." I snagged one of the empty beer cans and prepped it with my scissors. At four twenty we pulled over to the side of the road and hit Louise's roach, then the B.C. floss roach; man, it tasted good! Two tokes each of *our* bud were almost equivalent to one of Louise's whole *doobs*. We got real stoned, back-at-home-stoned; it was marvelous. Just then, those two chicks whipped by in their jeep. I said, "Dude, what was up with you back there? That brunette was a babe!"

"They were jeep chicks? Why didn't you tell me they were jeep chicks? That changes everything!"

"What? Why?" I scoffed.

"Jeep chicks are hot man!"

"That's retarded! You saw them before! So now just because they drive a jeep they're hot?"

"Yeah! Jeep girls are wild! I would have even taken the short one for you."

Graham was crazy. I decided he didn't have a clue what he was talking about and was just too scared to talk to them back at the station. Though in all honesty, if it were the other way around I would have been too. I don't think either of us had ever actually asked a girl out; no, our romantic pasts were much too strange and complicated for that.

High and content we drove across the Arizona border. "Yeah dude," Graham said. We cruised for an hour or so then stopped at a station to fill up and buy a twelve pack of Milwaukee's Best and some smokes. Graham called his mom from a pay phone and said I'd better do the same; he always wanted to do the responsible thing, even though he was drinking under age and driving across the U.S. stoned.

I talked to my sister first, told her to pray for our wretched souls, and then she put mom on. I was really baked but focused hard enough to tell her we were in Arizona and doing okay.

It was my turn to drive and Graham accidentally left the trunk open. The way an '86 Tercel is designed makes it hard to tell the difference through the rear view mirror, but when I did my first shoulder check to merge back onto the highway I noticed. We pulled over and Graham checked if anything had fallen out. He lost his water bottle and some smokes, but I still had lots of both. We almost argued over whose fault it was but agreed it would be better to just enjoy our high.

I tore down the highway at full speed, chain smoking and sipping beer until twilight. The Joshua trees were long gone and in their place stood giant cacti, desert like you see in old Road Runner cartoons. We *had* to get out and smoke a bowl. It was beautiful. The sand still burned from the day's heat and the sky faded into gold and purple while we relished Louise's roach and sat cross-legged in front of an enormous spiky cactus. They were everywhere. I had to see how sharp they were, so I poked one and a small piece of needle got stuck in my middle finger. It hurt but in a good way. I wanted to inhale the entire desert, to soak in everything around me before it was gone forever. Graham teased me while I laughed and spent fifteen minutes trying to dig it out with another cactus needle. At last it came out and we sped southward in search of Yuma, our last stop before the Mexican border.

Sometime after nightfall we arrived in Yuma tired and burnt out. The first thing we saw was a huge white cross glowing with cheesy neon light. Graham laughed and snapped a picture saying, "Ah, the perfect advertisement for American Christianity!"

Burger King had a special on that summer: one dollar for a *whopper*. "Sweet!" We ate two each before going to the neighboring gas station for gas, smokes, and directions. The kid working the register told Graham there was a lake ten miles out of town where everybody went camping. I was amazed that a lake could exist in such an arid place. When we found it, it was too dark to see anything, so we drove until there were no cars and cruised down a trail right into the bush. Graham started drinking beer and studying his English/Spanish dictionary by flashlight while I put up the tent. It was hot and uncomfortably grimy, so when I was done I wanted a swim real bad. I went on a hunt with our left over wine to find the water and could hear the waves splashing against the bank, but every turn I took was overgrown with reeds and brush. It quickly became an exercise in frustration and I actually got lost for a half hour or so. Pissed drunk at this point, I wondered back cursing and stumbled across what looked like the remains of an old shack. I tossed my empty bottle then dragged two big planks from the debris back to camp to start a fire.

"Are you going to pee your pants if I light a fire?" I teased Graham.

"No dude, fire would be good. I think my batteries are dying."

Within minutes a raging fire like the kind we had back home was eating the planks and we smoked our remaining weed in hopes of finding more over the border. Thankfully high again we chatted excitedly: tomorrow we'd be in Mexico.

CHAPTER 11
So Close, Yet So Far Away

Sunday, September 5, 1999

You're supposed to purchase traveler's insurance before taking a car over the border, but it was Sunday and *Triple A* was closed. Plus, it just so happened to be Labor Day weekend so Monday was a write off too! Yuma was not only butt-ugly, it was also even hotter than Joshua Tree and we were stuck there for two more days! It was like a prison sentence. Mexico was right there waiting for us with its promise of cheap booze, cheap drugs, and cheap women, and we didn't have the right paperwork! So we went back to the lake in the dead heat of mid-day Arizona and found a better spot on the water. I spent the entire day sitting in the lake drinking beer, smoking Marlborough, and listening to a band I loved called *Lotion* while Graham sat stubbornly working on his comic and smelling like a wet dog. In the late afternoon he drove back to town to buy more supplies. It was the first time I'd been alone since leaving home so my thoughts turned to Lori and my heart began to ache.

"Aw, forget this," I said out loud and started fantasizing about the hot jeep chick to take my mind off it. A guy's hormones can take over and kill any sentiment; I got real horny and regretted not bringing any magazines. Suddenly, a fat American floated out of the reeds in a little rubber dingy with a fishing rod. If it weren't for his long cast plunking in the water and alerting me he would have caught me in a very embarrassing moment! *Phew!* He said a friendly "Hello" and floated on by with a flick of his wrist. I hadn't dealt with my hormones in six days.

"Damn!" I cursed knowing Graham would be back any minute.

No weed meant twice the drinking. By nightfall we were just smashed and had our best talk yet, the kind we used to have when Graham would come home from Hong Kong for Christmas break and we'd walk around for hours in the cold December air trading stories, philosophizing and conversing fervently about life, music and books. We went off about *Led Zeppelin* lying by the fire and agreed that they're easily the greatest rock band of all time. I spoke with grave earnestness, explaining how their tunes had gotten me through the year as I wallowed around our island in confusion and hurt, basking in the gloom of my secret obsessions. Then Graham finally got around to telling me about this cool chick named Becky he'd been mixed up with before we left:

Roy Milner

"I've dug her for a few months so I don't know why it happened. We were sitting in the field behind the greenhouses watching the sunset, and she put her hand on my knee, so I made my move and we finally kissed; and it was the longest, sweetest kiss. But when I stopped and looked at her she just looked...stupid, you know? Like a lost puppy with those dumb loving eyes. So I walked away without saying anything and just left her sitting there; like with Wanda—"

I nodded knowingly and fell silent. I don't think either of us felt like pulling that skeleton out of the closet without weed...

CHAPTER 12

You Gotta' Be Real Careful

Monday, September 6, 1999

It was Labor Day and Yuma was starting to grow on us like a fungus. Graham finally took a swim with me because he couldn't handle the level of griminess he had achieved. The thought of facing one more day with the mosquitoes and the life-sapping dry heat did not sit well with us, so we decided to find the cheapest hotel in town. Thirty bucks later we had a decent room with two beds and a TV. I finally got some alone time in the shower.

The air conditioning in our room was a sweet relief, along with a fresh bottle of whiskey and some more one-dollar *whoppers*. We got drunk and Graham, always dead set on truly experiencing his social surroundings, thought we should do something American. So we watched wrestling, more wrestling then either of us had ever been subject to. It gave us a good laugh until the early evening when we decided to go weed hunting. The main strip was long, wide and laden with every corporate logo in the book, the perfect picture of commercial *"Generica"*. In contrast, the sky was spectacular with clouds of pink and purple, and a blissfully golden horizon beckoned us southward. We were buzzing with anticipation because tomorrow would finally bring us to the Promised Land.

A big Puerto Rican kid sauntered past and we asked if he knew where we could score.

"There's a guy in my building that sells everything," he said with a surprisingly girly voice. So we followed him home as he launched into his life story.

"Yeah, my dad killed my mom when I was seven and I haven't seen him since. He's serving a life sentence in San Quentin so I haven't seen him in thirteen years. My Grandma raised me and now she's got some weird disease I can't pronounce, but she's got like a year to live or some shit, so I gotta' find a job 'cause her pension will be gone." Unbelievable story. We asked him if he wanted to get high with us but he said his Grandma would know and she'd have us all arrested. He was still kind enough though to take us to "Jason's" door in a loud, festering apartment complex. After he introduced us to Jason's buddy "Mo" he went up to make his Grandma dinner. Mo was a tough looking black kid who snarled when he spoke: "Shit boy, you hippies or somethin'?"

"No, just purebred Canadian stoners," Graham joked nervously.

"Ya'll are from Canada? Well shit white boy,

welcome to the desert. What are we looking for today?"

"Just some weed," I said.

"Weed! Hell, I don't know 'bout dat! Jason don't carry too much green shit know wha' I'm sayin'? You interested in anything else?"

It was clear from his aggressive mannerism and the state of the apartment that we were smack in the middle of a small time crack operation. I answered, "No, we don't smoke much more than weed."

"Well, Jason's gonna' be back in half an hour or so; he *might* have something or know somebody. You can chill if you want."

Neither of us knew what to say. The idea of hanging around was more than daunting; the place reeked of trouble. It didn't matter because Jason showed up at that instant, a bald little black guy resembling a pit bull. He grunted in our direction, said he didn't sell "the green shit" and sent us on our way. Sad and *weedless* we wondered back down the main strip and asked one more kid. He just kept walking, so I resigned to buying a big bottle of wine at a grocery store. Dusk fell and Graham pointed across the street saying, "Check out that little hick bar with the neon cowboy hat! We have to have a drink with the locals!"

Now in Canada the drinking age is nineteen and we frequented bars, clubs, and pubs all the time, but in the states it's twenty-one and Graham was only twenty. I tried to restrain his dire need to experience every social opportunity that crossed his path, mostly so I wouldn't have to suffer the eyes of alcoholic cowboy judgment: "Dude, that's a bar for good ole' boys! I bet no one under thirty-five goes in there, let alone under-aged hippie punks! Let's just go drink in our room."

"C'mon," he rebutted, "it'll be sweet! *Carpe Diem* right? I have to see the inside of that place!"

"Do you always have to use Robin Williams against me? You're under age man! They'll kick our ass and throw us out!"

"They won't kick our ass, they'll just throw us out, if they even bother to check our IDs. Go back to the hotel if you want."

I said it before, Graham was crazy, but I went in with him to make sure he didn't get snapped in two. We stepped inside where ten rugged regulars immediately turned and stared at us like we were in the wrong movie. We sat on the far side of the room next to the bar and looked around nervously. It was a classic saloon like the ones you see in old spaghetti western flicks, and we had absolutely no right being there. The waitress, a pretty but weathered forty year old girl who dressed like it was 1985 looked us up and down totally bewildered and said in a thick southern access, "Hey sweeties, ya'll got some ID with ya?"

I kicked Graham's leg and we presented them to her. She looked at mine first and said, "Where the heck ya'll from?"

"Canada," I said.

"Canada? Wow. Is it true ya'll live in igloos?"

We both laughed. "No," Graham said handing her his license, "that's the Eskimos *way* up north."

She was so amused by our presence that she plumb-miscalculated Graham's birth date and asked what we wanted to drink. Graham kicked me back and ordered a bud; I ordered the same. She brought us our beer then noticed my bottle of wine: "Sorry hun, you can't have that in here, it's state law."

"It's not opened, I just bought it to take back to our room with us."

"It's still state law, we could git in a lot of trouble."

"Well what am I supposed to do with it?"

"Mike will put it in his truck for ya 'til yer done yer drink. Hey Mike? Could you take this guy's wine out to yer truck?"

A tall scruffy hick with hazy eyes rose and staggered towards the door motioning for me to follow. I went out with him and he stashed my bottle saying, "Just grab me before you leave."

When we went back in the waitress was leaning on the bar flirtatiously close to Graham as he related our travels. She was all starry eyed and thought we were both brave and crazy for wanting to cross the border.

"It's real dangerous down there hun," she said. "You gotta' be real careful! Lord knows what kinda' crazy thangs can happen t'ya!"

One of the regulars sitting with Mike overheard the conversation and said, "You boys gotta' gun?"

I laughed out loud and asked, "You got one I can buy?"

Jen, the waitress, went and served someone else and Graham exclaimed, "Dig this place man! Imagine what these guys' lives are like! I bet all ten of them get plowed here every single night after herding cattle or whatever the hell cowboys do now. What a life, eh?"

"Yeah man, I bet they could care less about anything."

Jen kept running back and forth between customers, a piece of paper she was mulling over behind the bar, and our table, where she'd lean towards us and say, "But yeah, you gotta' be real careful..." She did this about three times, "Yeah, yeah, you gotta' be real careful..." It was pretty cute. But then I noticed her behind the bar one more time trying to work something out with her pen. She kept looking back and forth between Graham and the paper, and then she went wide-eyed. I knew before it happened. She dropped everything and ran over to our tables with her arms in the air.

"Okay guys, sorry, sorry, you gotta' git out right now!"

Everyone in the bar looked over at us, and two guys in cowboy hats actually stood up ready to drag us out. Graham apologized profusely and I tried to pay for the beer but she just said, "No, no, you just have to go! Mike, could you see to these boys please?"

Mike staggered back out the door behind us swearing under his breath. He gave me back my wine and said, "Watch the bullshit in Mexico or you won't be coming back." Then he stumbled back inside and slammed the door shut.

"Graham, you're an idiot!"

Sinning Man's Heaven

He just laughed and said, "How did a chick with such poor math skills get a job as a barkeep?"

We walked back to our hotel room, drank my wine and watched a documentary about Alexander the Great. Our conversation swayed from history, to modern events (which Graham always criticized me for not being up on), to stupid waitresses, to beautiful women in general. We quickly changed that topic and I began to reflect on the solo album I planned on recording when I got home. Nothing in life meant more to me than my music and, for whatever reason, it came to new life right there before me as I lay in that creaky bed in Yuma, Arizona discoursing with one of God's strangest prodigal sons. I leapt off the bed and grabbed him in a big bear hug proclaiming, "DUDE! This is so awesome! We're about to embark on a journey shunned by all! After all our talk it's actually about to happen!" I was elated, even without weed. My mind throbbed with new ideas. We were ready for anything.

Graham chuckled quietly at me, "Yeah dude, I know, we're finally here, and we're gonna' get some *real* perspective."

CHAPTER 13

The Entrance

Tuesday, September 7, 1999

There was a whack of stuff to be done before we could leave Yuma but I won't bore you with the details. Basically, we got all our papers together at *Triple A* where they told us we would have to give a five hundred dollar deposit at the border to get a foreign car traveler's sticker. We ate our last one-dollar *whoppers* at Burger King, then Graham withdrew the five hundred and we hit the road. We agreed to never visit Yuma again and to risk returning through Tijuana despite what the foul-mouthed Californian hick had told us.

Forty minutes later we were approaching the border and it was the strangest experience, not at all like I had envisioned. There was absolutely nothing for miles, just sky and sand and a big cement wall stretching across the horizon. As we drew near the border the highway turned into a narrow road that led into what looked like a little hole in the wall. My guts swelled in nervous anticipation, then, we popped through the unguarded hole and it was utter mayhem! Busted up old Volkswagen bugs whizzed down alleys, guards and civilians and hustlers and whores swarmed the streets and sidewalks with no visible purpose whatsoever. Dirt-stained kids ran by begging everyone for money, large trucks screeched to a halt in front of rickety old shops and unloaded all kinds of goods. I felt like I could see and hear the entire town from that first parking lot we pulled into. It was tremendously loud, and the first person to greet us was an obese hooker with gray skin and enormous rotting teeth. She pulled her raggedy hair back and shook her hairy tits in the most disgusting fashion, saying something in Spanish that I'm sure was no invitation to meet her grandmother.

"Holy crap!" I exclaimed. "This place is a zoo! Where are we supposed to go?" Graham pulled his shorts up and spat, "I guess we'll have to ask someone."

Now I'm not kidding, I've mentioned that Graham was the smartest kid I'd ever known, and he'd only been reading that English/Spanish dictionary for a couple of days, but he marched right up to a guard and said some crazy thing I'd never heard before. Whatever it was, the guard didn't like it. He yelled real loud and pointed his gun at us, then motioned for us to go into the adjacent office. Scared stupid, we crept inside at gunpoint and he sat us down in front of a tiny wooden desk. He pointed at Graham's wallet then tore it out of his hands, looked inside, and pocketed the five hundred dollars! Out of the blue an older guard stormed in and yelled something at the first guard who cowered and handed the money over to him. The older guard spoke decent English.

"Welcome to San Luis, I am sorry for Rodolfo, he like to steal. Here is your money." Rodolfo put his gun down and smiled sheepishly, embarrassed more than anything. The older guard pointed to another office trailer across the parking lot behind a big gate and told us to ask for "José". So we went to the trailer and a sign on the door told us to wait. We sat there for half an hour still shook up from the first guard until José, a well-dressed bureaucrat, showed up with his lunch and his secretary "Maria." They both spoke decent English and explained *almost* everything we needed to do. So with their paper work in hand we ran back to our car to retrieve the insurance papers and fill out all the required information. Then we marched down the street a couple blocks, overwhelmed with the language and the people hustling and slinging, and found an exchange table to turn our five hundred American dollars into pesos. We wondered back to José's office and gave him the paper work. His secretary asked, "Do you have the seven hundred and fifty dollar deposit for your car?"

Graham startled, "What?! *Triple A* said it was five hundred!"

"No, no, that's something different. It's seven fifty or you can't drive here!"

"Bullshit!" we agreed, but were forced to drag

ourselves back out onto the street to find a bank. Graham found a bank machine and withdrew the extra two fifty then we ran back to the exchange table for more pesos. With pesos in hand we booted back to the office. On the way a young Mexican packing vegetables in a big muddy truck yelled, "Hey pretty boys!"

I chuckled anxiously as Graham whispered, "We're gonna' get raped and killed and it'll have cost us seven hundred and fifty bucks!"

But there was no turning back now. We had dug our graves and owed it to ourselves to jump in.

Back at the office Maria said, "What's this? This is in pesos, they want American money!"

"WHAT! Why didn't you say that? This is Mexico! This is Mexican money!" Graham squeaked.

"It doesn't matter, they don't want pesos, the bank won't hold it for us unless it's American. Sorry, that's the rules!"

"Damn lady, why didn't *Triple A* tell us that?"

"Oh, they don't know anything."

"No shit!" We were getting right pissed off, Graham more so; he was going to loose even more money in a third exchange. I figured all in all he lost about sixty bucks just changing money he didn't have to in the first place. But once more we were forced to run back to the exchange table, much to the delight of the toothless old man running it who must have been in cahoots with José and Maria.

So after two exhausting hours of running around the nasty little border town of San Luis, we finally got our two inch by three inch hologram sticker which gave us the right to drive "freely" through Mexico, and stuck it on our windshield. José told us that to get our deposit back we would have to return to the town with the car. Graham swore he'd never return and said, "That's worth seven hundred and fifty bucks!"

Irate but relieved to be back on the road, we sped south swearing over and over at the ridiculous complications that had christened our foreign adventure.

"This calls for beer!" I proclaimed. We stopped just outside of town and bought our first twelve-pack of Mexican beer: sweet, sweet Tecate! Tecate was about to become my new best friend. I took the wheel and slammed one while Graham sipped his reverently, when to our horror, we came across a roadblock. One ordinarily dressed Mexican and two soldiers in green army attire with a big army truck waved us to the side of the road, and the civilian asked in broken English if we had any drugs or guns. I answered, "No way man, we just crossed the border and we're not stupid!"

He could tell I was legit but noticed Graham trying to hide his beer can. "You drink cerveza too?" he asked me.

"No, drinking and driving is totally illegal where I come from!" I answered.

" Is bad here too, but okay for him," and he sent us on our way with a smile, "Adios amigos!"

"Sweet!" said Graham. "Passengers can drink in the car here!" That didn't stop me. It was all desert lands now and we wouldn't be seeing anyone for a while, so I drank a couple more.

After two hours of driving, listening to *Smashing*

Pumpkins and *Blue Dog Pict*, I pulled over to visit our first Mexican gas station. Every station in Mexico is full-service; it gives each member of the family a job. When this particular family saw us and heard me trying to ask for a full tank of gas they lost it! They whooped and howled like we had driven out of the circus in a clown car. Graham ate it up: "This is hilarious man! They must think we're totally insane for trying this!" He was right. They laughed while our tank was being filled. They laughed while Graham went in to pay and buy smokes. They were still laughing when he came back out, beat red with embarrassment, wearing a big stupid grin on his face. He lit a smoke as I pulled back onto the road and said, "We're vulture food man." We both had another beer.

The next few hours driving over the lonely hills of the desert were a lesson in Mexican driving etiquette. People don't use their signal lights to signal a turn, they (especially big trucks) use them to tell you if it's safe to pass. I must have been signaled to pass eight times before evening fell, when oncoming traffic started flashing their high beams at me for no apparent reason. For twenty minutes every car we passed flashed us.

"What's that about?" Graham said.

"I don't know. I hope it doesn't mean another roadblock."

It was real dark at this point and I could barely see the road. I was going about 110 kilometers an hour when suddenly a gigantic black tire lying smack in the middle of the passing lane zoomed into view!

My reflexes jumped at the last possible second—we skidded around it and slid through the sand on the side of the road, narrowly missing a truck following close behind us in the traveling lane. I heaved a huge sigh and Graham patted me on the back: "All props man!"

I felt so cool right then; Graham's praise made you feel real good. The vultures would have to wait.

Around ten that night I rolled into a small desert town much quieter and welcoming than San Luis, and we decided to find food and sleep. A little motel rented us a room with one bed for eighty pesos (roughly eight dollars American) then we walked across the street to a little taco stand a family had set up in their front yard.

Now I've gotta' tell you, my stomach was churning something fierce, not just from hunger, but from sheer anxiety. New settings have always given me butterflies and now I was about to try conversing with people whose language I knew nothing about. In high school I took Japanese but Graham took French, French being closely related to Spanish, and he was incredible! Three days with his dictionary and he was already making small talk with the fat smiling Mexican behind the grill, ordering us *tortas* and tacos and cokes. The kid was phenomenal, just diving right in there, starving to learn more from the people and to experience every taste and smell. I was so impressed and told him so. After biting into my first-ever *torta* my uneasiness lessened. I thought I'd lose weight on the trip and in that instant I knew I'd be gaining! Those sandwiches were amazing! We stared at each other wide-eyed like we had discovered the good Lord's fallen manna and ate like starving Hebrews. Graham and I loved to eat, especially Graham. Back home we'd sit around his kitchen table and eat entire batches of his mom's chocolate brownies. It was hilarious watching him because he was so skinny but ate like a rabid horse.

I asked Graham how to say 'good' then gave the fat smiling Mexican a thumbs up in praise: "Buenos mi amigo!"

"Gracias," he bowed his head humbly. Those first few folk we met seemed so gracious, the native-born people of the land who worked it and loved it and knew what it was to really sweat for their bread. I felt like a spoiled brat.

Graham pushed the dictionary across the table to me and said, "You haven't even looked at this yet! Are you going to at least *try* to learn some Spanish? I'm not going to order everything for you the whole trip you know."

I thought this was pretty harsh but I knew what he meant. I said, "Jeez, don't worry about it man. I'm a musician! I'll learn the important stuff as we go. Cerveza por favor, see?"

Graham had the upper hand as the more traveled linguist and therefore dealt with most of our transactions, which to some degree gave me the excuse to avoid those social situations I found unnerving. Though I'm not sure just how aware Graham was of the latter fact, it gave him what I considered to be

Roy Milner

an imprudent sense of power; one I was not looking forward to contending with.

CHAPTER 14

Mexican Chiba and Ms. Lorenzo's Little Sister

Wednesday, September 8, 1999

When I woke up the next morning Graham was already gone. He returned with a bag of pastries yapping away excitedly: "Markman! This place is so awesome! Forget Tim Horton's; there's a little bakery down the street—I've never seen sweetbreads like this!"

There were powdered donuts and juicy hot cakes with jams and jellies in the centers. We devoured them greedily, licked our fingers and laughed and cooed like kids in a candy store. Then we decided to relax a little before hitting the road and flicked on the TV. An old made-for-TV-movie from 1983 called *Prototype* was on, sort of a modern day retelling of *Frankenstein*. We sat through most of it until our room time was up, then loaded up the car and made for wherever we got. Back on the highway we started talking about

Frankenstein and old horror classics. Graham asked, "Did you ever read that Vampire Encyclopedia I gave you for Christmas three years ago?"

"Some, mostly the stuff about movies though. I was coming out of my 'dark stage' by then so I didn't give it the attention I would have when I was sixteen."

"Yeah dude, you were pretty messed back then. I remember when I first started hanging out with you, people would say, 'Look out for that guy Mark, he's demon-spawn!'"

"That was sweet," I snickered.

He lit a smoke and continued, "But what do you think made you go from being a good little church boy to 'demon-spawn?' I mean, we almost had the same lives growing up and I was pissed off too, but I never got into all that dark stuff."

I thought a moment then answered, "It probably *started* in grade seven when my parents made me go back to school. I remember sitting on my mom's lap like a sniveling five year old, shaking uncontrollably with fear all that morning, begging to be home-schooled. And then before I got in my dad's car I was so nervous I puked all over the carport. Of course they knew they had to stay strong and make me go, so on that drive I remember clenching my fists and deciding right then and there to give into my anger. And a guy as sensitive as me is already predisposed to that kinda' stuff, you know? I always found creatures of the night alluring, and I got that first taste of mystery when I started getting into my comic books and horror movies, but that shit's all cliché—it's hard to make anyone really get it. Obviously the more I got picked on the angrier I got, but by high school it developed into this glorious, all consuming rage, which made me feel so strong...to the point that I was possessed by it, and I knew people were scared of me, and I knew I could draw in the girls I liked, and then when I started creeping around at night I started to see things—"

Graham interrupted with noted interest, "Yeah, was all that real or were you just putting on another show?"

"*Honestly* honestly? Both. Obviously when you guys were around I was doing it for kicks; like Brendan would get so scared he'd have to go home, which you guys always thought was hilarious. A lot of that crap was for attention I admit, but seriously; I didn't just dream that stuff up! When I was alone at night walking through the forest summoning things... I swear there were times I heard and felt another presence! Voices promised me power and put visions in my head. I was so raw and hungry, and those demons filled the void for me, you know? And I still considered myself a Christian!"

Graham shook his head, "That's messed up dude."

"Yup," I agreed.

He chuckled, "Good thing you became a pot-head instead!"

"Yeah, now we're friends with most of the people we hated because we're all a bunch of stoners!"

At that point I wanted to get high so bad. Spidey's mix tape was playing again and that *I Mother*

Earth song was making my now nostalgic heart bleed with sentiment and desire...

We rolled into a town called Los Mochis around 5:00 p.m. and got lost trying to find a place recommended by Graham's Lonely Planet that was supposed to be "a family friendly hotel with clean rooms at good rates." Mexicans are so funny. They're so eager to be helpful that they'll give you directions even if they don't know what you're talking about. After an old newsstand clerk sent us south in the wrong direction and a delivery boy sent us north in the wrong direction, we finally stumbled across our hotel: "Los Tres Burros," or, The Three Donkeys. Behind the front desk were the three brothers who ran the place, a pegboard with keys hanging on it, and a big fridge full of beer. They sold us a six-pack and gave us the key to our room. I loved it: Mexico was so cheap! It was only seventy pesos for the night (about seven bucks) and just thirty-six pesos for the beer. Back home it costs four times that!

"This is bloody marvelous," Graham sang. "I'm gonna' get so pissed tonight!"

Our room was three stories up on the lower level of the roof and consisted of four white walls, two bumpy single beds and a cockroach. That was it, like a mental patient's cell.

Los Mochis was swarming with party people and it was only Wednesday night. It's a fairly large town and we couldn't wait to experience as much of it as possible during our one night stay, so after slamming our beers we hit the streets as the stars came out with the bright neon lights of the warm Mexican evening. The first place we hit was a taco bar across the street where we gorged ourselves. *U2* was playing on the radio and we noticed half the people in the restaurant knew the words.

Our hotel had a bar built into its left wing, so we wandered back to check it out. The inside was much larger than it appeared from the street, with a spacious stage and a decent light show whirling around the tables. They weren't serving yet and nobody was around except a sound guy playing with a mixer. We figured a band was playing that night and asked him who. He didn't speak a word of English but his gestures were crystal clear: he stuck his hands in the air and shook his ass. Graham laughed out loud and said, "Awesome! Lonely Planet rules dude, definitely a family friendly hotel! We *have* to come back here tonight!"

I hesitated, "I don't know man; I don't think I'm up for the strip-club thing."

"What? Isn't this the kind of stuff we came down here for?"

"I came to get drunk and high for cheap man; I don't do strip-clubs."

"What about the magazines under your bed?"

"That's different."

"Um, no it isn't dude."

I knew he was right, but neither of us had ever gone that far, and I wanted to keep it that way. If I saw any naked chicks it was going to be for free and for private pleasure, not some *skanky* venture with a bunch of fat, drunken perverts. With that in mind we took off in search of more "cantinas" (bars) and had a shot of tequila and a beer in every place we saw. After four stops, a fat middle-aged Mexican reeking of garbage and urine stepped in our path and told Graham in Spanish that he had missed his bus and wanted us to buy him a beer. Graham politely lied that we were broke (his Spanish was improving by the second!) and the brute grabbed me by the hand without warning, squeezed it with tremendous strength and opened his eyes real wide with the creepiest smile you ever saw and shouted, "I'M SINGLE!" I tore my now stinking hand from his solid grip and said, "Sorry bud, I'm straight!" and we ran like hell from his demented cackling. I ventured onward already disturbed...

Our next stop was a dungy little cantina with twelve or so tables and a classic bar with one old man serving. Two whores, one tall and sickly, the other short and fat with freckles all over her body, sat in the corner scanning the room and laughed out loud when they saw us. This was not a place for skinny white boys. We bought a beer each then searched for an empty table. Everyone was over thirty and stared at us indignantly as we wormed our way across the room. In the middle of it all we passed by this wiry, long limbed Mexican who sat alone hunched over the table with his shoulder blades jutting straight up in the air like he once had wings that were sawed off. He gazed up at us with fiery red eyes and giggled maniacally as he stretched his skinny arm out to shake Graham's hand. Graham took his hand and said, "Ola," and the psychotic skeleton-man dug his long yellow thumbnail into the back of Graham's wrist and drew blood with a gurgled snicker. Graham winced and jumped back as I dodged around him and made for the far corner. We sat down and Graham rubbed his hand saying, "That guy's gotta' be on acid!"

I said, "He's on a mescaline binge and he's fucking possessed is what he is! Did you see his eyes?" We both looked back and he was rocking back and forth over his bottle of Tequila talking to himself in a muddled, high-pitched winy. The fat freckled hooker in the opposite corner kept making eyes at me and giggling to her friend. Her smile revealed a huge gap between her buckteeth, which she licked as if she was the best lay in town. I chugged my beer in one go and said, "Okay I'm done. Let's get the hell outta' here!" Graham wholeheartedly agreed and we made for the door.

Back out on the streets we came across an arcade that served alcohol, so we blew some change on *Street Fighter 2* and pinball games for an hour or so. Drunk and hungry for more we headed back the way we came on the other side of the street intent on having a drink in every bar in the neighborhood, when we smelled it. I grabbed Graham by the shoulder and exclaimed, "Dude! Where is that coming from? Where is it?!" We glanced frantically in all three hundred and sixty directions trying to pin down where the sweet smell of marijuana was coming from. "There!" Graham said with a nod. A handsome young Mexican dressed in jeans and a white dress shirt stood on the corner leaning against a street light with smoke oozing from his mouth and swirling slowly all around him like Humphrey Bogart. Mexican chiba at long last! We crept up to him to ask if he had any more. He grabbed his crotch and pulled with a big cheer, "Morta mi amigos! Si, si!" It was the only time in my life I enjoyed staring at another man's bulge.

Our new hardly-English speaking friend introduced himself as "Alfredo" and told us to follow him. We entered a building, climbed a thirty-step staircase, and found ourselves in the middle of a large club with loud cheesy dance music and two hundred people having one hell of a good time. Alfredo led us to the baños (the bathroom, pronounced *banyos*). We all squeezed into one of the stalls where he undid his zipper, reached between his legs and produced a big bag of green. Graham took his cigarettes out of the pack and gave them to me to put in mine then Alfredo jammed a heaping hand-full of bud into the empty package. Better yet, Alfredo refused our money, saying something about growing *morta* at home and how selling drugs is wrong. What a dude!

I couldn't understand a word Alfredo was saying and just wanted to go get high, but Graham thought we'd better be polite and chill with him a little after such a gracious offering. He was very interested in Canada and talked Graham's ear off for about twenty minutes while I drank and watched the girls on the dance floor. Finally, he said he had to go and we started to leave, then out of nowhere, two cops grabbed Alfredo, pulled his shirt over his head and threw him down the stairs! The poor guy toppled head over heals down all thirty steps! Before I could see what happened next Graham grabbed my arm and exclaimed, "Let's book!" We ran through the crowd back to the bathroom. Graham went to flush the weed and I said, "Dude, wait, just stick it behind the toilet and we'll wait it out!" Luckily we had both drank a lot, so we stood at the urinals and had a good, long, inconspicuous pee while our hearts thumped wildly. Four grueling minutes ticked by when suddenly, to our unimaginable relief, Alfredo walked back in with a big smile: "No worry amigos! No worry!" He explained to Graham in Spanish that someone down the street had been shot and they were searching for someone with a gun. Lucky for him they thought his bulge was real because if you get caught with marijuana in Mexico you go straight to jail. So now I was really ready to get high. In just one night I had already had three heart attacks!

Giddy and finally holding, we headed back to the hotel to roll up. On our way we saw the fat freckled whore with some poor *shmuck* crossing the street and she yelled in Spanish, "Hey little lambs!"

Back in our room Graham started cutting and I had to run back down to the car to find some papers. There was a gorgeous young *señorita* in a tight black leather skirt lying on our windshield talking to who I guessed was her boyfriend. I said a casual "Ola" and retrieved our *rollies* from inside the Tercel. As I locked the door the girl stared at me with this darkly seductive look that said, *Wanna' fuck me for money?* And her boyfriend gave me this neutral but cocky look that said, *Wanna' fuck my girlfriend for money?* She spread her legs a little and gave me a glance of her panties. I paused for just a moment, and then went back up stairs.

Graham rolled three tight *doobs*, one for each crazy event of the evening, and we climbed up onto the hotel's roof to look out over the dirty neon lights of Los Mochis. Our car was directly below, three stories down, and I pointed out the girl and her pimp to Graham. They were still waiting around hoping one of us would go down and take the bait. Believe me I was tempted. We stared at her longingly and passed the joints back and forth between swigs of Tecate.

Graham frequently entertained the idea of getting into politics, particularly diplomacy. He turned away from the girl and said, "Do me a favor and don't ever tell anyone what we were up to out here, okay? What if I get into office one day and I have to speak on drug policy or sexual rights? Here I am pissed out of my gourd leering at prostitutes in a foreign county! We're a fine pair of hypocrites Markman. You wanna' go check out the family friendly *titty-bar*?"

I giggled nervously, "Can't do it man, sorry." Of course part of me wanted to, but the idea of all those dirty men getting hard over the same girl made me ill. And besides, I was too scared. So Graham went for his first strip-club experience by himself. I went back down stairs to buy another six-pack and, much to my surprise, discovered five very scantily clad *señoritas* hanging around the office. Two of the brothers were whooping and groping them and hardly noticed as I paid for the beer. It dawned on me as I returned to the room that our Lonely Planet was slightly outdated and that we were staying in a brothel. It was only our second day in Mexico and I already wondered how much longer I could resist its temptations.

Back in our room I turned off the lights and lay down with Arvo Pärt's *Te Deum* playing in my headphones. There in the darkness, drinking in the purity of that sparse and sacred work, I began to pray with a grave numbness, while two floors beneath women degraded themselves in the filthiest of all professions before bestial men and my best friend.

When we were in high school there was this ridiculously hot teacher named Ms. Lorenzo who taught Spanish. Some guys actually chose her class over French or Japanese just so they could ogle her for an hour every day. Anyways, as I lay there in my holy moment Graham burst into the room and exclaimed, "Dude! I just saw Ms. Lorenzo's little sister masturbating!" I burst out laughing and asked, "So what was it like ya' perv?"

"Definitely a visceral experience, but it was so unnatural. These people are messed up dude! I couldn't take anymore because they *actually* brought a donkey out on stage for her to play with... Look, I think I grew another chest hair!"

CHAPTER 15

Cockroaches and Machine Guns

Thursday, September 9, 1999

Breakfast that morning was pretty gross. I had drunk way more than Graham and was pretty hung over, but Graham insisted we'd both feel better after runny eggs and stale toast in what seemed like a nice place. It made me even more nauseous, so I lay down in the car and tried to write while Graham checked in at an internet-café to see if Philippe had e-mailed back. When he returned to the car he said, "I always drive in the mornings, can you take the first shift?" I wanted to oblige him but my head hurt too much, so I said, "Sorry man, I don't think I can do it; I feel like crap."

He almost got cross, "Are you going to be hung over every morning? We've got a lot to do you know and that doesn't really help things along."

"Sorry man, jeez, I just didn't drink any water

last night. Let's smoke a joint when we get on the highway and I'll feel better, okay?"

"Okay. Find the map. Where am I going?" I directed him out of town and we sparked up once we were back in the desert. It was terribly hot and still quite dry, but the weed fixed all that. We drifted along digging on a Canadian band I loved called *Glueleg* and Graham told me he had to find a copy if we ever returned to Canada. I said, "If? You planning on getting a job here or something?"

"Maybe, why not? The idea's to stay as long as we can, right?"

"Yeah, for sure, but I'm not working here man, no way! You can't make anything!"

"You don't need anything to live here. You can fly home and I'll sell the car and see how long I can stretch it out for." He was being cocky because he'd spent more time in the third world than me and he wanted to see how far I was willing to go. I chuckled and teased him, "Yeah dude, you're real pretty; you could work as a gigolo for some fat old mompo!" (Mompo is Spanish for homosexual.)

"Screw you pretty boy, light me a smoke!" he joked. I lit a Camel for him and he practiced blowing smokes rings against the windshield. I was feeling great again. We reminisced about our first wild night and agreed we were brilliant for making the trip. Sill, I laid my hands on the car and prayed every twenty minutes or so that our little engine would hold up.

In the early evening we arrived in the beautiful seaside city of Mazatlán. So far all we'd seen was sand

and the occasional green shrub, but Mazatlán had palm trees and rich people's beach houses and rickety, dumpy little poor-people-huts. Some streets were almost decadent, with intricate stonework and clean white rock walls, while other streets weren't streets at all; just long stretches of thick, goopy mud. The town was a living paradox with crippled, hard-done-by brown peasants and white wealthy tourists from all over the globe. You could stand in one spot and see the setting-sun sinking into distant ocean waves of orange and gold, doctors and lawyers gallivanting around the beach-front stores with their silicone wives in their white v-cut sweaters and real leather sandals, then turn your head and see men in army-green with machine guns standing at a bank entrance, or a group of children caked with mud selling smokes and dirty comics. Graham said, "Okay, so where do we fit in?"

Graham got us lost on a steep hill, so I took the wheel and sped back down to a grocery to buy more beer, then drove to the outskirts where we'd seen a "decent" looking place on the way into town. Our original plan was to sleep in the tent but it seemed unlikely that there'd be a place safe enough to risk it in or out of the city.

The hotel was pretty disgusting. The beds were almost clean and at the very least the TV worked, but every square inch of the place was crawling with huge cockroaches. You literally had to kick your way up the stairs.

Once we were settled we sipped Modelos (another Mexican beer) and kicked the sack around out in the courtyard. The manager's two little kids came out and marveled at us, or rather Graham; he could conjure miracles with a hackey-sack even loaded.

It was only about ten but we were both worn and just wanted to keep rolling south, so we turned in early and fell asleep watching *The X-Files* in Spanish.

CHAPTER 16
Independence!

Friday, September 10, 1999

In the morning we realized we hadn't eaten in twenty-four hours and our bellies were roaring! So after ditching the crusty hotel we found a diner across the street from the gorgeous ocean-view and ate a towering stack of hot cakes with "fresh" fruit and syrup I'd never encountered. Graham enjoyed it much more than I did.

After breakfast we agreed the impressive waves deserved our attention before we moved on so, with Modelo in hand, we sat on the beach and dug on the mid-morning sunlight pouring over the sparkling ocean waters. Satisfied with our beer-buzz we took to the highway and I drove for half an hour before pulling over to smoke the weed I had stuffed down my underwear. There were but three roaches and a chunk of bud left so Graham cut up a can and we smoked all of it; the perfect amount to get us just blazing. Then as we sped southbound and chain-smoked Pall Malls (Mexican cigarettes) in an effort to keep our highs afloat, the landscape began to turn lush and green. It's pretty much springtime year round in Mexico and on this particular day it was absolutely stunning, like the pictures you see on the sides of coffee bean packages. In the hot afternoon sun we stopped in Tepic and bought more beer (yes, there's a bit of a pattern to this trip). Barely out of town I finished my first drink when suddenly there appeared another army roadblock! I had just enough time to throw it out the driver's side window. Three soldiers armed with M-16s stood in my path as a fourth came up to my window. Graham was smart and played dumb, pretending he didn't understand a word of Spanish as I kept saying, "No habla Español! No habla Español!" The soldier put his fingers to his mouth as if smoking a joint and said, "Drogas? Morta?" (Drugs? Marijuana?) I shook my head intensely and laughed, "No, no; no stupido!" (No we're not stupid.) The soldier gave me a big smile and a thumbs-up then sent us on our way. *Phew*! Graham heaved a huge sigh of relief, "Yeah dude, all props!"

"I'm still pretty baked man, that was intense!" I laughed nervously.

"We're gonna' have to start being real careful," Graham cautioned.

One hour down the road in the late afternoon we crossed a small stone bridge and found ourselves stuck in a little valley town behind a caravan of big rigs

101

and Volkswagens. For twenty minutes we sat without even budging until Graham finally said, "Okay, this could take hours. I'm going to go ask around and see what's up." So he jumped out of the Tercel and disappeared. I probably only advanced another thirty feet when Graham returned rejoicing, "I just talked to some pigs up there and they said today is the beginning of their ten day Fiesta de Independencia (Independence Day party)! The trucks are hauling in equipment and supplies for the fair! We've gotta' get a room man, there's gonna' be one hell of a party tonight!" So after a lengthy struggle to park the car down an alley we finally got out and rented a room for eighty pesos. The hotel was clean and had a cozy feel with lime-green walls and large windows that let the sunlight fill the rooms. We threw our stuff on the beds, discovered the toilet was broken, fixed it, then hit the streets at dusk.

WHAT A PARTY!!! I had never seen anything like it in all my life! The entire village was out to get ripped and the streets were ablaze with celebration. We made our way up a couple blocks to the center of town and couldn't believe our eyes. The entire plaza was packed with hundreds of merry, riotous Mexicans! All the girls looked gorgeous, every guy whooped and hollered in falsetto with their tongues flapping against the roof of their mouths, "Ailelelelelele!" And everybody had a beer in hand. Mariachi bands and marching bands and even mariachi-marching bands whaled in every corner of the village, beating bass drums and snare drums, blowing trumpets and plucking guitars and acoustic basses. Folks of all ages danced and jumped and screamed. The younger crowd rode on fair rides and ate cotton candy and hotdogs and *tortas*, while the older folk got drunk and made fun of each other at the games tables and bars. And literally every fifty feet you could stop at an umbrella cart and buy a Corona. They'd crack it open for you, scrape a chunk of salt over the opening then squeeze lime inside, turning the cheap beer into a delicacy! We drank and walked and dug, and drank and walked and dug. We drank at every stand and whirled around with our jaws to the floor in amazement.

"These are my people man!" I sang.

"Oh yeah dude, this is too much! We've got to stay another day at least! Look at that!" We kept turning, and reeling, and grabbing each other excitedly and pulling one another to look at different rides and people and bands and lights and colored lanterns and piñatas and firecrackers. It was heaven. All the girls wanted us and all the guys wanted to be our friends and drink with us. Los Mochis had been a harsh, evil city of whores and bums, but Ixtlán del Rio was a friendly farming village of good, hard working people wanting a good time. I can't relate everything from those first few hours, mostly a lot of eating and drinking and shaking hands and smiling. At one point we were surrounded by six little cuties and Graham was managing to have a conversation with them while I stood there sucking on my beer. Now I was really wishing I spoke Spanish and I started to feel kind of stupid. He translated for the prettiest girl and she asked why I was so quiet. *Damn* I thought. I could have done anything I wanted but I couldn't even tell her she was beautiful.

Graham kept talking with the girls and I ran over to a grocery to buy more smokes, when suddenly two cops rushed past me and dove on a guy trying to get away with a poster he had lifted. Of all things, they beat the crap out of him right there in front of half the town just for stealing a poster! I couldn't imagine seeing anything like that at home.

When I found Graham he was talking to this good-looking kid in a blue baseball-cap named "José." He was probably about seventeen and seemed like the sweetest most contented little Mexican in Ixtlán. He shook my hand vigorously as if I was a celebrity then led us through the mob of merry-makers to a shadowed, cobble-stoned alley where some of his buddies were lighting off firecrackers and having a hoot. They greeted us like old friends and gave us high-fives wearing giant grins. You could tell that the four of them had been tight friends for years, like Graham and I were with our crew when we were in high school. They took off their hats and introduced themselves. There was Ivano in the white ball-cap, a wormy little guy with a runty face but a warm smile; Alex with the slicked hair, the tallest and oldest of the bunch who was jovial on the outside but kept a deep sorrow behind his dark-brown eyes; and a shiny little fat kid whose name eludes me. We just called him Smiley because he was so pudgy and grinned like the Cheshire Cat. The six of us, all good and drunk, had a nice long pee on the wall then went back to the plaza to fill up for more. Graham asked if they knew where we could score some *morta* and Ivano got real serious for a second. Speaking in Spanish only and using his hands he explained that it's real dangerous to carry dope in Mexico, but said that if we really wanted some they knew a guy from Los Angeles who could hook us up. So we were introduced to Pepé behind the tilt-a-whirl and he told us he'd be back in half an hour. While we waited amongst the festooned piñatas and colorful rides two things happened: first a group of cops tore through the crowd frisking everybody in the square for drugs. A couple of people got beaten with sticks and a couple more got hauled off to jail just for refusing to cooperate. I thanked God we weren't holding anything...yet. Second, I saw the strangest, most exotically beautiful *señorita* I'd ever seen operating one of the rides. Something about her was incredibly mysterious; this traveled, streetwise air about her that made it clear she was traveling with the fair. She looked almost like a sleek, graceful bobcat with both strength and mad sex appeal. Her glistening emerald eyes and dirty blonde hair suggested that one of her parents had been white. When she looked at me I immediately thought, *Wow, she could teach me a few lessons*! I was under her spell and couldn't pull away from her gaze—it was almost frightening. I wanted to go talk to her, language barrier or not, but there was something in the warm breeze that felt off, something foreboding. She kept staring at me, beckoning me to come over. Her eyes pierced right though my being and at that moment I felt for the first time that my soul wasn't nearly as weathered or as dark, or even as powerful as I thought it was all my growing up years. This was witchcraft. I was so frightened of this girl yet I wanted her so bad, to discover what alluring poisons she might have in store for my lusts and desires. Graham suddenly patted my shoulder, "Dude, this guys' not gonna' show. Let's get out of here before the cops come this way."

I felt really strange. Super-drunk, exhilarated, and anxious—anxious like when I was twelve and my bowels would do weird things. Graham tried to drag me off to a discothèque where José and the *muchachos* wanted to introduce us to some girls, but I had to go to the bathroom so badly I ran back to the hotel and locked myself in the can. Afterwards, I didn't feel much like trying to find everybody; besides, the hotel had a curfew at midnight when they locked the gates to keep out thieves. So I lay in bed and had a smoke. Every time I closed my eyes I saw my sorceress. Her image was burned into the fuzzy lightning behind my eyelids. I breathed deeply and tried to think about anything else, but every bone in my body wanted to go back to the fair to find her.

Graham came back with a couple of beers just before twelve and told me he had made arrangements to score some weed the next night. Both of us were bombed and passed out to the distant sound of drunken Mexicans whooping in the streets.

CHAPTER 17
The Love Of Mexico

Saturday, September 11, 1999

I woke up dead tired. Graham made himself get out of bed saying, "It wouldn't be right to skip breakfast on our first morning in Ixtlán." So he dragged himself downstairs and found a place to eat. When he returned I was still asleep dreaming of witches and shadows, so he went back to bed too. Around twelve thirty in the afternoon we made ourselves get up for lunch. I suggested hamburgers and fries and Graham started again with a sermon: "We can't eat North American food man, we're in Mexico so we have to eat Mexican to fully experience the culture!" to which I responded, "Well, I wanna' fully experience a burger with fries in Mexico!" I loved the *tortas* and tacos, but it was all we'd eaten in four days and I needed a taste of home. Graham begrudgingly followed me into a little diner and we ate dry burgers with soggy fries.

107

As we stepped back out into the street a middle-aged Mexican of average height and average build (apart from his beer belly) came bursting out of a cantina wearing glasses and a bright red flower which stuck out of his white dress-shirt pocket. He stormed down the stone steps towards us shouting, "Ola amigos! Hello American friends! I love America!" He shook our hands and put his arms around us as we explained that we were from Canada.

"Si? Canada? Que bien! I have been everywhere! I traveled all of America, all of Europe, never before Canada! Que bien! You let me show you Mexico! 'Dis is *my* Mexico; Mexico is beautiful! Come, come! First cervezas!" We followed him up the street to another cantina and he told us, "I am Gerardo but everyone call me *El Amor* because *I* am 'de love of Mexico! I love Mexico, and Mexico loves me!" He kept smelling his little red flower then stuffing it back inside his pocket.

At the cantina there were only two *muchachos* sitting at opposite ends of the bar stewing in their depression and tequila. One of them looked over like he wanted to kill us for even entering his private bar. The other one slapped the bar right in front of the bartender and gave a loud bellow. The bartender snickered at all three of us and asked in an annoyed tone what we wanted to drink. We each slammed a Modelo then Gerardo ordered us three more and said, "Is fiesta time! Is just starting! I drank all day and all night no sleep, still we drink mucha cervezas!" Buddy was ripped and I mean *R-I-P-P-E-D*! We were there no more than three minutes before he hauled us back out onto the street to buy a six-pack from the adjacent market. With six-pack in hand he waved down a taxi and said, "Come, come, I show you Mexico!" I paused and said, "Oh man, we can't afford a cab; poquito dinero man, we're on a budget."

"No worry; is okay, I know him!" So we climbed in the back and slurped beers as the indifferent driver whizzed us out of town and up a small green mountain overlooking the town. It was, as Gerardo proclaimed over and over again, simply beautiful. I already used my coffee bean package simile so I'll just let him take it from here:

"'Dis is Mexico, Mexico is beautiful, see amigos, I told you... 'Dis is Mexico," and he waved his hands around like Vanna White, pointing at the lush vegetation and vast green slopes dipping into the surreal valley of Ixtlán. It took a lot of effort to convince "El Amor" that we were blown away by the valley's splendor. We told him repeatedly, "Wow man! Holy shit! This *is* Mexico! It's gorgeous El Amor, gorgeous!" He made us take pictures of him with our arms around him then led us back down the other side of the mountain by foot, all the while waving and whispering, "'Dis is Mexico, 'dis...is...Mexico..." At the bottom of the hill the cab was waiting for us and took us back into town. The cabbie asked for two hundred and fifty pesos and Gerardo didn't have it. Graham wasn't carrying enough cash so I swore out loud and had to pay: *'Dis is Mexico.*

Our six-pack was dead so Gerardo dragged us inside the first cantina he saw. The second we walked in twenty men raised their cans and yelled, "EL AMOR! HEY! HEY!" Graham and I were beginning to gather that El Amor was the town drunk. He made us sit down in the middle of the madness and ordered more beers saying, "See? See? 'Dis is Mexico. 'Dese are my amigos! Everyone loves El Amor!" He started talking more in Spanish and even Graham could barely understand what he was ranting about. First he was telling all the *muchachos* not to worry because we weren't gringos but Canadians, then he mumbled something about being the future mayor of Ixtlán like his grandfather and picked up my half full beer can and threw it to the ground saying, "No, no, 'dis is Mexico! In Mexico mis amigos drink full cervezas!" Of course now I was paying for the beer. When Graham put his can down on the table El Amor batted it with the back of his hand half way across the room and the bartender, friend or not, flipped his lid and kicked us out.

    Curious to see what our new loony friend would do next, we followed El Amor to two more bars and made sure not to set our drinks down, after which he insisted we visit the church. I felt kind of bad being drunk in a holy place with such a letch of a man. Inside he started muttering the craziest nonsense and wrapped his arm around Graham and sniffed his flower over and over again: "'Dis is beautiful, *my* Mexico..." Graham turned to me wide eyed and whispered, "Dude, this guy's completely loco, it's time to ditch!" So we told him how beautiful the church was and said we had to go get some pictures developed.

He plopped his beer down right next to the Virgin of Guadalupe and said, "Come, come, I know 'de best place, come." He made us buy another six-pack next door, threw his arm around me with a new beer in hand and led us to the photo shop. Inside he lost his balance and spilled beer all over the floor in front of the display case. The poor lady running the shop stood up and said in Spanish, "Please, get your friend out of here!" I made El Amor follow me to the market to buy cigarettes and Graham finished filling out the photo-return forms. I could tell El Amor had no intention of leaving us alone, so I told him we were meeting friends for dinner.

"Muy bien! I know 'de best restaurante!" he exclaimed.

"Sorry El Amor," I said gently, "we already have plans, but don't worry; we'll see you tonight in the plaza!"

"Promise? I have more to show you!"

Graham lit a smoke and said convincingly, "Of course El Amor, you're our new amigo!"

"Okay amigos, see you at 'de fiesta!" And off he stumbled. He must have crashed hard before the evening's party even got underway because we didn't see him again. It was a sweet relief to finally be rid of Gerardo; you never know what these kinds of people are going to get you mixed up in—we'd find that out soon enough.

Graham decided we needed to find a good spot to kick the sack. In a quiet corner behind a grocery two little kids saw us lighting our cigarettes and asked

111

us to light their sparklers. Then they danced around us waving their fiery wands as we spun and hopped and glided around the hackey-sack like we were in some third-world street ballet. It was mid-day and we were already drunk, so after the sparklers burnt out Graham said he wanted a nap before the fiesta broke out. We hacked our way back to the hotel and Graham slept while I wrote about The Love of Mexico.

Sometime after six Graham came to and we found a restaurant. Now if you've never tried *real* salsa *verdi* you haven't lived yet! This spicy green salsa smothered over *real* Mexican beef in a *real* corn tortilla was the limit! There was going to be a lot more drinking that night so we made sure to fill our bellies. After trying to dig on the soccer game on the television with the other patrons we hit the now swelling streets at dusk and started in on the salt, lime and beers. Two drinks in we caught sight of Ivano with his white ball-cap and he ran to greet us with the same warm smile. We headed to the plaza to meet the rest of the crew before going to the pick-up spot to get our weed. There was José, Alex and Smiley with two other *muchachos*. We all high-fived and shook hands tightly then gathered around a table under the marquis. Alex pointed out the drummers in a passing marching band and said, "They okay," then pointed to his self with a thumbs-up and started to drum in the air.

"Buenos!" I said. "I play too!" We laughed and started beating along with the band on the table. Graham was so fantastic. He managed to carry on a confusing conversation with Ivano and José and still translated the key words for Alex and me. After half an hour of difficult but worthwhile conversation we figured out that Alex and I had both lost girls to other drummers in the same month! It was wonderful, our worlds coming together there in the middle of that gigantic frenzied fiesta. We toasted to each other's pain and squeezed hands tightly and taught each other to swear.

"Puto!" he said and spat.

"Fuck!" I yelled banging the table. We took turns cursing in each other's language and agreed that women are all evil. At that instant, I kid you not, the green-eyed sorceress I had been bewitched by the night before floated by our table and kept her enchanting gaze fixed on my soul. I became hot and cold at the same time and shivered with intoxication. Graham looked her up and down and said, "Dude, follow her!" I couldn't. It was like I was tied to the chair, probably by my guardian angel. The *muchachos* didn't even seem to notice; they were too caught up in the bizarre travels of two tall white Canadian stoners. I shook my head and chugged the rest of my beer so I had an excuse to get another. Graham followed suit, as it was almost time to meet our contact. The eight of us rambled over to the spot, all the while struggling to understand one another. We entered a large bar intended for the younger crowd. It was built like a classic saloon but with twice the space and a jukebox playing. We sat in the only available table in the center of the room and carried on our conversation. Periodically, another *muchacho* would come in and give us an update as to the whereabouts of our *"morta"*. At that point there were seven young guys all trying to help us score. It was exceedingly unorthodox, but they so desperately wanted to help us out.

Meanwhile, the conversation between Ivano and Alex started to get heavy. I knew they were still talking about old girlfriends but everything was in full-throttle Spanish now. Both of them hung their heads low and started to tear up. Graham looked over at me and whispered; "I don't know what I'm supposed to say to them right now."

"What are they talking about?" I asked.

"*Both* of their girlfriends had abortions, against their will..." I turned to them wide-eyed and said, "What? Oh man...Lo siento (sorry)," and put my hand on Alex's shoulder. They seemed so moved to be able to share such secrets with people from a first-world country, like it meant more when we heard them than even their priest. What were we supposed to do? A few awkward seconds dragged by as we sat there uncomfortably longing for a way to give them peace. I prayed silently under my breath and Graham whispered to me, "This just got really weird man, any suggestions?" I looked over at the jukebox and motioned for Alex to come with me. He wiped his eyes and followed. Together we looked over the list of songs and Alex pointed out the ones he loved. The only thing I recognized was *The Bee Gees* and *Ace of Base*. Ouch. At least they had *Night Fever*, and it was Saturday night, so I popped in my peso and let the disco roll.

Sinning Man's Heaven

It took another half-hour while the *muchachos* ran in and out of the bar, until finally a ninth kid arrived and whispered in Ivano's ear. Ivano asked us for eighty pesos and strutted casually out the door with it. He came back in, sat down real close to us to block anyone's view and unfolded a balled up map of southern Mexico to reveal a huge clump of dry Ixtlán dope. Graham rolled it up, stuck it down his underwear and whispered, "Holy shit, that's like half an ounce for eight bucks!"

"And just think," I laughed, "it only took two hours and nine guys!"

The eleven of us left the bar and most of the *muchachos* disappeared into the crowd. Alex shook my hand in farewell and said he had to get home. I was sad to see him go, though at this point all I cared about was Graham's shorts. Ivano, José and Smiley stayed behind and we invited them to come back to the hotel to get high. They were such great kids. They didn't want to get high at all but came back to our room to show us the safest place to hide it. I found the whole thing rather absurd but Graham took them very seriously, like at any moment the cops would burst into the hotel. Ivano kept doing laps of the room looking under every nook and cranny while José nodded in approval and agreed, "Si, si," over and over again. Smiley just stood there shining and smiling, thrilled to just be a part of everything. When Graham and Ivano finally agreed on a hole in the mattress they all cautiously crept from the room as if it was now off limits. I was getting annoyed. It was 11:00 p.m. and no one was in the building. I wanted to sit by the window in our bathroom and smoke a joint but the *muchachos* insisted we lay low in the plaza for a while, so I begrudgingly followed Graham and the kids back to the square. On the way, Graham—now quite loaded—accidentally bumped into a big angry *hombre* who threatened to kick his ass if he saw him again. Smiley said he'd fight for us, cute little Smiley. Jose and Ivano clenched their fists and said in Spanish, "Yeah, don't worry, we've got your backs!" Graham told me what they said in amazement and said, "Man, these kids are so awesome!"

In the plaza José disappeared then returned with three young girls he wanted us to meet. They stood there like dogs in show and Ivano said in Spanish, "Do you want any of them?" We both shook our heads; it was embarrassing. The fatter, meanest looking of the girls curled her lip at us and stormed away. José took off, probably to find more girls, and Ivano and Graham communicated by sign language at a table. I just sat there drinking shots of tequila waiting to get back to our dope. Everyone around us was whooping and shouting and Ivano did the same then pointed at me.

"Mark, he wants you to try," Graham said. So I cocked my head back and, using my falsetto, yelled strong and true in the direction of a little cutie trotting by: "Ailelelelelele!" Ivano yipped and laughed and clapped his hands together, "Que bien! Si! Si! Hahaha!"

Graham stoked, "Yeah dude, nice pipes!" I felt

cool for all of three seconds until my mind turned back to the green.

Graham checked his watch, "Damn, we gotta' get back to the hotel before curfew!" It was time to say goodbye to our dear friends knowing full well we'd never see them again. In the morning we'd be on our way to Guadalajara. We thanked our gracious hosts then bolted to buy smokes and hotdogs before the hotel gates were locked.

In our room I jumped excitedly onto the mattress to find the weed. Graham tried to stop me: "Let's just go to sleep man, we've had lots to drink."

"What?" I protested. "You can't be serious! We've been waiting two days to get high and now we've hit the mother load! What the hell, go to sleep?"

Graham said, "I don't wanna' get busted here man. Those kids were scared to death of even being around weed!"

I argued, "That's 'cause there's a big party with cops raiding the crowds out there! What, you think they're gonna' come in a hotel past midnight and search every room? The gates are locked dude!"

"Yeah, but the owner, or someone in another room could smell it and—"

"And what? Turn us in? Yeah right Graham. *Nobody'll* even catch a whiff if we smoke it out the window and you know it. What's up with you? I'm usually the paranoid one. I don't wanna' get caught either but there's no way it's gonna' happen, okay?"

He yawned, "I just think we should save it for tomorrow."

I couldn't believe it! This was not the Graham I knew. I paid him no mind. "Sorry bro, I'm going to roll a fatty; you can join me if you want." I unfolded the map and sniffed the dry weed. It was leafy and bunk, more like actual weeds than the fat buds we smoked back home, but it was drugs—cheap drugs in abundance. I pulled out my scissors and performed the ritual. In the bathroom I swung the window wide open and sparked my jay. Man it smelled good, especially because somebody didn't want me to have it, which didn't last long. Graham smelled the sweet aroma and couldn't bear it any longer. He came in the bathroom and said, "Well obviously I have to hit it now." *Obviously.* We huffed it back in all its majesty and I even made him smoke the roach. But just to give you an example of Graham's fickle nature, the following night in Guadalajara he was snorting lines of cocaine off the bed in our new hotel room.

CHAPTER 18
Coke

Sunday, September 12, 1999

Despite getting smashed the night before, we both woke up feeling refreshed after a delicious sleep and packed up to say farewell to Ixtlán. As we drove out of town I kept my eyes peeled for one last glance of my sorceress. She wasn't there.

The drive to Guadalajara was gorgeous, with long yellow-green grasses and gnarled trees blanketing the rolling hills of Jalisco. Of course we were thoroughly baked and listening to Antônio Carlos Jobim, which made it all the more serene. I hardly even remember passing through yet another army drug check with half an ounce stuffed between my legs. It seemed so easy.

It didn't take long to get lost in Guadalajara. It's the second largest city in Mexico and it was more than overwhelming in our condition. Sometime that afternoon we found a taco stand run by a family who claimed to have the greatest secret recipe. On my word, those tacos were without rival! The old woman explained to Graham that they soaked their lamb meat in Tequila then buried it under ground to marinate before cooking.

After our delectable late lunch we tried to find Philippe's house but couldn't make sense of the map; Guadalajara was a maze. After two frustrating hours we finally found it and no one was home. I wasn't too interested in staying at Philippe's parent's house anyway, what with the desire to have a room we could smoke and drink in, so we consulted our Lonely Planet for the most agreeable hotel and I drove us to the heart of the city. It was madness. The dirty streets of downtown Guadalajara are a frightening place, one of those dungy whore-infested crack-dealer-ridden third-world cities plagued by hustlers and bums that you see in foreign films on *Showcase* late at night. We were fixin' to have a hell of a time...

To our dismay the "Hotel Hamilton" was full up. It had the best rates for the most decent rooms, the ideal place for us to shack up for our three-day visit. The pretty *señorita* at the desk told us to please try again the next day. So we undertook a strenuous search and all we could find were disgusting brothels and ritzy suites for rich tourists. The last place we came across was called "Hotel Reno" and it had to do. It was the same price as "Hotel Hamilton" but the rooms were appalling. Wallpaper hung from the walls in shreds and all the bedding was stained. The odd cockroach would crawl by but we were getting used to those. I brought our sleeping bags up to cover the beds and Graham parked the car on the street behind the building. When he came back up with our bags he said, "The manager lady is pretty nice, or completely indifferent. She says we can do whatever we want so long as we don't make *too* much noise!"

I immediately rolled some *doobs* and we explored the ugly four-story building up and down. The room above ours was vacant and unlocked so we made it our little playground for an hour or so. With no one below we were free to romp around in all disregard, drinking, smoking, and kicking the sack off the walls. The maid heard us messing about and opened the door for a quick glance then shook her head back and forth with a cynical grin.

When it got dark we both did a little writing back in our room then went out to buy more supplies. Down the street there was a little hole in the wall with iron bars where they sold liquor, so we bought two six-packs of Tecate. On the way back we were relieved to find that our hotel's bar was just a regular bar and grill. Still, the owner wanted to make sure we enjoyed our stay and said we could take the waitress upstairs. She was entirely indifferent when we declined and ordered the chicken instead. After eating the owner asked if we wanted any cocaine. I said no thanks and Graham said, "Why not? We came here to try new things right?"

"Don't bring that on us man," I said. "I just know something bad is gonna' happen if you do!"

The owner insisted, "Is good, real good señor!"

Graham smacked his lips, "Yeah, I'll try some," then followed him behind the curtain. When they were done the transaction Graham ran upstairs to divvy up some lines. I went back to the car to get my headphones and my smaller case of tapes, the one I kept all my mix-tapes from friends in. When I got back to the room Graham had already snorted a bunch and was cutting more with his bankcard. I sparked a jay and looked on disapprovingly.

"Man," he said rubbing his nose and licking his teeth, "this shit's good! I gotta' get more! There's three lines left there for you," and he handed me the rolled up dollar bill then ran out the door. I couldn't believe it; Guadalajara had suddenly possessed Graham. The stuff scared me to death. I'd done every drug under the sun except cocaine, crystal meth and heroine because I had such addictive tendencies that I knew they'd kill me. But those white lines lay on the bed and I wanted them, bad. I got down on my knees and drew closer thinking *this is it. This is the line I promised myself I'd never cross.* I put the rolled up bill to my nose and slowly bent over the bed. Then, as I was about to inhale, I felt an all too familiar presence. I jerked back, threw the dollar bill on the bed, and cracked open a beer instead. Graham walked back in.

"Aw, what the hell man? Why didn't you snort it?" he said bending over to do my lines. Then he diced up his new batch. "Are you going to make me do all this coke by myself?"

"You don't have to snort it all now," I said.

"I'm not carrying this shit around tomorrow! I'm surprised; I thought you'd be all over this!"

I refused, "Nope, can't do it. I promised myself I'd never go that far. I tried while you were gone... it was weird man. I could feel things battling over me, like when I got stuck up at Cowichan last month."

"Hey yeah, you mentioned something about that. Tell me a 'Marky-Mark-story' while I get blitzed!"

I went into it: "Okay, bear with me, this is kind of embarrassing. I had this fantasy of finding someplace where I could be completely alone under the night sky to trip on *E* by campfire and look at porn. I figured somewhere up on the logging roads behind Cowichan Lake was the best bet."

"Dude man, that's some elaborate jerking off!"

"I know; it's pathetic. You know I want to wait 'til I'm married, but I'm so horny dude! I'm always thinking of the next best thing."

"But you already did it!" he smirked.

"Yeah, for barely two minutes when I was sixteen! And then I felt so embarrassed and guilty. Don't get me started on Vanessa or we'll be up all night... Then there was Kate two year back."

"Was she that hot Quebecois chick?"

"Yeah man. Did you know she broke up with me after I told her I wanted to wait? And she was crazy about me too. She was so fine; I almost wish I slept with her when I had the chance—"

"Dude you're drunk," Graham interrupted louder than usual from the coke, "you're supposed to be telling me about Cowichan!"

"Right. So I drove to the lake in the van and just kept going up the logging roads for another couple hours. I drove and drove and got totally lost, which I guess was the point, and almost made it all the way to Port Alberni driving through forest 'cause I had to be absolutely certain I was miles from anybody. Around eleven I found the perfect spot right in the middle of the forest. I ate my *E*, rolled some joints and built a fire. When the drugs kicked in, obviously, I felt incredible, and I put on *Zeppelin One* and started moving around the fire as one does on ecstasy. Everything was perfect, but when I pulled out a magazine I couldn't shake the feeling someone was watching me. Every time I'd get settled my heart would jump with paranoia and I'd have to go take a look around. Obviously no one was there, I mean, it was the middle of the night in the middle of nowhere! So I finally worked up the nerve, and I was so horny and feeling so good, then *How Many More Times* came on. You know how creepy that song is right?"

"Yeah dude," Graham said, now just reeling with his high.

"Well this horrible sense of dread, not paranoia, but pure evil just consumed me! I could feel it coming out of the ground trying to pull me in. I got really scared and it made everything even more enticing. I started to war with myself: 'C'mon Mark, you've spent all the money, you're here, let's do this!' Then another voice would say, 'No no! This is straight from hell. Pack up and leave now!' and on and on. Now, yes I was high, but I was all there man—it's not even a hallucinate drug! I started to actually see shadows come out of the fire and the dirt, and as they did, these huge shards of light started to fall from the sky and swing at the shadows, like huge radiant creatures soaring down from the stars with swords warding off these dark shapes. I was seeing this! Angels and demons warring over my mind, trying to lay claim to my soul! I freaked dude! I kicked out the fire, threw everything in the van, and I was outta' there!

Graham snorted a line, intently listening to my story and said, "That's insane dude! Total 'Marky-Mark-story.' Tell me another one."

"But wait; that's just the first half! I went back the next night!"

"Ha ha!" Graham laughed shaking his head. "Dude, you're messed!"

"I know! But I was so annoyed the next day for not enjoying myself the way I had imagined after all that effort, so I did everything again! I bought another cap of E, more weed, more smokes, more wine, and gassed up the van."

"Oh yeah!" Graham exclaimed. "Terry was asking about you. He told me he sold you E two days in a row but I told him not to worry 'cause you're just a regular-old-stoner."

Graham didn't know I had two other guys, aside from Terry, that I bought E and other goodies from on a regular basis, and here I was pretending like I was a saint for not doing coke.

But I continued, "Yeah, I just had to try again. I was so stubborn and horny I made myself forget all about the night before and drove back up. There was no way I was going back to the same haunted spot, so I drove even higher up the mountains past the logging roads. There was this perfect spot and I got out to set up, but a voice in my head said, 'Keep going, there's something better.' I had to be sure I had complete privacy so I got back in the van and kept going. I found another spot further down the other side of the mountain and thought *sweet*. So I got out and started setting up again. No joke, I felt that voice again, 'No, keep going, there's something better.' I got real excited and kept driving until I came to a trail with that orange surveying tape stretched across it. Dumb ass that I am I drove through it convinced something spectacular lay ahead. It was around 11:00 p.m. when suddenly the van jarred and came to a sudden stop with a thud. I was actually sober at this point too, and I had my eyes on the trail the whole time. Everything seemed normal so I stepped on the gas, but the van wouldn't budge. I figured it was a big pothole so I put her in reverse and stepped on the gas. Nothing! So I finally opened the driver-side door to take a look: I was hanging in mid-air and it was twenty feet down to the river!"

"What!" Graham exclaimed, now thoroughly engaged.

"Yup! That's where the voice was leading me, over the edge of a cliff so I could learn my lesson. The ground had fallen out from beneath my front-left-tire and the front bumper was just barely holding on to the other side. My front-right-tire was kissing the last

Sinning Man's Heaven

bit of earth still clinging to the road, and both my rear-tires were in the air. I could feel the van slowly sliding forward, trying to pull the last bit of dirt away so it could tumble to the left and fall the twenty feet with me inside. I punched the stick into park, kicked in the emergency brake and scrambled to the back of the van to shift its weight. Then I opened the trunk and luckily found a stack of rocks that had fallen from the cliff above, so I stretched my legs out and managed to roll a few over to lift inside. I had some rope but none of it was long enough to anchor to a tree so I packed in more rocks and prayed the earth would hold until morning."

Graham bellowed, "That's so classic dude! All props! So what did you do?"

"What was I supposed to do? I took my *E* and enjoyed myself without any more creatures of the night appearing. It was great 'til morning when I had to walk in the scorching sun for five hours all burnt-out, but some folks in a jeep finally picked me up. They got me back to Cowichan and I somehow managed to retrace my steps with the tow-truck guy. It was awesome though, he charged me ninety-seven dollars to pull it out and I had exactly ninety-seven bucks in my wallet!"

Graham snuffed, "You always come across the most random coincidences! What is that?"

I answered, "They're not coincidences man, its God, I'm telling you!"

"Maybe; I think I might have changed my mind about being an atheist. There has to be some all-powerful being pulling the strings up there. I'm not turning back to Christianity just yet, but there are definitely some intense forces at work. I don't know about angels and demons like you saw; everybody interprets experiences in different ways—"

"Interpret nothing man! I friggin' *saw* angels swooping down on me from the sky and demons trying to pull me under!"

He laughed, "You were on drugs dude!"

"What about just a few nights ago?" I argued. "We both woke up shaking on Devil's Pass right? That was no coincidence!"

"Who knows what that was? It was the middle of the night and we were both hosed!"

"C'mon Graham, you can't possibly pass it off like that!"

He reasoned, "Don't you find it a little strange that all this shit happens when you're high?"

"Trust me, I saw crazy stuff like that way before I even started doing drugs! Like the stuff I was telling you on the way to Ixtlán. Lot's of people have had supernatural experiences. There's so much out there we can't explain!"

"I'm not arguing that! There are millions of unsolved mysteries we can't account for, but to say there's *one* truth to it all is just naïve isn't it? Like you said, there's so much out there! How can you subscribe to just one idea?"

I was at a loss. The boys asked me this question all the time. But there's no tangible answer you can give someone who refuses to believe that there can only be one way things came to be. I lit a smoke and said, "Look dude, we're all born of woman, we all breathe, we all need to eat and drink, and we all encounter things we think we can't explain. I'm telling you, it all came from *one* place bro. There can only be *one* beginning, and there's only *one* truth whether we follow it or not. Everything is tied together and whatever happens, happens for a reason."

While Graham and I continued debating in our smoky hotel room, someone broke into our car.

CHAPTER 19
Gilbert

Monday, September 13, 1999

A small mob pointed and laughed at us back on the streets that morning. It seemed they had gathered to see our faces as we discovered that their friends had smashed in our passenger-side window and taken all our stuff. Graham said, "Don't say this is because I did coke last night." My ghetto blaster and fifty plus tapes were gone. My bag of batteries and my favorite sunglasses were gone. Some of Graham's clothes were missing and a little emergency money he had stashed in the glove box. Graham chuckled nervously, "Awesome, everyone gets to laugh at the stupid white kids who left their car in the street overnight. Shit…"

I swore in unison, "Shit! My tapes man! All that great music…" Almost instantaneously four policemen on bicycles appeared from behind the corner of the hotel and rode over. Graham whispered, "Dude, don't tell them anything is missing okay?"

"Why? I want my shit back!"

Graham was way ahead of me; I was straight up mad but he knew what the score was and replied, "Because I don't want to hang around to fill out police-reports! Our stuff is history dude, and they're probably the ones who did it!"

This was very likely. It felt like everyone on the block knew it too. Someone had even been kind enough to tie Graham's blanket around where the window used to be and all four cops denied doing it. Only one of them spoke decent English and he asked a bunch of jumbled questions as the other three tried to look professional while whispering to each other. I was so pissed off I didn't speak a word while Graham kept shaking his head saying, "No, everything's fine thanks, nothing is missing, no, no, we don't care, it's all good thanks, nothing is missing, thank you, we have to go..." They finally wished us good day and rode back the way they came. We hopped in our sad little car and tore out of the neighborhood to find a more private spot where we could clean out all the broken glass. Ten blocks up next to a public garbage can we performed the tedious task and cut up our fingers while drinking Tecate from the adjacent store. Graham fumed, "This blows! I don't even wanna' bother trying to replace the window. Let's just leave it; we came to chill with Philippe."

"I don't know dude," I contended. "Can we drive

through all of Mexico without a window? There's gonna' be rain forests and crazy people and…"

He cut me off, "Let's just get another room and worry about it later." So we went back to our first choice, "Hotel Hamilton," and were lucky enough to find a vacancy. Before that though, as we parked in the street beside the hotel, a tall, well built middle-aged Mexican washing a row of taxis strolled over and said, "Hola mis amigos, you should let me look at your brakes, 'dey don't sound too good!" He introduced himself as Gilbert and said he ran the car-washing racket in the neighborhood. We talked with him a bit and he also said he could get the window replaced for cheap. Graham decided we should trust him. I whispered in his ear, "This is just some guy off the street! I don't think there's anything wrong with the brakes."

"Dude, neither of us knows anything about cars and I don't wanna' crash *yet*!"

"Exactly!" I said. Gilbert raised his hands and took control of the situation, as I presumed he had countless times before.

"Don't worry amigo, you can trust me! I take good care of you and make sure your car is safe, okay? Come see me in an hour and I be done washing."

So Graham and I went and smoked a nice fat bowl in our new room, which was much nicer than "Hotel Reno." The hotel was run by two pretty *señoritas* in their late twenties and owned by their father. The spacious yellow rooms were clean and the large windows made for a decent view of the streets below.

Sinning Man's Heaven

An hour flew by and Graham left to meet Gilbert despite my protests saying, "No, you were right before; we can't keep driving in this place without a window. Don't worry man, it's my car."

Gilbert took Graham to the other side of town and introduced him to some shady characters in a dumpy little garage that informed him Toyotas barely exists in Mexico, and in order to replace the window they'd have to make it themselves. They made him pay up front then took the driver's side window out and traced it on a piece of cardboard for the measurements and said it would be ready in seven days. Graham was not happy about this; he wanted to leave in three, but Gilbert insisted.

Afterwards, Gilbert took him to a strip-club and made him buy dinner. On the way there some creepy *muchacho* threatened Graham, so Gilbert knocked him out with one punch. The guy lay there twitching as they entered the club. While they ate, Gilbert talked about his wife and son, then he left for the night with a hooker. Graham drove back to the hotel mystified and educated thinking "'*dis is Mexico.*"

Meanwhile, I took a walk around the block and bought some smokes. What a sleazy neighborhood! I had never imagined myself hanging in a place like this. When I got back to the hotel there was a tall good-looking blonde guy about my age getting a room. I heard him speaking in English so I introduced myself. He turned with a casual smile and said in an Australian accent, "G'day mate, I'm Miguel. Good ta' meet cha'!"

"Hey Miguel, I'm Mark. You wanna' come up and smoke a joint?"

"Awe, ye, that'd be great! I was gonna' have a nap and that would be just beauty to knock me out!"

We shared travel stories and got nicely baked. Before he retired to his room we agreed to meet for dinner.

Around 6:00 p.m. Graham got back and told me about the garage, the fight, and the strip-club. When he said it would take six days to get the car fixed I startled, "Six days stuck here? Jeez. Maybe we should just forget about it like you said."

"I already gave them the money. Besides, this place is crazy man! We can party hard and hang with Philippe a bunch while we wait." He had a good point. I warmed up to the idea of getting bombed in the city for a week and told him about Miguel and, Graham being Graham, he was game for a second dinner.

I could tell Miguel didn't smoke up too often because when we got him from his room he looked exhausted. But we got him outside and the three of us strutted down the streets checking out the girls and the food. First we ate some tacos none of us had tried yet: cow tongue (I think it was cow) and cow brains. The tongue was kind of creepy, I mean it was an actual fat juicy tongue ripped out of some animal's mouth, fried up and slapped on a tortilla! And the brains reminded me of *Night of the Living Dead*. But they were both surprisingly tasty, especially the tongue, which was a lot like tenderloin.

We spent the rest of the night at a swanky jazz bar

drinking and chatting. Miguel was cool enough but Graham and I agreed afterwards just a little shy of interesting. His head was screwed on tightly though, and he had a solid view on people and the places he'd traveled. I found myself thinking that Graham and I both came off a little jaded because he nodded his head a lot without responding.

After a while I just tuned Miguel and Graham out and had to give the band their due. Their take on *Footprints* stoked me out. When they were done their set I had to go over and praise the drummer.

Later that night we returned to the hotel with a twelve-pack of Tecate. Graham rolled some joints and we laid around our room talking about the U.S. Even Miguel couldn't help but be a little jaded about Americans. You have to understand, Canada, Australia, and the U.S. are the three largest English speaking countries in the world and sometimes you can't help but feel like the U.S. is the big bully brother who tends to forget about his younger siblings. Miguel loved our stories about the hicks we met cruising south. He laughed out loud when I told him we were asked four times if we lived in igloos, and even louder when Graham said we were asked, "You gotta' gun?" four times. In the end we agreed we all loved Americans but wished they had a broader education system. Miguel went back to bed fried as anything, obviously not the elemental veteran Graham and I were. I sparked another *doob* and wheezed, "Well, here's to Guadalajara and a hell of a start to the week."

"Yeah dude," Graham raised his beer. "Amen."

CHAPTER 20
The Ghosts of Guadalajara

Tuesday, September 14, 1999

Graham retrieved the Tercel from the lock and pay parking lot across the street that morning and met up with Gilbert to "tune the engine." Gilbert took him to a dumpy diner and made him buy breakfast. It almost made him sick: a cow's hip with bone marrow floating in boiled goat milk. After "breakfast" they went to a garage and Gilbert fiddled around under the hood and said in Spanish, "It'll run smoother now."

Graham came back around noon and woke me up for lunch. We went for tripe tacos (much tastier than it sounds with salsa *verdi* on it) then bought some pens in a corner store. Back at the hotel we got baked and Graham went down stairs to kick the hack. I was super mellow and a touch hung-over, so I laid on the bed listening to mix-tapes and passed out. I awoke to a sudden quiet madness: Graham whisked in the room with a skinny little Mexican who hardly noticed me sit up as he looked around doggedly and grabbed the big mirror from off the wall, threw it on Graham's bed, and started dicing cocaine on it. Graham rolled up a bill, inhaled a couple lines then handed it to his new hyperactive friend. He snorted his share in mere seconds and handed me the tube. No one had spoken a word. I took the tube without hesitation, bent over the bed and had my first-ever lines of coke without even thinking. "Is there more?" I asked. My angels must have been on a bathroom break.

"No," Graham said. "This is Mike." I felt a slight rush of synthesized vigor course through my skull as I introduced myself. Mike shook my hand and said, "Ola." He was short and skinny as any hobo, with tight sinewy muscles and glazed red eyes that spoke of incomprehensible strife and weathered, cursed years of uncertainty. His red ball cap, green button-up shirt and blue jeans were ratty and smelled like the desecrated sidewalks, and when he blinked I noticed two small fish tattooed on his eyelids. I had no idea we were about to become such good friends.

The three of us hit the streets so Graham could talk to Gilbert, and Mike and I could find more coke. Mike and a few of the other street folk washed taxis for Gilbert so they could earn his protection and buy food and drugs. They all had nasty coke habits and there was always a bottle of tequila on hand. Mike introduced us to everybody and Gilbert told me to go buy some beer. I bought a twelve-pack and we all sat around the Tercel and drank while Graham and

Gilbert talked business. I was pretty sure Gilbert was playing us, trying to make up reasons why we needed him so he could keep milking us for meals and beer for his friends. Graham even said it that night, but we were stuck there and needed protection. There were all sorts of crazies running around and we knew we needed to join a family, so that afternoon Graham and I bonded with the gang. There was Gilbert (The Godfather), Mike (the right hand man), a tall skinny kid named José with a little white mutt-of-a-dog (we called him Monkey Boy because he had enormous eyeballs and ape-like limbs), an oddly well-dressed kid named Tony with shifty eyes and a goatee, a cute little fourteen year-old girl named Juana who dressed like a boy to keep her parents from finding her, and a few other *muchachos* who just sat around drinking all day.

Mike's English was scant but good enough that we could almost follow each other. I sat in the back of a cab with Monkey Boy and Mike sat in the front with Graham while Gilbert went to use a phone. We got to talking about the drugs we had tried and Mike said, "De guy give me de, de PCP in de cigarette, you know? And, I try, and, nothing happen! But time go and, I sit on de street and dis car, was der, and den it was mucho poquito you know? Mucho mucho poquito," and he held his fingers close together. He was trying to tell us that he once smoked PCP and when it kicked in, a car shrunk to the size of a pea right before his very eyes.

Gilbert came back and told Graham he had a friend across town that would charge us much less to keep the Tercel in his lock-lot. Since we wouldn't really need the car until we left town Graham agreed and, despite my protests, let Gilbert take the car to fix the brakes and store it at his friend's. Mike said not to worry and told me to meet him in the plaza in thirty minutes to buy more coke, then tucked his head into his chest and speed-walked down the street to take care of some other business.

Graham and I moseyed back to the hotel and saw a big old *Yamaha YZ 450* dirt bike parked out front. Inside there was a young, dark-haired white guy who looked too small to ride it. He was trying to get a room, but the sister on shift, the one who kept flirting with Graham, told him there was no vacancy. He was about to leave when Graham said, "Hey, cool bike. How far did you ride from?"

"Canada," he said. "I rode around the States for a month and decided to just keep moving south."

"No way!" I exclaimed, "We're from B.C.!"

"No way! Me too! I came down from Pemberton!"

We couldn't believe it! You just don't expect to run into someone from home when you're getting wasted in the gutters. Graham said, "Crazy man! Well hey, you can bunk with us until a room opens up if you want."

"Aw, that'd be great, thanks. The other places around here are so shitty!" He introduced himself as Brendan and brought his bag up to our room. Now, usually travelers from B.C. are big potheads and love to reminisce about the sweet *crystally buds* back home, but Brendan wasn't that type. He was more of a *silky-boy*, with the nice clothes, the spiky hair and the straight-shooter facade. Still, he seemed pretty cool and was happy to smoke a joint with us. We talked about Mount Whistler where he said he worked as a ski instructor and made fat cash off the Japanese tourists.

    Before long half an hour had passed and I ran to find Mike in the busy plaza. I had no idea how to find him amongst the hundreds of people hustling and scurrying around, but I stuck out like a soar thumb amidst a crowd of short Mexicans. Mike grabbed my arm in the crowd and told me to give him fifty pesos. He took my money and disappeared. Five minutes later he gave me a tap and said, "Vaminos!" I followed him down two streets, a filthy alley, and into a dull-lit cantina. He asked the bartender (whom he obviously knew well) if he would watch the door for cops while we were in the bathroom then led me into a stall. Mike was a pro. In thirty seconds flat he taught me all about coke and how to do it fast and undetected. He asked, "Credit card?" and I gave him my bankcard. He wiped the back of the toilet with his sleeve, diced the rock with my card in three seconds flat and whispered, "Lick 'de card. Policia always look on card." This was serious business and Mike had getting high on the streets down to a fine art. We quickly snorted our lines and he shuffled over to the sink to stash the rest behind the plumbing. "Hey," I said, "I wanna' take that back to the hotel now."

    "No, no," he said, "We amigos! I get de coca and you share. We have more after cerveza, 'den you go." I was learning, my money for his connections.

We returned to the bar and I bought us each a beer. Mike educated me: "We put 'de coca in 'de baños because 'de policia come in cantina all 'de time! You be careful mang, mucho careful! Comprende?"

"Si, gracias mi amigo!" I thanked him for looking out for me. He went on to tell me about his times on the street and in prison. He said we had to be extra careful with our drugs because the *policia* would stick us behind bars for as long as they wanted if they caught us with anything suspicious. I didn't understand everything he said, but gathered that he had once lived in California with a wife and a son. She left him for a bigger man who kicked the crap out of him when he tried to bring her back home. After that he said he was dead to the world, and I could see it in the way he carried himself, like a tormented ghost hovering around the streets trying to keep his fellow lost souls high enough to forget the past. I asked about the eyelid tattoos and he said it meant he was sleeping with the fishes. What a sad, wise old bum. He confided in me like Alex and Ivano did about their girlfriend's abortions; it was almost like he felt a spark of life again to be able to talk to an outsider who just shut-up and listened.

Our beers were empty and he said it was safe to go back in the baños. We snorted our lines then made for the street. There was just a pebble left for me to stick down my underwear and still a big wad of weed back at the hotel, but I figured while I had Mike on hand I'd be wise to score more of both. He told me to give him another hour so I gave him fifty more pesos

141

and made my way through the back alleys in search of a vision. As long as I live I shall never forget that walk, my first blazing experience on cocaine. When you're high on weed you become wary of everything and get real paranoid, like everyone is staring at you and judging you for being stoned. But on coke you become the Holy Ghost. You could care less what people see or say, like an invisible god marching through your kingdom, radiating the majesty of your un-crushable ego. My head felt like a blimp pumped full of pomp and circumstance just floating down the sidewalk dragging my compliant body behind it. My city was all washed in gold as the sun tried to burn through the gray clouds muffling its late-afternoon rays. I rambled along, not with any sort of purpose or consciousness; I just floated through Guadalajara, and it was glorious. A while later I recognized a street I was on and found myself two blocks from our hotel, so I went up to our room to check out the scene. Brendan was lying on Graham's bed reading a book and Graham was nowhere to be found. I sat on my bed and started drumming on the nightstand.

"I just did coke for the first time," I said to Brendan.

"Oh yeah? Never got into the stuff myself."

I spoke quickly, "I wasn't ever going to either but Graham went on a binge two nights ago after I warned him something real bad would happen, and it did. I figure we already paid the consequence so I might as well take advantage."

He obviously had no clue what I was talking about

so I jumped up and said, "I gotta' go get some more," then ran out the door. The streets were busy and I feared once again that Mike would be impossible to find, but he was sitting on the sidewalk in the street next to the hotel where we were earlier. I sat beside him and he passed me a rolled up piece of tinfoil. Then I went inside the adjacent corner store to buy a bottle of tequila and returned to drink with Mike on the curb. Five minutes later Monkey Boy showed up with a clean-shaven, spiky haired kid who slipped me a brown paper bag and asked for ten pesos. I was stocked up.

Mike and Monkey Boy weren't interested in marijuana but they helped me polish off the tequila while we took a turn each snorting lines in the back seat of the cab they were supposed to be washing. I was deliciously high and wished Graham was there so I could thank him for bringing me to this crazy place. Monkey Boy sat there with his big eyes spaced and wide as saucers while Mike and I traded stories, when Juana, the fourteen-year-old cutie who dressed like a boy, ran over and knelt in front of us. She conversed a moment with Mike and put her hand on my knee. I sat there casually thinking she was just being friendly when Mike turned and asked if I wanted her. I sat stunned for a moment and she began rubbing my leg. I took her hand in mine softly and said, "No, lo siento, I'm okay, gracias." She didn't even flinch, just smiled and carried on down the street. I turned to Mike and said, "Isn't she fourteen?"

"Si," he said sadly. "Is hard to get dinero here."

"Wow," I said stunned. "I don't believe in money for sex man, no way!" Mike patted me on the back and said, "'Das good man, das good. Is wrong, I 'tink 'de same." What a guy, the angel-hobo of Guadalajara. The three of us got real quiet while dealing with reality in our blazing heads. Finally, Mike smacked Monkey Boy and they jumped up to wash the cab. I said adios and walked down the street to mull over my pathetic existence. *This is so weak*, I thought. Here I was feeling sorry for myself because some naive pianist-chick had broken my spoiled little heart back in easy-life-BC, when these unthinkable real-life tragedies had maimed and crippled all of the wonderful people I was befriending. I thought of Mike with his cheating wife and long-lost son; little Juana who would rather sleep with perverted strangers than live with her family; Ivano and Alex –teenagers with dead babies. What was I doing in Mexico?

Somehow I found my way back to the hotel as night fell. Philippe had finally shown up and taken Graham to party with his friends on the other side of town, so I was left alone with our new roomy Brendan. When I walked in he was already passing out. I opened a beer and said, "Here, you better drink this." He sat up without objection. I pulled out the new weed I scored and we compared it to the old stuff from Ixtlán. It was a touch better. Brendan got droned real fast as I threw beer and weed at him and he opened up. I have to say I did not like him. He told me about all his escapades as a ski instructor. He got his kicks meeting chicks in the clubs and making them feel like they were everything he was looking for in a relationship, then he'd bed them and throw them out the door like used Kleenex. I didn't even bother telling him about my romantic ventures. He would never have understood. Miguel knocked on the door and came in with a six-pack of Tecate at the perfect time—we were almost out of beer. He shared a couple then asked if we wanted to go for dinner. Brendan was now a zombie and I wasn't hungry, so he went on his own. Brendan, on the verge of collapsing, laid his sleeping bag down between the two beds and crashed. I sat in bed smoking Camels and writing furiously until Graham got back. We shared the events of our day like an old married couple and smoked our nightcap *doob*. I had a difficult time sleeping with all the coke in my head but finally dosed to the hum of Graham's snore.

CHAPTER 21
Hooky

Wednesday, September 15, 1999

Brendan had a small bruise on his forehead in the morning. He laughed sourly and said he had tripped over me in the middle of the night on his way to the bathroom to puke. *That's what you get for being a dick* I thought.

Graham was naturally worried about the Tercel and went to meet Gilbert to make sure everything was cool while Brendan and I lay around feeling burnt-out and miserable. Around eleven Brendan got up and went down stairs to see if there were any rooms available yet. They only had a room for two but luckily (my luck to be rid of him) a twenty-something Englishman named Nick arrived and said he'd be happy to share. So Brendan came back up and moved his stuff.

Graham returned and said Philippe had all sorts

of plans for the day, but after coming down off the coke I didn't feel at all like being social. I didn't actually feel as bad as I made myself out to be, but sunk low enough to play hooky on my best friend:

"I don't feel up to it man, I'm starting to feel pretty sick. Go on ahead and don't worry about me." I think he bought it because I'd been spending so much time on the can and attributed it to the spicy food, but that always happened to me in new situations; those nervous bowel-reactions from grade seven would return to haunt me. I'm sure Graham was happy to not have me slowing him down anyways, so he left to meet Philippe and I was free to do what I really wanted: spend some quality time doing cocaine and looking at naked girls.

After a quick visit to a newsstand and some alone time in my room I was guiltily satisfied and super-wrecked. My head pulsed with the new chemical and I had to drag myself out to the streets to find food. I ate some tacos, bought a six-pack and found Mike scouting the street for police. When he saw only me he poured a line right there on the curb and put his nose to the ground in one swift motion. The guy was like the Batman of snorting coke. We walked a while and shared my beer until he disappeared to buy us another rock. He came back with my share before running off to wash another cab, so I returned to my room to chill for the duration of the night.

Graham showed up to pick up some of our weed and I met Philippe for the first time. I wondered what his first impression of me was as I lay there like a stain on the bed gunned on my vices. I told them both not to come too close because, "I might be contagious." So Philippe stood in the doorway and smiled. He seemed like a really gentle, quiet sort of kid and looked much geekier than I had expected with a mushroom shaped haircut and glasses like John Lennon. His blue t-shirt was tucked into his jeans and revealed the beginnings of an impressive beer belly you wouldn't expect to see on such a young Mexican. As they left for a party up town he said in flawless English, "When you're feeling better we'll go to a football game." I felt guilty for staying behind in my gluttonous den. Evil thoughts started to enter my mind. I was drunk, I was stoned, and damn it, I was lonely, sad and horny. Cocaine was already changing me, filling my being with determination and squeezing morality out of my ears. Magazines were useless; I wanted a girl. I put my sandals on and strutted down to the now darkened streets to find a hooker. Three girls stood in front of the hotel in black dresses waiting for a trick. *Too skanky*. I wandered further down the street and saw two more. *Too fat*. I walked five more blocks then I saw her—my sorceress from Ixtlán! I froze in place, devastated by her beauty. Suddenly I realized I was out of my skull and that it wasn't really her, but this girl could have been her twin sister. Then out of nowhere, just as I was about to invite her to my room, shame fell from the sky and showered me in reality as the cocaine wore off and my cheeks filled with blood. I became utterly embarrassed and spoke out loud, "What the hell am I doing!" I fled back to the hotel in fear and the three hookers

Sinning Man's Heaven

standing outside didn't even look in my direction. I felt like a baby, a big, lost, inexperienced baby. In my room I rolled a *doob* as if against my will—I was getting sick of it all. The urge to get laid was unbearable but I thought to myself, *one day I'll find the girl of my dreams and I'd have to tell her I slept with a prostitute in Mexico, then she'd never marry me.* Still, I must have been the horniest guy on the planet. Why was it so easy for other guys to go and do those things?

Fireworks began going off right in front of my window. I turned off the lights, cracked a brew and pushed the window open to watch the independence celebrations still ransacking Guadalajara. Everyone was going crazy outside while I sat alone in that dark hotel room. I wanted so badly to join in the madness but felt too ashamed to leave the shadows of my guilt. Spidey's mix tape, which thank God I still had, kept me feeling the pulse of life as cops screamed around in their trucks whooping and throwing tequila bottles; hookers fell over one another laughing and primping and trying to look presentable to the poor *shmuck* businessmen in gray suits who stumbled drunkenly down the dirty streets and alleys of the festering toilet bowl city. That wonderful *I Mother Earth* song brought me to tears as I witnessed the mayhem and took in the line, "I can tell the time is right to find the legs to deal with this alone..."

CHAPTER 22
More

Thursday, September 16, 1999

More of the same I'm afraid. I guess I wasn't really lying when I told Graham I was sick. He was still off with Philippe in the morning so I succumbed to the disease, despite the inspired thoughts I had had the night before, and plunged back into the coke, the beer, the weed and the magazine.

Late that night Graham returned to find me where he left me. We smoked some bowls and he told me about the band he'd seen the night before at Philippe's amigo's party.

"Dude, you would have loved it! These kids were probably eighteen years old and they played *Radiohead* covers flawlessly all night!"

I realized we hadn't seen much of each other since arriving in Guadalajara. Heck, Graham didn't even know I had started a nasty little nose candy habit on the side. I lay there and wondered to myself why I was always so secretive and then crashed hard.

CHAPTER 23

A Day And Night On The Town

Friday, September 17, 1999

Coke will put you in a *pissy* mood real fast when you don't have any left, so that morning as Graham and I walked to the plaza trying to decide how to spend our day I said, "Let's find a bar." Graham stopped dead in his tracks and blurted, "You really don't want to remember this trip do you?" He had sorely underestimated me; my ability to absorb substances and still take everything in somehow eluded him. But I was too out of sorts to explain this and argued back, "Hey, I'm on vacation and I came down here to get right messed, okay? Don't play babysitter!"

"Dude, you can sit in a bar back at home any time you want but we need to take this place in before we leave! C'mon!" I was in no position to argue and kept my bitter mouth shut like a good little boy and followed my friend all around town. We scoped out

Sinning Man's Heaven

what is considered a mall in Guadalajara but I perceived it as a three-story parking lot jammed to the hilt with shacks, huts, stands and decaying markets right out of a post-apocalyptic 1980's sci-fi film. I half expected Mel Gibson to saunter by in black leather pants. I'd never smelled so many odors at the same time: salt water, rotting fish, scalding pig flesh, jasmine, oregano, burnt hair, melted wax, animal intestinal fluids and sweat all mixed to create a foul-gutter-potpourri.

My head was swollen from the hangover and the lack of chemicals in my blood, so I bought a pop and slugged it back as Graham led me out into the open roofless square to kick the sack. Suddenly, two hundred pairs of eyes were locked on us and we were putting on our tall-white-boy-hippie ballet for all of Mexico. Within seconds we were surrounded by at least fifteen children and they hopped and skipped around our hackey-sack as if we were all in the football (soccer) playoffs. It became so amusing I almost forgot my headache. Graham wowed them all, even the old women sitting on mats knitting clothes and making tortillas by hand. The brilliant contrast between those kids laughing and chasing the ball with the walls of the cramped, dank and sinister complex surrounding them caught me off guard. I stepped out of the circle, sat on a bench to finish my soda and just watched my friend dancing gracefully in the blinding sunlight with the snot-nosed youth of nowhere like an angel of the earth. Graham was beautiful and it

153

seemed like the entire planet knew it. I felt so far from everything.

Later in the day two little *hotties*, I'd guess around seventeen, started following us around and making eyes. Graham whispered, "Those chicks are into us man. Which one do you like?"

"Both, but aren't they a little young?" I said.

"Yeah, and they probably have boyfriends or dads that would love to cut our dicks off, but dude, the taller one is digging you big time, look!"

"I know, yeah, she's cute all right."

Graham paused then said, "Hey, we haven't talked about this yet. What do we do if we *both* score?"

"Yeah, I was thinking about that... Do we just do it in the same room?"

Then I knew he shared the awkward recollection of a moment we had never talked about. Two years before Graham had come home from Hong Kong for Christmas vacation. He showed up at a party I was having and we were both so drunk and excited to see each other that our embrace turned into a long kiss.

"I don't know," Graham rejoined after a long silent pause. "Wouldn't that be kind of weird?"

I nodded, "Probably; let's just take it as it comes."

I got caught up digging on four guys playing marimbas while Graham saw a *Rage Against The Machine* shirt he had to go buy. The girls grew tired of waiting for us to make a move and disappeared.

We ended up back at the hotel after much wandering and eating to shower the heat off and get ready for some dinnertime bar hopping. Night came with a refreshing warm breeze and we set out. First we bought a phone-card to call our mothers and assure them we were safe. I told mom we had been robbed and that we were waiting for our car to be fixed. She immediately began to worry about the guys I told her were working on it. I just said, "I know." Then she told me some horrible news: "You don't have a job anymore."

"What?!" I gasped.

"Business was too slow so your uncle had to shut down the bakery. I'm sorry honey." What a downer. I loved that job and the late-night hours hanging with my uncle. Finding new work is the worst. Graham handed me a smoke, "Don't worry about it man."

I moaned, "But by the time we get home I'll be completely broke and I won't have a source of income! The bakery's gone and Lori's new boyfriend will have my spot in the jazz quartet. I don't have enough students to make anything teaching."

"You can start selling weed!" Graham joked.

"Not in a million years!"

"Just think of it as starting with a new slate, and until then all you have to do is have a wicked time!"

"Yeah... Let's get pissed."

"Indeed, let's."

So we got pissed. We ate tacos, guzzled beer and slammed multiple shots of Tequila. The Lonely Planet pointed out an old bar called "Los Fuentes" which was supposed to be some sort of landmark, so we asked our way around until we found ourselves stumbling through the doors into a Clint Eastwood flick. Fifty ripped old Mexicans turned and laughed as we found a seat, but it seemed more this time like they were laughing with us instead of at us. Waiters and waitresses shuffled around the room in a frenzy trying to keep up with the reckless consumption and one took our order with a hint of spite. Graham laughed out loud, "Oh my god, this place is insane dude! Check out the old guy with three chicks over there; he's the loudest one in the room! I'm so glad we came here."

Just then a skinny little white guy in his mid twenties sitting directly behind me asked, "Hey, are you guys American?"

"No," I said turning around without thinking, "we're Canadian, thank God."

His eyes narrowed, "I'm American."

"Oh, shit. Sorry man, I didn't mean it like that."

"How did you mean it then?"

I hesitated, "It's just... we just spent a week cruising through the states and everyone seemed kinda', naive."

"You mean stupid?"

"No no, dude, I'm sorry..."

He cocked his head, "I go to the University of Virginia. Where do you go?"

I changed the subject, "All I mean is, in general, it seems like Canadians know a lot about the U.S. while Americans seem to think we all live in igloos."

He got real intense and said much louder than he had to, "Oh! So I shouldn't know that Canada had ten provinces and two territories until just this spring when Nunavut was declared the third territory for

Sinning Man's Heaven

the Inuit people who actually *do* live in igloos? Can you tell me how many states are in the U.S.?"

Wow. I didn't even know Canada had declared a third territory that year. Graham applauded him cynically, "Great! So you're smarter than the rest of the people in all fifty states!"

The now furious American said, "They speak French in Canada don't they?"

"In the east," I said. "We're from British Columbia so it's really only taught as a second language in school. I took Japanese."

"What about you?" he said to Graham.

"Yeah, I speak French."

"Great! Well this here is Marie and she's from Paris. Say something in French to her."

Across the table from him sat an attractive, plump French girl who was getting the biggest kick watching her date embarrass us. Graham hesitated for a moment and said something in French to her, "Bonjour, <blah blah blah>..." She answered him as only a *hotty* from Paris could and asked a question back. Graham sat dumbfounded. The American slapped the table, laughed and said, "That's what I fucking thought!" and went back to his girl and his drink. Graham cursed in embarrassment and chugged his beer. I followed suit and we left. Outside Graham laughed, "Yankee prick... Damn man, I've been so busy wrapping my head around Spanish I got it all mixed up with what she said; especially because our Quebecois French is different than in France."

"Yeah, but he wouldn't know that. Americans are

retarded!" I joked. We had ourselves a hardy laugh and wandered a while more admiring the nineteenth-century architecture and talking Graham/Mark nonsense. We ended up back in our room with a bottle of tequila and smoked our weed until the can tasted of aluminum.

CHAPTER 24
Celebrate The Great Divide

Saturday, September 18, 1999

We rose early that morning and took a taxi to the lock-lot where we jumped in the Tercel and sped to Philippe's parent's house. I had another hangover. It was almost a shock to the senses to be back in the suburbs in a neatly kept middle class house with a warm, doting mother who couldn't help but worry about us. She made us breakfast and prattled on in exceptionally good English trying to convince us to stay until our car was fixed. Graham would have stayed out of politeness but I insisted we stay at the hotel where we had our freedom and habits; besides, our new car window was going to be ready in two days. Mom was great but I wanted to get out of there and I'm sure Graham felt it too when we got back on the road and lit our smokes. Philippe came as tour guide and spent the afternoon showing us the attractions.

One of our first stops was an elegantly decorated cathedral that was in service. We stood inside for a few moments gazing up at the solemn figures gleaming in the candlelight, saints and martyrs looking both holy and grotesque as the people bowed their heads before the priest and chanted prayers in unison. At first I was awe inspired, then as I listened to their devoted worship my swollen mind turned not to my faith, but to my relationship *with* my faith. Guilt overtook me again as I thought how much I already missed cocaine. The bloodied eyes of the church's grim statues seemed to burn through me and I had to get out. *Beware of false idols.* I dared not talk about it as Graham searched the rickety market stands for Jesus key-chains, holy cross trinkets and postcards of the Virgin of Guadalupe. I asked him, "Why are you buying that crap?"

"For the novelty of it," he replied. I felt my stomach knot even more and needed to find a bathroom. We passed by a butcher shop just as a pick-up truck pulled up to deliver some beef, and when I say beef I don't mean neatly stacked cases of steaks and roasts, no, I mean a freshly slaughtered cow with it's head chopped off and it's wet, bloody innards sloshing around the back of this dirty beat-up truck for all eyes to see. It was disgusting. Two guys hopped out and simply threw the remains of this cow onto the front porch of the shop, making a bloody mess. This did not help my current state and I was lucky enough to find a toilet behind a curtain across the street before it was too late. Philippe laughed afterwards and said,

"You look like you need a Pepsi!" We each bought a bottle of pop where the clerk poured the contents into plastic bags then handed them to us with straws. Philippe explained that the owners were too poor to let customers take the bottles. "Damn…" I whispered wide-eyed.

Later in the afternoon we visited what once was the chamber of commerce. It had been transformed into a memorial sight with huge murals painted over the walls and ceilings—nothing short of spectacular. Gruesome images of furious battles, fallen soldiers, and terrifying, abstract mayhem filled the corridors and archways in reds, oranges, browns and blacks. Philippe's little tour of Guadalajara seemed to be soaked with blood and sent my conscience spinning with questions of morality and the human condition, historical events weighted with brutal realities and messages far beyond our tiny worlds. I wanted a beer.

Suddenly I was in my mode and couldn't turn off the music in my head. It came out of nowhere, a great juxtaposition, a song weighted with the fabric of ancient dramas and my own experience, a song both mine and yet not mine, like God himself planting a blue print far more advanced than my own designs in my skull and saying, "Use this." Graham noticed me dragging behind, lost tapping on my legs and trying to count the bizarre time signatures streaming through my brain when the title suddenly came to me: *Celebrate The Great Divide*, a centerpiece for some great musical work still gestating inside me.

Our next stop was the bar.

In the early evening we took our car back to the lot then taxied back to the Hotel Hamilton with Philippe and two six-packs to watch football. Philippe loved the sport more than life itself and promised to take us to the "Chivas" game in the morning. As we watched the game in our room I couldn't help but notice the evening sky radiating outside. I'd never seen anything like it. It may have been the smog but everything was lit with an uncanny lime green glow; the clouds, the buildings, the streets, even the air itself was a green you could reach out and touch. I opened the window wide and stuck my head out three stories above the quiet street to breathe it in, and for the first time on our journey I felt pure tranquility. I wasn't stoned, I wasn't drunk, yet suddenly everything just lined up: my blood sugar, the hum of the city, the frothing mellow green engulfing it all in its cool gentle breeze and the new song in my head. I began to sing softly, cooing to myself just enough to embrace the moment without disturbing the guys and their football game. It was my favorite five minutes in Mexico. I had to get out in it and slipped out the door where the colors and shades wooed my wanderlust. While I drifted through the streets bedazzled by an otherworldly Guadalajara, the green skies grew darker and then slowly morphed into wispy purples over starry black.

When I finally turned back the street was barren until I happened upon a shoe store where two shadows lying on a large piece of cardboard in the alley shifted and one whispered, "Mark?" It was Mike and Monkey Boy. Mike motioned for me to lie down and asked for a smoke. I lay next to him and they both gave me a high-five before I handed Mike the rest of my pack and Monkey Boy handed me an open bottle of tequila in a brown bag—classic. I'd spent a lot of time hanging with street kids back home beating drums and buying weed from them but I never imagined myself this close to the dumpster. There I was, invisible with the bums, and I loved it. An hour or so later we had finished the bottle and I promised to buy them more in the morning. They high-fived me once more before I made my way back to the hotel. The boys were mid-joint when I returned.

CHAPTER 25

Swearing In Spanish

Sunday, September 19, 1999

There's something about mixing tequila and beer that pretty much guarantees you'll wake up with a hangover. Mom always said I like to learn things the hard way. Regardless, Graham and I were pretty stoked to see our first football game, so we hopped in a taxi with our host and sped across town to the stadium. Oh the food! They were selling spicy *tortas* in every corner and we grabbed lunch. The only thing that bothered me was the greasy broth they poured all over the bun and I'm picky that way, especially with a hangover and a weak stomach. Graham ate two and told me to suck it up.

The game was a blast! Mexicans friggin' LOVE football! The stadium was packed and everybody was flipping out like Canadians do at the NHL playoffs, and this was just regular season! Philippe was a riot.

Sinning Man's Heaven

He was cheering for the visiting team from Neza, his home town, and they were getting there asses kicked by the Chivas, so he kept yelling at the top of his lungs, "AWWW PUTO! PUTO MADRE!" which Graham had figured out was pretty much the most vulgar thing you could say in Spanish. My personal favorite part of the game was the beer, the best way to cure a headache. It seems the further south you go the bigger the drinks get. The beer vendor would come around and you could buy these MASSIVE cups of "Sol", I mean like those 1.5 liter cups you get *slurpees* in at 7/11. The drunker we got the more Philippe screamed at his "USLESS" team: "PUTO! AW PUTO! PUTO MADRE!" and he spilled beer on the seat in front of him. I would never have guessed that the quiet, gentle Mexican kid who had shown us around the day before could put on such a display. Graham and I laughed our heads off. After his team was destroyed we taxied back to the hotel and he had to split. I was beginning to really like Philippe and it was sad to see him go. That was the last time I ever saw him.

Graham left to get his film developed and to see about laundry. Mid-afternoon found me looking for Mike and Monkey Boy with a bottle of tequila. They were up a couple of blocks crouching behind a cab they were supposed to be washing, snorting coke off the curb. Monkey Boy's *googley* eyes lit up when he saw the bottle and Mike told me he could get me more weed. He disappeared for ten minutes to find his guy while Monkey and I drank. He came back with a small dollop of bud, which he gave me for free (loved that guy!), and said to wait around for the real package. I helped them wash the cab and waited but the guy never showed. "Mañana," Mike said (which means tomorrow). Graham arrived with a *sixer* and we lied around until dinner.

Dinner must have lasted three hours. It was our last night in Guadalajara so we strapped on the old end-of-summer-feedbag and just walked and ate and walked and ate. Tacos here, *tortas* there; hot dogs, churros, oh the churros! We ate every kind of taco available: cow brains, cow tongue, tripe, all smothered in that green salsa. What a great night. There was one restaurant though where our very gay, very snot nosed waiter, we were sure, tried to mess with Graham (we had nothing against gay folk it's just that this guy really wanted you to know). He brought him out a *torta* with a big old pig's foot lying on the bun; I mean hoof and all! Graham raised his right eyebrow and looked at me with disgust, "Um, oh my god. Am I actually supposed to eat this?"

"I don't know dude! What the hell is that?"

"It's a foot! It's a fried...pigs...foot! Is that gay waiter trying to make fun of us 'cause he thinks we're American?"

"What did you order?" I said.

"I don't remember, I just read something off the menu."

I scoffed, "That looks pretty sick dude, I don't know if you should eat it."

He laughed aloud, "But it could be what I ordered!"

"But *how* do you eat that? It's all bone!"

"Damn, I dunno'," and he proceeded to strip what little flesh there was off the hoof and lay it on the sandwich as he remarked, "Maybe gay-waiter's trying to see if I'm man enough to eat it."

"It's your stomach bro," I chuckled as Graham sunk his teeth into the charred, tough meat. The waiter neither flinched nor gave any sign of foul play. To this day I have no idea whether it was a joke or not but later that night Graham got a brutal stomachache. We fell asleep watching one of my favorite movies, *Flatliners,* in Spanish.

CHAPTER 26
B.S.

Monday, September 20, 1999

A week had passed and we were finally going to get our stinking window so we could leave Guadalajara! This made it easy to get up early and Graham's stomach was feeling better. Against my better judgment he had given the car keys to Gilbert who promised to pick us up at 8:30 a.m. But Gilbert arrived on the dot and whisked us off to buy him breakfast.

At the filthy little diner he ordered that weird calf-hip and bone marrow in goat milk thing again and made Graham get the same. I stuck to coffee. I actually believed Graham was enjoying his second attempt at it. Gilbert, made happy, sprang from his seat as if he had a plan and started the car while Graham paid the bill.

At the garage (if you could call it that) he told us to wait in the car and got out to talk to the mechanic.

They stood some distance from us for more than a moment until Gilbert strolled back over to Graham and said, "It's not ready yet." I could hear Graham swallow before he half laughed half gagged, "What? Why?"

"We have to wait until Friday."

"Friday? That's four more days, man! Why isn't it ready?"

Gilbert didn't give a reason, instead he motioned for his mechanic buddy who didn't speak English to explain and it all became clear to me sitting there in the back seat. I felt the blood rush to my brow and I nearly shouted, "The fuck four more days! It doesn't take ten days to make a window, that's bullshit!" Gilbert looked at me sternly and Graham whispered, "Chill dude, let me hear this..." and he listened intently to the excuses in Spanish, trying to make sense of them. I was pissed and whispered back, "They're trying to keep us here man!"

"Yup, this is fucked," he agreed. By this point Gilbert and friend were heading inside pretending to argue over something. I punched the seat and cursed, "Shit! I knew he was scammin' us!"

"Sorry man, you were right, we should have just left the window."

I took a long breath, "Shhhit... Don't feel bad dude... I was the one all paranoid about it originally remember?"

"Well do you want to wait around 'til Friday?"

I spat, "No way! Gilbert just wants to keep us around buying food and beer for everyone; let's bolt!"

"Yeah dude, but we can't tell him. We'll say we're using the car for the day and drop him off wherever he wants. I'll get the refund for the window then we'll jet."

"Sweet man, it's like you've got some wicked escape plan!"

"Nice; that rhymed," Graham said casually as Gilbert got back in the car and started towards our hotel. Graham redirected him, "I think we're gonna' use the car today Gilbert, just drive wherever you need."

"You're not going no? You need 'de window," he said in an almost threatening tone. "I take care of you guys!"

"No, no, we totally appreciate you watching our backs man! Thanks a lot, we just have to run some errands, get our laundry done and stuff."

And the Oscar goes to...my boy Graham! Gilbert dropped himself off at the taxi depot by our hotel where some of the gang was washing cabs. It dawned on me that they were all always really quiet around him and why: he was big, smart and crazy.

We sped down the street excitedly making plans for our escape. Graham asked, "Do we have enough weed?"

"We've got a little left but Mike's supposed to get more for me today."

"Cool, so what all do we need to do here— you should get your laundry done while I get my film developed and pick up the refund for the window, then we'll meet at the hotel to check-out and meet up with Mike before we book it."

Sinning Man's Heaven

So I grabbed my clothes from our room and Graham dropped me off in front of a sad little shack he had found days before where an old woman did laundry by hand for a living. She took my bag with a toothless grin and said it would be ready in three hours, so I walked back to the hotel to get drunk. Graham showed up an hour later with bad news.

"The bloody mechanic didn't have the money and said he'd have to get it from the bank after work. We're stuck here another night man!"

"Well screw it!" I said, "Let's go without it!"

"It's sixty bucks man, no way!"

I groaned, "Awww! Why can't we get out of this fucking town?!"

"I just hope that guy doesn't tell Gilbert— I need a beer."

I passed him one then we smoked a *doob* before I left to meet Mike. Graham made a point of saying, "Don't tell Mike we're leaving okay? I know you guys are pretty tight but I don't want the risk of Gilbert hearing anything!" I could tell Gilbert was really getting under his skin and felt a little bad that I'd spent all this time chilling with the gang while Graham did the dirty work, but he'd gotten us into it.

I told Mike. How could I not? We'd never see each other again and I had to say goodbye with a bottle of tequila and a pack of smokes. He promised not to tell anyone we were leaving and said, "I know, I know, Gilbert is loco! But he take care of us." I thanked him for all the hook-ups and even gave him my phone number saying, "If you ever make it to Canada you call

171

me!" and I knew he knew I meant it, which made us sadder still knowing it would never happen. Monkey Boy showed up with two packages for me asking for 50 pesos. It was like buying a quarter ounce for only $5 and I had to tell him, "In Canada that would cost 800 pesos!" and I gave him 200. I knew I'd miss his big ear-to-ear smile.

Around 2:00 p.m., with two green wads tucked down my pants, I walked through the city to pick up my laundry, tripping out on legless hobos and old deformed women lying in the middle of the street begging for change. It was hard and made me wish I had something to say or do. I settled for going back to the room to get loaded and think about it. It was boiling hot, so I took off my shirt and started writing until I fell asleep with a few beers and a nice fat bowl in me.

I half woke sometime later to Graham lightly grazing my back with his fingers. It was soothing, and without thinking about it I fell back into a heavy sleep until I was woken again by the sound of him returning with the refund and the pictures. The sun was beginning to set and he dragged me out to the golden streets for another "last night in Guadalajara." While we ate tacos and drank beer at our favorite place he told me one of the *señoritas* that managed our hotel had just offered him a bit of the naughty and he sheepishly declined. I said, "She's pretty hot though. If she was just a little thinner I'd do her."

He laughed, "Yeah, but she thinks you're stupid 'cause you can't speak Spanish."

"She said that?"
"Uh huh; in so many words."
"Little bitch," I muttered.
"Ha! But she is pretty hot."
"Yup. You should go for it."
He didn't. We got fried and watched something with William Hurt on the tube. Then I remembered, "Were you touching my back when I was passed out?"

He answered coyly, "Oh, yeah; I was tripping out on your back hairs because your skin's gotten so dark that the light coming in from the window lit them up like gold. Did it bug you?"

"No, it was super relaxing. You knocked me right out and I'm still so tired."

"Aw man, me too. What a week! We better get some sleep so we can sneak off before Gilbert shows up."

CHAPTER 27

The Great Escape

Tuesday, September 21, 1999

7:30 a.m.—we didn't have much time. After a quick breakfast two blocks down we snuck ever so cautiously back to the room for our stuff. Graham ran downstairs with his bag and peered out from the hotel's entrance. The coast was clear so he booted across the street to the lock-lot we were now parked in, paid the fee, then zoomed back to the entrance where I could see him. Once he was in position I grabbed the rest of our stuff, tore down the stairs, tossed the room key to the *señorita* who liked Graham, and leapt anxiously into our trusty, windowless Tercel with a quick prayer under my breath for it's health. No one had seen us and we were highway-bound at long last. The sun was shining, the sky was blue and clear, and I had three fat joints rolled from our new stash. Guadalajara still didn't want to let us go though, and we fought to find our way out of the city. Every road we took led to a dead end or a roundabout and Graham cursed, "This fucking city's determined to make us permanent residents! If this isn't a metaphor for our week…" It took us an hour, a long, frustrating hour to finally find an exit onto the highway, and as we passed the last few buildings and rolled out onto the open plains I sparked the first jay and sang, "SWEET, GLORIOUS FREEDOM!"

"YEAH DUDE!" Graham chimed. "If I never see that city again…"

"Yeah dude!" I echoed.

He blew a smoke ring, "I vote we take a different route home."

"Of course, we have to see as much as we can anyways right?"

He laughed, "And we definitely saw ALL of that shit hole. I'm gonna' miss Philippe though. I'd go back ONE day to see him."

"Tell him to come see you," I coughed.

"No doubt. You gotta' give Guadalajara it's props though, this is probably the best weed we've had since we left."

"Yeah it's pretty good, eh? Glad you brought Mike up that day, he was an awesome guy."

The weed *was* good. I started to feel tingly and sublime as the pasturelands and mountains streamed past us in every shade of green and brown imaginable. Then Graham asked, "Mark, have you been praying for us this whole time?"

"Heck yeah man!" I nearly shouted in surprise.

"Not even exaggerating, every morning I lay my hands on the car and beg God it'll get us home; and quite literally every half hour I ask for his protection."

"Cool man. My mom does that; you know, little silent prayers throughout the day? I was just wondering if you do it too."

"Totally!" I exclaimed. "I'm so glad you asked that. Do you ever pray?"

"No, but I'm glad one of us is. We need all the help we can get out here."

I thanked God he had even mentioned it as we chain smoked our Camel Straights and shared the silent moment. It was strange driving without music while our thoughts bounced around the car, and I didn't want to mention any of them for fear of disrupting that lingering solace of brotherhood. Graham spoke, "Too bad your ghetto-blaster got stolen... But it's kinda' nice to have silence too."

"Yeah, I sure miss *Mojave 3* though," I said mournfully.

"Do you ever *not* listen to music? I know you're a musician and music's your life but do you ever just sit in silence?"

This was weird. He was right. I always had music playing, I mean always. But for some reason, maybe because I still had that urge to be cool, or maybe because I felt Graham would judge me otherwise, I lied: "Of course I do, you gotta' have that quiet time, right? Sometimes late at night when I'm writing in the studio I'll turn everything off, dim the lights and just sit in the middle of the room to think."

Why did I say that? Awkwardness sunk its ever

so familiar teeth into me as I struggled to understand why I lied to keep my friend loving me when he would no matter what, save dishonesty. I tried to resign myself to the notion that it was because Graham had a certain way of stating things.

Around noon we drove past a rickety old stand with a sign that read "*TORTAS*" propped up against it.

"A lunch-stand out in the middle of nowhere!" Graham marveled. "We have to eat there!" He turned around and parked next to the splintered picnic table. A 13-year-old-girl was the only person in sight and she looked reluctantly at us from behind the counter as we got out of the car with eyes glazed. Without a word she whipped up two *tortas* and we sat to eat.

"Oh my god," Graham exclaimed with his mouth full, "good sandwich little girl!" He ordered another and while he was waiting for it said, "Imagine, you travel all over the world and the best thing you've ever tasted is made by a kid on the side of the road in the middle of nowhere. You should have another one." I still had the munchies and should have eaten more, but I was too scared to approach the little girl again, high as I was with my still paranoid thoughts binding me in stasis.

A few more hours down the road our high began to fade, so we sparked another fatty and got in but two tokes before Graham spotted an army truck and yelled, "Oh shit!" I coughed out my toke panic-stricken and tossed the mid-burn joint out the window.

"Light a cigarette!" Graham said now pulling up three cars behind the road check. As I lit a Camel

177

and handed it to him he whispered, "Same routine as before." This was scary. We'd done this before but now the car reeked of marijuana. I lit myself a smoke as the car in front of us was pulled over by a fat man in civilian clothes for inspection. Graham whispered, "Are you praying?" Then an army dude with a uniform and a machine gun sauntered over with a smoke in his mouth. He took one look at Graham, another look at me, and then motioned for us to drive on without a word. Graham's watch was *velcroed* to the steering wheel—it read 4:20.

"Wheeew..." breathed Graham. "You keep praying so that that happens next time too!"

"Yeah baby! Yeah! Holy crap that was freaky! What a waste of dope! Two more minutes and we would have passed those guys!"

"I know, the second we light it and boom!" he cackled nervously.

I smacked the dash, "Can you believe it's 4:20?! What is with that number on this trip?! I'm sparking another!"

"Do it! Probably the safest bet now, eh?"

"Yeah baby!" I repeated. *Austin Powers* came out that summer. Graham rejoined, "I thought we were totally screwed there man. It's the baby faces, we've both got baby faces and that guy thought we're just stupid kids. We *are* stupid kids."

"Yup," I agreed and handed him the newly lit joint. We got stoned fast and after a few kilometers he yawned, "I'm cut man, you okay to drive?"

"No worries; stoned driving is my specialty!"

Sinning Man's Heaven

I took the wheel while Graham kicked back and did some drawing. We chain smoked and cruised until dinner time where we found ourselves surrounded by broad sloping hills covered with beautiful purple flowers that stretched to the horizon where the sun was poised to set. The road ended in a gorgeous little village outside of Mexico City and we pulled up to a cantina to ask about accommodations. The barkeep sent us down a dirt road and into an open field where a family lived and ran a convenient store with a loft above for rent. It was pricier than we were used to but also the nicest place we'd stayed in Mexico, with a spacious marble floored bedroom, a clean all-marble bathroom and a smooth white-stone staircase leading up to the roof where you could look out over the rolling green and purple vista.

After we had showered and settled in, one of the four sons knocked on our door to tell us dinner was ready. I felt a little nervous and had to go to the bathroom before we went down. Graham said, "Why do you have to crap twice as much as normal people?"

"You know; I've been like that since my nervous breakdown in grade seven."

"What are you nervous about?" he asked.

"I don't know, being around new people I guess."

"Well I don't think we're eating *with* them, just at their table."

Down stairs they had a homemade chicken dinner spread out for us. Grandma sat behind the store register reading while Momma wiped the counters and her daughter swept the floor before closing. As we sat

179

to eat, Graham fixed his gaze on the crucifix above Grandma then noticed she was reading a Bible. He whispered, "Don't order any beer tonight, okay?"

"Why?" I asked.

"Because they're full-on Christians and I don't want them to think they have to worry about us." Just then the daughter asked what we wanted to drink and Graham said, "Coca-cola por favor," and I said the same. As she got our sodas and Grandma and Momma watched us eating I whispered, "See, you're making me nervous man." Graham swallowed a bite of chicken and grunted, "Huh?"

I explained, "You're making me think they're going to judge us."

"Look, it's their house and I just want to be respectful, okay? You can go one night without beer... Why are you being so weird about this? We were around new people all the time in Guadalajara and you seemed fine then."

I rejoined, "See but that's different."

"Why?" Graham challenged stuffing a spoonful of potato in his mouth. I caught myself. I didn't want to admit it even if he knew it was partly because I was drunk the whole time. I stuck to the social end of it: "Because street people don't matter. I mean they matter to me but nobody cares, you know? It's like we were ghosts together; there was no judgment or anything."

"Yeah dude," he reminisced. "Everyone was real cool, except for Gilbert."

"Gilbert, man! It already feels like weeks ago."

Graham speculated," I betcha' he's the one who broke into our car too, probably set the whole thing up. He did look out for us though."

"Yeah, gotta' protect your investment," I joked polishing off my plate. Graham forgot his wallet and headed upstairs for it, but I told him I'd pay and be right up. As soon as he was gone I grabbed a *sixer* of Tecate from the fridge and paid Momma at the till. Grandma looked at me suspiciously but smiled warmly when I thanked them and said goodnight.

Graham was in the yard with the four boys kicking a soccer ball around. He saw the beer and kept playing without a word as I smiled nervously at the eldest brother, probably 19-years-old, and went up to our room. I'm sure there was no reason for the shame I felt but it kept me from hanging around to play.

When Graham came up I was one beer in and scribbling away in my journal. He cracked open a beer without mentioning it and said, "Those guys are so awesome! Even the little guy could school me at football, that's all they do here! They were stokin' on my hack though. Hey, where's the weed?" I was relieved to hear he was ready to get wrecked and pointed to my bag. "In the back pocket there. You roll better joints than me; have at 'er." I loved watching Graham roll; he'd been rolling his own cigarettes for four years and made the tightest *spliffs* in the quickest time. When they were ready everyone had gone in for the night, so we went up on the roof with our treats too take in the starlit sky and scenery. Graham sparked a *doob*, took a nice big toke then asked me

181

while he exhaled, "So were you nervous like that in high-school?"

I answered, "It's kinda' hard to explain; I guess all four years were different. When I was getting slammed into lockers by the jocks in grade 9, yeah. And the first couple days of school every year pretty much sucked hard."

"Oh I know, 'cause that's when you find out who you'll be hanging out with the rest of the year."

I nodded, "Aw, I fuckin' dreaded it! Everyone would get to school and gather in these little circles and I'd always be too shy to approach one and open my mouth, even with guys I knew the year before."

Graham remarked, "It's so funny we were both sitting in the library all those years without a single word. Why did we finally talk?"

"'Cause I noticed you were reading John Wyndham and I mentioned how much I loved *The Chrysalids*."

"Oh yeah, good book. But you were a senior then, you seemed more confident than anyone. "

I explained, "That was different, I was on fire by then! For the first time in my life I had awesome friends, and I met you and we had so much in common and you started hanging with all of us. Our worlds grew and melded together and we had so much fun judging and hating everyone else and dreaming up the crazy shit we pulled off…"

Graham took another huge toke and exhaled, "Those were good times. People are so easy to control. I grew my hair long and put on some weird clothes then suddenly everyone wanted to hang out with me after years of making me feel like shit."

"But that's just it," I exclaimed, "it was totally different from what I was used to so there was this underlying anxiety that nobody cared as much as me. I had so much love to give and it bothered me a lot. It made me feel this strange division from everyone, even if it was just all in my head, but it brought on those nervous waves again, especially at parties and performances and stuff. I was real nervous at grad."

Graham gasped, "I can't believe you were nervous that night, you were hilarious! The only sober person there, going around telling everybody what you thought of them. That was awesome!"

I coughed out my smoke, "YOU were hilarious, making out with Wanda, AGAIN!"

"Oh man, I knew we'd end up talking about her sooner or later."

"What a mess," I shook my head.

"Yeah, that's probably the meanest thing I've ever done."

Now dear reader, I must confess I've held out telling the story of Wanda so that you wouldn't despise your two main characters, but that night sitting on a roof in a field on the outskirts of Mexico City under that gorgeous night sky, Graham and I got smashed and tried to understand those string of events for the first time. He lit yet another joint and asked me, "You really liked her at first didn't you?"

I nodded, "Yeah, at the beginning of grade 12 I thought she was hot, plus she seemed different from her 'popular' friends. I was real lonely since Vanessa had moved away, so I had my eyes on a few girls, and she definitely stuck out. But then she started dating *whatsizface* and I forgot all about her. But then their drama went down and I guess she was ostracized from her friends or whatever. Then she started hanging around people I knew and I heard she was really into me; so I thought, *okay cool,* and we ended up having some awesome talks. One night she came over and I could tell she was waiting for me to make a move, so we drove to the park and I said some fantastically romantic bull-shit that sent her reeling, and at that moment I was stoked that we were about to make out, but then we did and—"

Graham snorted his toke out, "And she tasted salty right!"

I laughed, "Oh man! I feel so bad saying it now, but yeah! She'd probably been sweating from dance class that day or something, I shouldn't have judged, but her kissing seemed so…stoic. Maybe because I was used to Vanessa's passion but—"

Graham interrupted, "I thought she was a pretty good kisser but maybe I didn't have anything to compare it too."

"Well I tried to get into it and I just couldn't, but she was loving it! Oh man, and then I took her back to her mom's apartment and noticed that their door was number 9 and I foolishly mentioned 9 was my lucky number and she was all, 'Oh wow! Mine too! This is incredible, it must be a sign!' then I just wanted to get the hell out of there. She begged me to stay until her mom got home and asked what my favorite color was as if it was imperative to our destinies, and I walked out of there thinking I'd made a huge mistake."

I could tell Graham almost enjoyed hearing me speak poorly of her, even with the guilt. I continued, "I was so scared of hurting her feelings that everything I said or did that week just led her on. She called one night as if we were a couple, which I guess we sort of were, and asked, 'So should we do something this weekend?' and I kept making all kinds of excuses to not have to be with her, then I pretty much ignored her and *thought* she got the point. That's where you come in."

A sly grin took Graham's face as he blew a smoke ring then said, "Chick must have issues dude, amidst all that she corners me in the parking lot and starts kissing me out of the blue."

"I know! What did you think?"

"I thought, *what the hell*, right? She had great tits and she was pressing them up against me, so we fell into the back of Matt's van and made out the whole lunch hour."

"Yeah," I laughed, "I remember you were all tripped out because I told you I was done with her and it was your turn."

"I don't remember that," Graham said.

"Dude! I said that just a couple days before she kissed you and you said, 'What are you talking about?' And then after she *did* kiss you, you said, 'You're trippy Mark, you always know everything before it happens. What is that?' And I told you it was my prophetic gifting."

He thought a moment and replied, "Weird. Yeah, okay, maybe I do remember something like that…"

"Dude, c'mon! That's exactly what you said; word for word. You even told me Jimmy and Joey had commented on it. It was only like 3 years ago—"

"Anyway, she kept tracking me down to make out that week and I learned pretty fast that I wasn't interested. She was just sorta'… dumb."

"I know, I didn't think it at first but she was kinda' slow in the head. She must have done a lot of drugs before coming to our school."

Graham chuckled, "Probably. I didn't give her any reason to think I was into her, but she still wanted to fool around and I was all for fondling her chest more."

"And then she came to *my* window at 2 a.m. 'cause of course she knows about my late night travels and asks if she can join me. So we walk through the park and she's still trying to make me love her. I couldn't stand it, though I have to admit I got a hard-on staring at her pants while we were sitting across from each other on that bench."

Graham reflected, "She did have a nice body; voluptuous."

"I don't think I was into our plan 'cause she was two timing us, I think it was simply because I abhorred her deliberate refusal to face facts."

"Totally," Graham agreed, "but they went hand in hand. She was asking for it."

It came to us late one night while we were prowling

around the forest: our vindictive little plan to "crush Wanda's soul." Graham would spend an afternoon with her and act all charming and romantic, giving her the illusion that he was ready to take things to the next level. Then he would bring her to his house a couple hours before his mom got home from work and lead her up to his bedroom. As they passed through his kitchen there would be a surprise waiting for her: I would be sitting at the kitchen table holding a large mirror and a butcher's knife with a pool of blood dripping onto the floor. As I carved her name in the blood Graham would say the following words:

"Wanda, look into the mirror. Look at your reflection. That's all you are, a reflection, a flat surface with no depth or perception. You're not a living, breathing creature, just a hollow image." The idea cemented our brotherhood and we couldn't help but embrace one another in anticipation when we concocted it late one night.

Yes, dear reader, I know. We can't afford to get into it much in this book, but I was dabbling with some dark forces back then. Don't worry though; it didn't go quite that far. I was prepared to do it, but Graham was walking with her the day before execution and couldn't take her anymore. They came across a puddle of water and that's when he struck: "Wanda, look into that puddle. Look at your reflection. That's all you are, a reflection, a flat surface with no depth or perception. You're not a living, breathing creature; just a hollow image." And as he walked away she stood there dumbfounded.

187

He told me everything the next day and I was relieved we wouldn't have to do the kitchen-table thing. But that night, around 4:00 a.m., I was awakened by a knock on my window. I expected it to be Graham; he joined me on my excursions from time to time, but it was Wanda again! I yawned and whispered irately, "What?"

"Mark," she moaned, "you know that I love you!" She made me sick. I mumbled, "Its 4 o'clock Wanda. I'm really tired. Let's talk tomorrow, okay?"

I managed to avoid her the next day at school; then sure enough, I saw her and Graham making out in the parking lot. She was so stupid. Graham had gained a thirst for the power and was now just experimenting to see how far he could push it. He enjoyed a few more gropes then played the whole thing out again. They were at her house, probably about to go all the way, when he turned to the mirror and repeated the lines, this time with vehemence and poisonous detail. She burst into tears screaming, "How could you do this to me Graham?!" and he left without another word.

He called me that night and said it was finished. I walked to his house in the middle of the night to revel in the gory details. Sitting in his car, we discussed the whole thing with wicked pleasure and embraced saying, "We did it man! She's dead! We killed her!" We agreed it was fun messing with her head; no regret.

The next morning, Graham went out to his car to go to school. He lit a smoke, revved the engine, then as he checked his rear view mirror, Wanda popped up from underneath a blanket in the back and cackled like a witch, "Good morning Graham!" He jumped in his seat and almost burned his wrist with the cigarette! Unsure as to whether she had been back there during our discussion the night before, they drove to school without a word. Upon arrival Graham paced the halls trying to find me with the potentially lethal news that she had gone insane! I was in the kiosk picking up the high-school yearbook when Wanda found me first. She asked coyly, "Will you sign my annual?" I was stunned and said, "Sure." We traded books and she went down the hall to sit and write. As I began to pen some generic end of the year drivel in her book Graham found me and panted out of breath, "Mark, she's crazy! She slept in my car last night dude!"

"What!" I exclaimed basking in the drama. "Did she hear us?"

"I don't know!"

She marched back up to me as if Graham wasn't even there and handed me my annual with the most unusual smile on her face. As she turned away I opened to her page and read in bold capital letters, "I AM NOT DEAD!" A chill ran up my spine as I showed it too Graham. He half choked half laughed in revelry, "Oh my god!"

At graduation I avoided her at all costs, not for fear, but because I had so much else going on, which is another story. Quite frankly I didn't care. I caught her looking in my direction from time to time with evil eyes, then sad eyes, then soft eyes, then evil again. And you read correctly at the beginning of this little fairy-tale: that night Graham was at our after-grad party, and when I looked up from telling my umpteenth drunken class-mate off, there he was sucking her face again. He looked over at me from behind her head and winked. I laughed out loud as he gave me a thumbs up, still locked at the lips. Poor girl.

"Did you ever see her again?" I asked Graham as I passed him another beer up on our roof in Mexico.

"Nope. Just gave her the mirror speech one last time and left her crying. Did you?"

"Just once. Two years ago I went over to Ben and Nicky's for dinner with the gang when they told me she was coming."

"Oh yeah! You told me this; I would have been kinda' scared."

"I almost was, but then I thought, *ooh, this might be fun*! So I insisted on getting the door when she knocked. I opened it just a crack and said, 'Are you here looking for answers or a good time?'"

Graham laughed, "Ha-ha! Marky Mark, that's good!"

I continued, "And she meekly replied, 'A good time.' I said, 'Good answer, c'mon in!' Then I complimented her on her dress and told her she was looking really good, which she was, and she played the whole night out like she could care less about me. But soon after dinner I got bored and wanted to go home and get high with my guitar, so I bid everyone farewell. As I was putting my jacket on Wanda squirmed in her seat, then when I turned to leave she moaned longingly, 'Maaaaark?!'

"Oh man," Graham cringed, "that's so pathetic."

"So I turned back and said, 'Yes?' and she just sat there staring up at me with those dumb puppy-dog eyes again, hoping I'd throw her a bone. I just said I had to go and left."

"That's so perfect," Graham cooed, now utterly stoned and eating up the conversation. He cocked his head and asked, "Why do you think we enjoyed that so much?"

"I don't really know. Fuck that was mean. I didn't feel all that bad about it then, but I sure do now."

He nodded, "We were pretty harsh, but she was asking for it."

"Yeah, and it was fun, eh? Do you think part of it was 'cause in our eyes she came from the popular crowd?"

Graham finished my sentence, "And she represented everything we hated and was the perfect target for our revenge?"

"Yeah," I said.

"No," he replied shaking his head and lighting a smoke. "She was being stupid and we needed to put her in her place." He didn't mean "we" as in the present, he meant "we" as in the elitist pricks from high school, but I was glad he said it. We grew soul ties in our last year of high-school, and hearing him state so bluntly how much we shared the hatred of normalcy and stupid people back then erased any doubt in my mind that he would forever be my brother, in whatever twisted way. I loved him immensely. I'm so sorry Wanda.

CHAPTER 28
Pigs And Pyramids

Wednesday, September 22, 1999

Graham wanted to drop in on another old friend from Hong-Kong, a girl named Adele he had had "a little thing" with. Apparently she was really cute, daughter to one of Mexico's richest men, and currently studying in a town called Cholula outside of Mexico City. We made ready to head that way but the car wouldn't start that morning.

"What the hell did Gilbert do to this thing?" Graham grumbled. The two older brothers came out, all grins, and took a look while Graham kicked the ball around with the younger ones. I sat in the driver seat deep in prayer, begging God to give the brothers the wisdom to get our car going. Fifteen minutes later it started right up and I thought *this is a Godly home. They have to be the most amazing family in all of Mexico.* I said it to Graham as we waved goodbye and drove off, and he nodded saying, "There was definitely a peace in that place."

"I wonder where the father is," I said.

"Probably working in the mines with a big smile on his face," Graham praised the apparition. I wanted so badly to be a good man.

I drove most of the day while Graham tried to outline the best way to Cholula. We missed an exit without realizing it and ended up cruising right into Mexico City, much to my frustration. The traffic was ferocious and I began to sweat beads. A way out seemed hopeless, and as I stopped at a stop sign and waited for my chance to turn around, a policeman approached the car and knocked on the window. He sounded angry and said something about our license plate. I pointed at the travel sticker we had on the windshield but he didn't care. I couldn't understand what he asked next and Graham said, "He wants to see your license!" So I pulled out my wallet and before I could get it out he reached into the car and snatched the whole thing out of my hands. A greedy smirk overtook his face as he searched through it, pocketed my wad of cash, and threw the empty wallet back at me exclaiming, "Rapido!" gesturing to move on. I yelled, "Hey! What the fuck man?!" but he kept walking with a laugh. Graham said, "Dude! Just go! You're going to get us locked up!" I was so pissed and couldn't figure why he'd stopped us in the first place. "Fuckin' pigs!" I cursed. "Guy just walks up and robs me blind! That was like 40 U.S.!"

"This place is psycho dude. Get us out of here

before another pig sees us." It was a chore but I managed to get back on the highway and find the right exit. Adele told us later that in Mexico City the last digit of your license plate number dictates the days of the week you're allowed to drive in the city, it's their way of keeping traffic under control. Good idea; someone should have told us.

Sometime in the afternoon we found ourselves speeding up a windy road atop a lush green mountain. Dark clouds rolled in and turned the clear day's sunlight into shades of white and gray. Over the summit and a few clicks down the other side Graham peered down an overgrown slope and exclaimed, "That looks exactly like home! We've got to burn a *doob* there!" I pulled over excitedly and jumped out: he was right! It was a like a wistful slice of home and we ran down the bank like children in the park. Huge trees like slender giants towered over the rich green grasses and sweet smelling vegetation. Fallen branches and overturned stumps formed a damp glen for us to climb through and find the best spot to perch under the gloomy afternoon sky. You could actually taste the mist and I knew it invigorated Graham as much as it did me. As he rolled the joint I took a huge breath of the fresh cool air and said, "This trip is such a roller coaster."

"Yeah dude," Graham offered his token catch phrase. We smoked two joints then sat there in harmonious silence with our cigarettes, listening to the birds and the wind gently passing through the swaying trees. I wished it could have lasted forever,

Sinning Man's Heaven

but the light rain started to come down heavier and we wanted to get to Cholula by suppertime.

Graham took the wheel and another discovery of our poor car's new faults presented itself as we tore down the steep hills: the brakes were shrieking, metal on metal. Graham cursed Gilbert again. It sounded bad, really bad, so he tried to coast down the entire mountain without braking which was dangerous but not an option. At one point we almost flew off the mountain and I swallowed my guts, but good ole' Graham guided his sad car straight and true, and once we reached the bottom it was smooth sailing for another hour before we rolled into charming Cholula.

What a cool little town. The streets were pieced together with cobblestones that wormed through the close-set buildings. The homes, shops, and huts were jammed together forming an incredible labyrinth, their walls made mostly of smooth white stone, stained with the colors of life by the centuries. Lanterns and festooned lights hung from the railings and rafters, illuminating the sewage water that ran down the sides of the alleys and passages with a warm glow. It was dank and cozy at the same time. Graham loved it and told me to look in the Lonely Planet for a hotel. It suggested a place called "Hotel Reforma", which was situated between the central plaza and the largest pyramid in the world: The Great Pyramid Of Cholula. It was an amazing sight.

The hotel itself was a small plaza, which was really cool. We walked through the gates and found ourselves surrounded by doors and tourists from France,

195

Germany, Japan, and the U.S. Our room was small but clean, apart from the bugs.

After settling in we hit the main plaza to find *tortas* and beer. The plaza was absolutely beautiful, like the setting for an old romance. We strolled out into its spacious green gardens intertwined with cobblestone paths, fountains and exotic trees. The paths all joined in the center where an elegant black gazebo surrounded by neatly painted benches stood. Smiling couples passed to and fro amidst the humming streets as the first stars of the night broke out. The plaza was bordered by a surprisingly large, century old building that was now part cantina, part fancy restaurant, and part coffee shop. Perpendicular to that was another building divided into assorted shops, a large bank and a pharmacy. Across the street overshadowing everything stood a massive Catholic Church now faded gold, ominous and unyielding. It's bleak walls stood less than a stone's throw away from our hotel. On the opposite side, literally a few feet behind our room was what I thought to be a small overgrown mountain around 60 feet high, but Graham found out from the innkeeper that it was actually an overgrown pyramid. "Cool!" We climbed to the top of it and found the most incredible view of The Great Pyramid, which towered on the opposite side of the complex across from the train tracks evoking strange mysticisms and untold stories about which one could only begin to speculate. And crazier still, the Spanish had built a church on top of it in the 1500's that is now a major Catholic pilgrimage destination. The whole scene

Sinning Man's Heaven

was unlike anything I had imagined and both of us were completely enthralled. There we were, chilling on a pyramid, smoking good Mexican *chiba*, drinking *Bohemia* (the best beer in Mexico), and staring at the largest pyramid in the world. I slept well that night.

CHAPTER 29
The Famous Adele

Thursday, September 23, 1999

We both woke with hangovers but it was worth it. As we gorged ourselves on sweetbreads back in the plaza Graham beamed, "Man I love this. I think I've found my future home in the third-world."

I half agreed, "Yeah, this is the first town we've seen I could actually consider living in," and he added, "Probably because it's the least Americanized." An American overheard him say it as we entered the internet-café, and to our surprise he shrugged almost in agreement. Graham whispered, "That's how you tell a traveler from a tourist."

There was a message from Adele in Graham's email telling us where to find her dorm room. It turned out she was living just a few blocks away from our hotel.

"That worked out well!" Graham said. I was both

Sinning Man's Heaven

eager and nervous to meet Graham's little Spanish *hotty* of whom I'd heard so much about.

There was some time to kill before she got out of classes so we scoped out the Great Pyramid but opted not to spend the money on admission into the tunnels. Instead, we perused the little shops and trinket stands where I bought a cool little pipe in the shape of an ancient demon, which we proceeded to take up to our pyramid and test out. I call it *our* pyramid because no one else ever climbed up, which seemed odd since it was so enormous and offered an incredible view of Cholula from every angle. Fine by us.

A good mid-day bake accompanied us back down to the bank where my card got stuck in the machine. I left my wallet in the sun too long so the heat had warped the corners. This was an especially difficult problem to solve with my poor Spanish and my inebriated state. I fought to contain the paranoia as my red eyes fell on the guard's machinegun like I'd done something wrong. I turned to Graham and batted my eyelashes as he sighed, "Oh god, do I have to do everything?"

I said it before and I'll say it again: the kid was amazing. We stumbled our way up to the teller to explain and his Spanish had gone from basic to near comprehensive in just two weeks. A guard returned ten minutes later and handed me my card with a dopey grin. I could feel Graham stewing over my lack of effort to learn the language and as we walked out into the plaza he said, "Next time you do it yourself."

The guard at Adele's dorm wouldn't let us in.

Unaccompanied boys were not allowed and she still wasn't back from her class. Graham left her a note saying to meet us at the hotel and we returned sleepily to our room to lie down and chain smoke.

A couple hours later there was a knock at the door and Graham opened it to a tiny-silhouetted figure. Adele stepped in and kissed him on both cheeks with a perky "Olla Graham!" then hugged him tight. He introduced her to me as I put my cigarette out and rose from the bed half awake. She tiptoed over and said in perfect, unaccented English, "Olla Mark, you may not be used to this, but in Mexico we greet new friends with a kiss," and she kissed both my cheeks the same as Graham. My eyes adjusted to the bright light pouring in through the open door and I got my first good look at her. She wasn't what I expected—half as pretty, almost plain with shoulder length brown hair and skin lighter then our travel worn tans. Under her faded blue jeans and white t-shirt she had the figure almost of a small boy. Still, she moved with a delicate grace that made her quite attractive and I could see why Graham liked her.

She took us back to her dorm to make us dinner and introduce us to her roommate Tara. Graham and Adele were obviously going to couple off, so the awkward position that Tara and I would be put in was my main concern. It was flung out the door the moment we met. She was pretty with dark native skin, but not quite thin enough for my tastes, and I almost instantly pegged her for a prig as she glared coldly at me with black eyes that said *if you think I'm going to hang out with you just because you're here with my roommate then you're stupider than you look.* Still, I made every effort to be friendly and she ignored us completely; it was easy to tell she was trying hard to look pre-occupied. She packed her bag to leave and I said, "Nice to meet you Tara." She barely managed a half smile and replied, "You too." We didn't see any more of her.

The girls' room was lavishly decorated and way too big for two students. Adele's bed and most of her furniture was made of rich mahogany, and as she warmed us up some zucchini soup and stir-fry on the stove Graham rubbed his thumb and index finger together and whispered, "Daddy's got dough." It was hard not to be shocked after all the dirt-stained kids we'd seen collecting sticks outside their huts. Ready or not, we were about to see how the other half lived, and I was about to handle it very poorly...

CHAPTER 30

Rags To Riches

Friday, September 24, 1999

Adele took care of everything. She made arrangements for us to come home with her for the weekend, bought our bus tickets, and even hooked us up with a trustworthy pay by the day parking lot to stash the Tercel while we were gone. It was practically undrivable now and she promised to have her driver look at it when we got back. Graham told me it would be nice to feel a little security and breath easy again but I wasn't so sure. I knew he'd want me to tone it down around his friend's family and I felt really self-conscious about staying in someone's home with my desire to stay droned.

Three bus rides later we were in the heart of Mexico City. I won't bother to try and describe it except to say MAYHEM! I found the perfect metaphor for that place on the last bus above its driver's head: a cross dangling from the rear view mirror, a picture of the Virgin of Guadalupe, and the Playboy bunny emblem. I judged the entire country right then and there and the irony somehow eluded me.

It was a 10-minute walk from the bus station to Adele's neighborhood. The complex was well protected with a tall fence of black iron bars, security cameras, and armed guards. The contrast was startling. You felt an instant change in the air as you stepped out of the bleak streets of the city, through the towering gates, and into this luxuriant, colorful bastion of serenity and repose. The guards greeted Adele and gave both Graham and I friendly smiles as we marveled at the lush green trees lunging over the gardens and fountains, their warm scented leaves rustling in the golden sunlight. The old world houses, more like palaces, looked entirely cozy and inviting, almost natural nestled among the well-kept flowerbeds and cobblestone paths.

Daddy's house was the biggest. It was four stories tall besides the innumerable lofts built around the tall spiral staircase that climbed straight through the main passage. No one was home except the jolly old maid Maria. She fixed us lunch and we had a nice time, finally at rest from our crazy "vacation."

After lunch, Adele took us to the top floor, which had a spacious balcony overlooking the beautiful compound, and told us it was all ours for the weekend! The flat was very comfortable with a huge bathroom, and the balcony gave us the privacy and freedom to live the way we were accustomed. I felt like royalty after the conditions we'd seen and I couldn't help but feel a little guilty.

As we smoked and talked watching the sunset from our perch, Adele's dad pulled up and she rushed downstairs to greet him. Graham glanced at me notably overwhelmed with our change in surroundings. We made our way back to the kitchen to meet daddy who was busy conducting business affairs on his cell-phone. He shook our hands with a faint nod of acknowledgment as Adele tried to introduce us between sentences. The plan was to get groceries for the weekend, so the four of us climbed into his Mercedes. He was still speaking frantic Spanish into his phone when we arrived at the store. I was astounded at his ability to drive with such precise aggression amidst the insane city streets whilst planning the take over of some inferior company. It was a little intimidating, even when he told us to get whatever we wanted. He was almost as tall as me, with broad shoulders and a fair sized girth. His glasses and balding gray head marked him as wise and well lived while his constant lack of expression gave me the feeling of a cunning and indifferent man. Still, his generosity to his spoiled daughter with her two outlandish guests was appreciated no matter how genuine.

Maria chuckled back at the house when she saw the items we brought back: Smarties, wine, canned oysters, crackers, and other assortments that only a couple of North American stoners would hastily grab in an awkward moment. I was feeling really out of place, and the hunger pangs for some weed started to tug at my nerves as my body realized it had been without substance all day. We retired to our balcony with the wine and Adele told us we would be joining her for her mother's birthday the following day. I was suddenly panic-stricken. *Us in high society?* I rolled an extra big fatty after Adele went to bed.

CHAPTER 31

My Country Is Better Than Yours

Saturday, September 25, 1999

Graham was already downstairs eating breakfast with the family before I was showered up. At the bottom of the stairs I heard two new voices speaking perfect English and my fear of meeting new people struck my gut. I took a deep breath and entered the kitchen to find daddy had already left, while Adele's mom and brother were getting acquainted with Graham. I later learned that mom and dad were divorced, but mom still came and went as she pleased. She was a beautiful woman and on her fiftieth birthday: tall, thin and stately, with short black hair and wire-framed glasses, which to me gave her great sex appeal. What I couldn't understand was how she gave birth to Adele's older brother, ugly and emaciated, with pale white skin and unsymmetrical ears that stuck out, immediately bringing *Nosfersatu* to mind. His speech was lazy and slow as if every thought was an effort to keep in focus. Shaking his cold limp hand and trying not to compare it to a dead fish, I sat next to Adele as Maria brought me some toast and coffee. The family argued over the particulars of the day then all disappeared in a frenzy as I finished my breakfast.

Before we left for the party I said to Graham upstairs, "Adele's mom is hot dude!"

"Ha ha! I hadn't thought of it, but I guess she is attractive for an older lady."

"Weird, that's the first time I've ever found anyone over fifty attractive. Hmm... You wanna' smoke a bowl?"

Graham frowned, "We can't go to her party stoned. Just chill a while, okay?"

I was annoyed, and really anxious about a big social event. This was not the kind of thing I came to Mexico to do. Still, it wouldn't do to be rude or risk getting busted by some observant relative. I'd have to control myself.

Adele's dad had just bought her a new car, some nice shiny thing. The three of us climbed in and drove uptown to another rich-people neighborhood where a throng of shiny new cars lined an immense driveway. Glamorously dressed friends and relatives swarmed around the beautiful yard set up for a decadent outdoor party with a white tent sheltering elaborately decorated tables laden with white lace and plate upon plate of tasty treats. A bartender was just finishing his spread, so I watched to see if an aunt or uncle would go for a drink, and much to my delight, almost everyone made their way in his direction. Adele began introducing us and we were soon the center of attention as the tall North American travelers. Uncle Juan made sure we got a drink. I downed it and ordered another rum and coke. Graham whispered in my ear, "Not too much, okay?"

"Why?" I asked indignantly. "Everyone here's partying, it's free drinks!"

"I just wanna' be respectful in front of Adele's family," he said.

"It would be disrespectful *not* to enjoy their hospitality," I argued.

"Just tone it down a little. We've got plenty of time to get messed later."

I didn't want to wait until later, but I didn't want to get even more frustrated with Graham, so I got lost in conversation with Uncle Juan and his wife who spoke decent English. The dread of these kinds of events always subsided once I got involved, and I actually started to enjoy myself. I managed to get a few drinks in me too. It was grandma's house and she kept insisting we eat and drink more, like any good hostess.

Our discussion focused mostly on the differences between Canada and Mexico; they all wanted to hear what it was like north of the U.S. which they all seemed to have a distaste for. All I could think of was the Virgin of Guadalupe praying next to the Playboy bunny. Graham didn't want us smoking cigarettes in their company so my nerves grew tenser as

Sinning Man's Heaven

the conversation went on. Somewhere between the agitation with our circumstances and my increasing need to get droned I was developing a real sour attitude, and felt by the way Graham sucked back his first cigarette after we left the party that it was rubbing him the wrong way.

Off again in Adele's ride we picked up her best friend Daniel, and she assured Graham he was nothing to worry about because he was gay. He was a cool guy and we got along great at the club we went to, and I finally got to chug some Coronas and tequila. I caught a decent buzz but couldn't satisfy my thirst. My weed was still back at Adele's where I wanted to be, so I ordered round after round until I had to pee. The place was packed to the gills and jumping and it was exceedingly difficult to shove my way through the main floor, past the dance floor and down the stairs. Finally inside the bathroom I noticed there were no urinals, and once I was in the stall it dawned on me. A girl peeing on my left and another farting to my right set in the real panic. Five long seconds rolled by as I debated whether to flee to the guys' washroom and prolong the agony or just get it over with right there. I opted for the latter and took what must have been the longest, most audible pee in the history of that dungy little girls' room. Then the hard part: walking out. I took a deep breath and waited until it seemed the quietest...*and...GO!* Two girls walked in that second prattling on like drunken chickens and stopped dead in their tracks as I smiled nervously and scooted past them hoping they wouldn't scream. Instead they started laughing uncontrollably as I opened the door, only to find a big scary bouncer staring straight at me. He'd obviously seen me walk in and was standing there waiting to see what I was up to, but when he told me in Spanish, "That's the ladies room you know?" and I shrugged like an idiot, he knew I was just drunk and foreign and let out a huge howl of laughter. In my head I was screaming all sorts of obscenities. I hated when people laughed at me. My face burned red with embarrassment as I recalled the idiots in school slamming me into lockers and laughing like hyenas. I recalled the time I lost my temper at a crowd pushing and shoving like animals through the gate to see *The Tea Party* at *Edgefest*, and everyone who witnessed my explosive foul language pointing and laughing at me during the rest of the festival. *FUCK!*

As I neared our table I noticed Adele staring up at Graham as he spouted off on—I'm sure—some smart sounding quip to Daniel. The dreamy look in her eyes bugged me. Then when we were leaving I paid closer attention to the way she carried herself while passing through the crowds and it really bugged me: unaware and unassuming of the lives around her, floating down the streets with her nose turned up as if Mexico City was her own personal fairyland. *Rich chicks and their little worlds* I thought. The more she told us about her other rich friends, guys she'd dated, her social life inside and outside of school, and just what a fine education she was getting, the lower my opinion of her became. And I knew it was all hard for

Graham to swallow too; even Daniel raised his eyebrow at me when she commented on some guy she'd dated because he was an heir to one of her daddy's rich friends.

After we dropped Daniel off the conversation swayed back to the Canada/Mexico comparison, and whatever Adele had to say about anything at this point wasn't sitting too well with me. I offered my two bits: "The biggest thing I've noticed here is the blatant perversion."

"What?" Adele exclaimed. "What's that supposed to mean?"

"There's filth everywhere you look! Prostitutes on every corner, nasty comics at every stand. Compared to Canada Mexico's one giant brothel!"

"I'm not perverted!" Adele retorted.

Graham coolly said, "We've got all that stuff back home dude."

I argued back, "But it's not all on open display like here. This place is twisted."

Adele came to her country's defense: "Mexico is not twisted! This is where I live and I love it more than anywhere else in the world. I'm sure you feel the same about Canada because it's *your* home."

"Yeah, and because it's not a zoo like the crap we've been seeing. Have you ever been to Canada? I've lived there all my life and it's not even remotely comparable."

"How many times have you been here Mark?" she asked with hurt in her voice.

"Just this trip," I answered, knowing where she was going.

"Once? You've been here once and you can already pass judgment?"

Now I had her. I said, "That's my point! We haven't even been here three weeks and I'm already blown away by the amount of crap we've seen."

"I've lived here *my* whole life and I haven't seen anything different from anywhere else," she said quietly. I, on the other hand, was anything but quiet, and launched into it: "You haven't lived here you're whole life! You've lived in a big mansion with fancy cars and fancy schools and fancy friends!"

I went on in a drunken rage describing every detail of every bad thing that had happened to us since we crossed the border as if I was on a crusade to dispel her naivety. My verbal vomiting continued until we were standing back in her kitchen looking for something to eat, where Graham (who I think was in basic agreement with my original point but was simultaneously pissed at me for being a total jerk to his spacey love interest) marveled at her ability to carry on this stupid argument without so much as raising her voice. He finally managed to calm me down with the promise of a huge fatty before we watched a movie. And then, calm, cool, and deceptively collected, I managed to make matters worse. I took a deep breath, looked her right in her stupid brown puppy dog eyes, and ended the argument with one sentence: "I just want you to know how ignorant you are."

CHAPTER 32

Do You Believe In God?

Sunday, September 26, 1999

Adele wouldn't even look at me the next day—obviously—but Graham didn't come down on me the way I expected him to, even though I knew he was perturbed with my tactless treatment of our hostess. I guess he knew I was an angry kid back in school, but he hadn't really seen me lose my temper since then. Was it because that's when I started doing drugs? He must have figured to some extent—decreasing my dosage sure hadn't helped matters. In fact it quite possibly caused exactly what he was trying to avoid. I thought *does this whole "substance in relation to behavior scale" affect Graham at all?*

We spent the morning with Adele's dad and he took us to the university to dig on an exhibit about the Mayans. The man knew a great deal on the subject and I ended up getting along quite well with him as he

213

showed us around. I wanted to say, "You know, sir, I find your daughter quite annoying." I kept fantasizing about actually saying it and chuckling to myself.

Daddy had business, so we said goodbye and spent the rest of the day touring the sites of Mexico City while Adele pretended I wasn't there. We saw an Andy Warhol exhibit, some other art galleries and halls, then we got lost in one of those huge malls like in Guadalajara, but with only one level resembling a giant aircraft hanger jammed full of tents and stands. Somewhere amidst this sprawling frenzy we ate a scrumptious, super-spicy seafood soup made mostly with seaweed, clams, shrimp, squid, and whole baby octopus, which I thought were so bizarre with their little baby tentacles gripping your tongue as you tried to swallow. Nothing like I'd ever eaten but very agreeable.

At one point in the day Adele wanted to show us this massive, jaw-dropping cathedral with literally hundreds of people pouring in and out. She explained how it had taken close to fifty years to build about two centuries earlier; how many people had lost their lives in the labor and how the state had invested all of it's money into its construction. I was astounded, and then almost horrified at the brutal sacrifice, the cost to the poor people for whom this sacred spectacle was built. As Adele went in ahead of us I said to Graham, "Jesus doesn't want this!"

He immediately knew what I was on about and whispered sharply "Drop it now Mark, it's part of their culture."

I couldn't let it go. "Culture? Dude, this part of

Sinning Man's Heaven

their *culture* is messed! Imagine the good they could have done for the poor with all that money! Instead they kill them off to build this useless thing for the state."

"How can you call it useless?" he retorted. "Look at it, it's gorgeous! This is a place of hope for people."

"But it's so hypocritical! It defeats the entire purpose of Jesus' message."

"Leave it alone man, those people died for their Catholic faith. Its just part of the culture," Graham repeated.

"What is it with you and cultures? Like that in itself justifies actions? Were you listening to Adele's dad talk about the Mayans?"

"I heard it man," he answered calmly.

"Some of that stuff was sick dude! But that was their culture, right? And now they've got this Virgin of Guadalupe; what kind of twisted crap is that? Inventing a 'saint' to trick the poor people into buying Catholicism?"

As Graham told me to shut it for the third time I noticed Adele kneeling down in front of one of the holy shrines. She lit one of the candles with a stick of incense, kissed her fingers, and crossed her chest in the Catholic tradition. My immediate response was to think *could this stuck up richy actually believe in God? There's no way. She has to be one of those heady atheists who honors their family's traditions simply because they were brought up Catholic. How hypocritical!* Half of me wanted to call her on it, while the other half wanted her to be a real Christian so we could forget

215

the previous day and really talk. She rose and crossed her chest one more time then I asked, "Adele, do you believe in God?"

She turned away coldly and said, "Leave me alone."

I caught up to her and asked again, "No, I really just want to know. Do you believe in God?"

"I'm not telling you, you'll just attack whatever I say."

She was half right, depending on her answer. I checked myself and resigned to simply knowing as I asked once more, "I promise I won't say anything, okay? Please just talk to me."

"I'm not telling you anything," she repeated, and Graham told me quietly yet a fourth time to leave it all alone.

Back in our flat that evening Graham and I huffed a much-needed *doob* as he ignored my apology saying, "Don't tell it to me." It was hard. I knew I'd behaved like a pig and I wanted desperately to leave our hostess' home on better terms. Reaching down into my belly for humility, I breathed deep and made the long walk down to the library where she was reading.

"Look Adele... I feel awful. You've been so gracious letting us stay here and showing us around, and your family has been so nice, and I'm really ashamed. I honestly have nothing against your country; I don't want to make excuses, but we've just been through so much and I vented on you for some reason. I'm so, so sorry. I want you to know I'm not the guy you must think I am. Can you forgive me? I want us to be friends."

Her eyebrows lifted as she replied, "Okay; thank you Mark. I want to be friends too."

I continued, "Listen, the reason I was asking you about God is because, believe it or not, I'm a Christian. I know I wasn't acting it, that's part of why we came out here. I've got some things to figure out, and... stuff..."

"I believe in God," she said gently.

"But all the way? Really in your soul, not just 'cause you're raised Catholic?"

She nodded, "Yes, all the way, and not just because we're Catholic. I've always felt God."

"Aw, me too Adele; I've never doubted, even when I've been at my worst."

"Worse than this?" she asked.

Ouch.

Graham entered the room. They were going to visit her mom. As they left I climbed back upstairs with shame rotting in my gut, writhing and twisting beyond embarrassment into disdain, then into anger, and then, as I entered the bathroom and faced myself in the mirror to see my brown skin boiling to a demonic blood red, it turned to sheer, soul scalding rage. I held the hot air in my lungs and clenched my jaw. Every muscle in my body tightened and flexed, more than I had ever flexed before to the point where it hurt, to the point where there was no distinction between sinew and soul, muscle and mind, body or brain. My hand clenched of its own volition and raised my arm straight out in front of me. I stared at the reflection of my white knuckles in the mirror, my fist shaking as though it held the key between time and space. My entire being, past to present, thoughts and emotions, became a quivering contortion locked in fiery stasis, the old me held fast by some new conviction. I stared hard at my fist, then at my throbbing bicep, strong and unyielding to the pain, and then through the mirror, past my sharp furrowed eyebrows, and deeper into my own eyes than I'd ever looked before, so deep I saw a strength I knew only in my dreams but couldn't unleash; my fist—my arm—my eyes—my fist—my arm—my eyes. I flashed on the comic book heroes I so desperately wanted to be when I was young: impermeable, untouchable, powerful and wholly pure, just and good by choice. What had I become? How did I end up so far from the righteous creature I so long dreamed of being, to escape, to rise above the fears and struggles this world and all its petty, unloving, uncaring, simple minded inhabitants unwittingly birthed and prodded into my bitter fury and constant judgment?

You were running a good race. Who cut in on you and kept you from obeying the truth? That kind of persuasion does not come from the one who calls you. A little yeast works through the whole batch of dough...

I'd had it with the yeast in my life, wherever it had come from. I'd show them. I'd show those bastards who used to smash me into lockers, the "cool kids" who hacked me down, every girl I'd ever had a crush on. I'd show Shaw and the boys back home, I'd show Graham and his stupid chick of the week Adele, and I'd show fucking Lori! My passion was going to

Sinning Man's Heaven

burn hot as the sun and I would show the world! I was going to become a good man, a great man, a man of strength and success, and in my anger I foolishly believed God was going to help me do it. Me. Me. Me! My mind swelled with a familiar yet even stronger sense of power as time returned, turning my anger into superiority. *Please God make me a good man!*

When Graham came up for bed he found me listening to Ryuichi Sakamoto's *Anger/Grief*, stoned out of my tree.

CHAPTER 33
Back To The Real World

Monday, September 27, 1999

At 6:30 a.m. the three of us were on our way back to Cholula in Adele's car with her driver Alonzo at the wheel, a dark skinned, middle-aged workingman with the warmest smile you ever saw. Some people, you can tell just by the way their eyes shine, have real joy. Graham commented later that he wished we could have hung-out with him more.

Adele was in the passenger seat and I sat behind her digging on the orange morning light spreading up and out over the dirt-red plains and intermingled green pastures. As the dusty sun arose it came to an angle that cast Adele's reflection clearly onto her window, so that I could see her but she couldn't see me. There she sat with her rounded little nose and chin tilted snootily up, her thin lips bent up at the corners with that clueless *perma-grin*, staring dreamily at the horizon without a care in the world. I stared loathingly at her hollow brown eyes, those stupid puppy dog eyes, and I felt hate: the hate of her wanting my best friend and wiggling her way between us. Guilt struck me and I looked away, well aware that I was sinning, but her stupid dreamy face still shone in the light before me, and as I turned and saw it again I wished I could smash it in.

Back at the plaza in Cholula, Adele instructed Alonzo to stay with us as long as it took to get our Tercel fixed up, then left for her first class. I wondered if he felt any of the reprieve I did when she was finally gone.

Alonzo was the dude. He knew a guy just a few clicks away who ran a garage, and this guy dropped everything he was doing for us. The first thing he checked was the brakes, and when he mumbled something to Alonzo, who in turn told us in English that the last idiot had made a real mess, Graham spat, "Fucking Gilbert!"

Our brakes fixed and belts tightened, Alonzo's amigo charged us close to nothing and sent us on our way. We couldn't thank Alonzo enough but he declined when we invited him out for beers saying, "Sorry amigos, tank you, tank you very much, but I must get to de city. Be safe amigos," and he shook our hands, flashed that joyful smile and hit the road. So we got drunk, finished the last of our stash, and lazed around eating *tortas* and tacos, avoiding the topic of Adele, and reveling in our freedom once again. But a new (or rather old) dilemma presented itself as

Graham finished the last roach: we were weed-less again! I lit a smoke and said, "We gotta' find more."

"This isn't like the city," Graham informed me. "If you haven't noticed we're right in the middle of a quiet, church going community."

"Yeah, but somebody around here must grow it. Remember Ixtlán?"

"Yeah, remember how hard that was?"

But when it came to weed I was always optimistic. I replied, "What else have we got to do? It can't hurt to ask a few people."

"Don't be so sure about that dude. But hey, I'm not going to stop you. If you can find green in *this* place, then all props."

So as we wandered the dirt-streets and cobblestone alleys I asked almost every youthful looking person we saw: all of them stared at me blankly or said, "No, eso es malo! (No, that's bad!)." By the time Adele caught up with us we were still dry.

Together again in the plaza (to my dismay) the three of us climbed our favorite pyramid where Graham and I planned to camp and spare our now dwindling accounts. I dragged the tent up then found the most level surface, and as I set up, Graham and Adele walked to the edge overlooking the plaza, sat down, and began to snuggle. *Ugh*, I cringed. *Oh well, if Graham wants to bang this miserable creature then so be it. He'll break her heart, we'll hit the road, and then he'll be mine again.*

By the time the tent was up they were kissing, so I ran down the pyramid to the corner-store and bought some beer and tequila, all the while thinking of Wanda on grad-night. When I returned they were still necking and continued to do so as I wondered around the other side slugging my liquor and watching the stars appear one by one. I recalled the great droned nights of my life and pondered each stars' relevance to the friends in each memory—like Seany, Jesse and Jocelyn lying on the sands of Island View Beach, realizing that anything we could imagine had actually happened or simply *was* through the ineffectual portal of time which has neither past nor future, but just is. And more importantly, the soothingly painful emotion each star held fast for me when I was a teenager standing on my high-school's roof well past the witching hour, listening to my eerie tunes on headphones and pining after Vanessa, after redemption, after fruition of my heart's musical longings, the deepest undiscovered wants of my soul which I was still to young to understand but felt above and beyond all things: realms bigger then anything in my tiny world on the Saanich peninsula. The trees that loomed over and shadowed my haunts, the secret places I stewed in and willed the fantastic while the rest of the town slept in unawareness.

And so as Graham played his puppy-dog games I began to sing, the old spirits pouring out of me to meet my newest muse unbound. I flowed drunkenly from contemplative ramblings to transcendent melodies charged with their own dialects and meanings. I let myself go in a way I hadn't in months and began to soar, drowning out the street noise with long low breaths of Tibetan throat singing then swooping up to higher inflections and middle-eastern-like chants—until I was interrupted.

Three dark figures appeared on the opposite side and huddled around a tiny flame. *They're lighting something!* I thought and approached them, my blurred eyes squinting to make out who they were. I drunkenly sputtered, "Ola mi amigos... uh, do you have, or, do you know where there's any *morta*?"

The figure nearest me turned and said in surprise, "Drogas?" as his friend took a huge drag off his cigarette that made the ember glow bright enough to light the crest on his shirt. I painfully realized that I had just asked three cops on their smoke break for weed as the first one said, "Eso es malo man! You can't do dat here... is very bad..." The other two shifted their weight towards me and I immediately played the fool: "Oh really? Oh, lo soriento amigo! Where I come from it's okay."

"Not here, is very bad. Do not ask anyone okay gringo? You get in big trouble. Be very careful." His partners looked me up and down speaking in hushed Spanish, undoubtedly questioning what to do with me, then came to some sort of agreement and started laughing their asses off, either because they thought I was so ignorant about their country that I had to ask if drugs were allowed, or because they knew I was so drunk that I hadn't noticed they were police. Either way they left me for crazy and went back to their shift chuckling away, much to my incredible relief. The irony was so delicious I had to interrupt Graham

Sinning Man's Heaven

and Adele and share the tale, even if it meant making Graham more wary of my ways. Instead he had a good chuckle at me saying, "Ah Mark, good ole' 'Marky-Mark-stories.'" Adele wasn't even listening. She was lost staring dreamily at Graham's lips as he smiled and laughed at me. Finally the torture came to an end when she had to get back to her room and Graham walked her back. He returned with hot dogs and more beer and we spent the rest of the night enjoying an argument about sex before marriage. I asked him, "So do you really like her?"

"I don't know. Enough to fool around and get my kicks while we're here."

"You're not going to bang her are you?"

He shrugged, "I don't know, maybe. I've been carrying this condom around with me for quite a while; maybe it's time it got used."

"But with her? Dude, I know you're not a believer anymore but, don't you think there's still something to be said about waiting for the right girl, or at least someone you're in love with?"

"Don't worry about it man," he said. "I don't think I dig her any more than that anyways."

"Damn man, I hope not. I can barely stand her."

"Yeah, you've made that pretty clear dude."

"She must hate me, eh? Did she say anything?"

"Actually, not too much," he answered. "Just, 'Wow, he sure has some strong opinions. He must be really interesting to travel with.' And I said, 'Yup, he sure is.'"

CHAPTER 34

Please Bang Our Daughter

Tuesday, September 28, 1999

Graham wanted one more day in Cholula to see how things would play out with Adele, but she had school until three, so in the meantime we decided to take the car out of town and see where we ended up.

Acapatec was a tiny village just off the main highway; no stores or markets, just a small cathedral surrounded by huts and simple square houses of stone interspersed in and around the wide muddy road. Across from this cathedral lived a large family who claimed to have a one hundred year old family recipe for the best *tortas* in Mexico, which they sold right there under the huge tarp sheltering their front door. You couldn't argue: if a sandwich was ever divine it was the one they made me.

Nobody was around, just the two of us and this extraordinarily friendly family made up almost

Sinning Man's Heaven

entirely of women; except for one little boy and a cousin around our age named Pablo who was visiting from school, the only one who spoke any English. He introduced us to his Grandma, a toothless old hag as jolly as Saint Nick, his two Aunts and six little cousins, and lastly to his nineteen-year-old cousin Rosalita whom it was impossible to not notice was drop dead gorgeous: tall and thin with long black hair swishing low enough to graze the belt of her tight jeans which revealed her curvaceous figure, as well as her tucked in white t-shirt and unbuttoned black blouse. Rarely would anyone find this kind of beauty out in the sticks, and she kept stealing glances at me.

The three older women sat on pails around the brick-stove preparing food while she hovered quietly behind them trying to look busy, fiddling with an old tape player and looking through her tape collection. When we were done eating our *tortas* we settled into some difficult but enjoyable conversation (what with Graham's now semi-comprehendible Spanish, Pablo's scant English, and the translations in-between for the rest of the family and myself). Rosalita snuck behind her mother and whispered something in her ear. Mom giggled uncontrollably and said something for everyone to hear. They all began laughing and clapping, looking me up and down and raising their eyebrows. Rosalita went back to her tapes and blushed. I looked at Graham for a clue and he said, "She says her daughter likes you." I smiled shyly at her as grandma wheezed something loudly and they

227

all exploded into laughter again. Graham turned red as his smile reached ear to ear and I asked, "What?"

He chuckled, "Huh huh, oh man, grandma's a little perverted!"

"What?" I repeated.

"She's referring to your height and how high you'd make her granddaughter bounce, if you know what I mean?"

I looked back at the family and the women were staring in the general area of my crotch, giggling profusely and elbowing poor Rosalita. The aunt said something to the mom, who said something to Graham, who said something to Pablo, who said something back to Graham, who said to me, "So what do you want?"

"What do you mean?" I whispered nervously.

"Dude, what do you want? You can have her."

I looked over at Pablo who nodded indifferently, then whispered back to Graham, "I can just...have her?"

"Whatever you want man. They're offering her to you; you're tall and white. Color's like currency around here, maybe they want her to have a light-skinned baby."

"You mean like, I could just take her inside right now and do it?"

"Dude, whatever you want."

I sat there stunned by this sudden lewd proposal. The girl was hot, and of course I wanted her, but how utterly indecent to just jump her right then and there in front of the whole family! To break the silence in this awkward moment I said to the older cousin, "Tell Rosalita I think she's beautiful and I wish we didn't have to leave." He did and she smiled and then frowned, so I promised we'd stop to visit on our way back in a couple weeks. Grandma wheezed something and Graham translated, "They want you to give her a hug goodbye." So I hugged her tight and gave her a kiss on the cheek, to which her family responded with uproarious *"oohs"*, *"awes"*, and *cooey* giggles. She waved sadly as we drove away.

Graham at the wheel said, "Man, I can't believe you didn't do anything about that. She was fine!"

"Damn, I know... I wanted her too! But that was so weird right? I couldn't just take her inside and start *shaggin'*."

"Who says you had to? You should have stayed behind and hung out with her and I could have come back for you later."

I cursed, "Damn! I know! I wasn't thinking straight; it was such an awkward situation."

"Yeah," he laughed, "Grandma was freakin' hilarious!"

"DAMN MAN! I want her! Why didn't I stay?"

Graham instructed, "Go back! I'll be hanging with Adele tonight; take the car and pick her up!"

"I dunno' man," I roller-coasted; "makes me nervous. We can't even understand each other—"

"Dude! We're on our fantasy trip to Mexico and you just met a hot *señorita* who wants you! You don't have to understand each other, just drive back tonight and get your kicks!"

There's nothing quite like a friend's fresh perspective is there? That was it, I resigned myself to giving up this whole waiting until marriage business (which is incredibly easy to do when there's a dream-babe who wants you and you're horny as hell) and going back to Acapatec with roses and a bottle of tequila to steal away Rosalita for a romantic night in my tent on the pyramid. I told Graham my plan, then he reached into his bag and handed me his only condom. He said almost mockingly, "I guess you've changed your mind about some things since last night, eh?"

Eluding the topic I said, "You sure you're not going to need that?"

"If I need one I'll find it; besides, I'd rather see you score with that hot little number before me with Adele."

"Alright," I joked taking the condom, "but I'm only doing this for your own good."

We parted back in Cholula. Graham went on foot to meet Adele and I took the car to run my errands: a dozen red roses from the local florist, a two-six of tequila and a quick stop at a station for gas and smokes. Then it was time to make the hour long drive back to find my *señorita*. With every mile my heart beat faster and my stomach filled with more butterflies.

I have to do this I thought. *I've waited long enough! How can God expect me to pass this up? Why should I wait any longer? It could be years before I find the right girl, and I'm not ready for marriage! But I'm bloody-well ready for sex! I've never been so horny in my life! It is just sex. It's just harmless sex. Please God forgive me, I have to do this; my libido is going to explode!*

My nerves were so shaken I began to doubt my ability to go through with it, so I opened the tequila and had some shots. *Whatever it takes* I told myself, the lust outweighing the fear. No matter how bad my anxiety got I was going to get laid.

The hour was up and the orange sun was just beginning to kiss the horizon as I slugged another couple shots, ready to greet Rosalita with the roses. I found the highway exit. Acaptatec. The church. The house. And Pablo sitting there with three other guys... *Crap!* They were too engaged in their conversation to notice me zoom up over the hill and fly under their noses. I tore down the other side and parked at the end of the road where I could still see them in the rearview mirror.

Now what do I do? That could be her dad and uncles, or worse yet, her boyfriend and posse! Time melted away as I sat waiting to see if they would leave or if Rosalita would appear. My heart beat furiously and I slugged another shot counting the seconds. As my nerves churned and flexed I recalled the first time I went to Vanessa's window at two in the morning and I had to crawl through her neighbor's back yard on the Native reserve. Luckily he hadn't cut his lawn in awhile because his huge dog heard me and started barking savagely and I dove down into it. The neighbor came out onto the porch with two of his big hairy beer-drinking buddies to see what was up. They stood there drunkenly questioning the dog and peering into the darkness, looking for any trespassers for the longest twenty minutes of my life. That was when I was sixteen. Now I was twenty-one, but for some reason I was twice as afraid. One more shot of tequila and I drove away.

Ten minutes later I turned down a dirt path that took me into the heart of a cornfield. I pulled over for another shot and a smoke.

I can't give up yet. I'll go back and maybe they'll be gone, then I'll get my girl. Anxiety gripped me tenfold as I searched for the stones to try again. My stomach began rolling like a rock-polisher. The tension was too much—I jerked off. Then the ever so familiar waves of scalding shame crashed over me.

WHAT AM I DOING??? This is not what I want! I want to wait for marriage! I don't want to honor a few random moments of lust, I want to honor God eternal!

I felt in my heart as if I *had* just done it with Rosalita; if those dudes weren't in front of her house I would have. It was worse than the guilt I felt when I was sixteen and went too far with Vanessa—but I loved her. This was something different, and everything finally came together. There in that cornfield, after years of keeping the distant memories of my babysitter at bay, the key source of my afflictions became clear:

I was only seven years old when it started; she was twelve. "You show me yours and I'll show you mine" turned into heavy petting, which then turned into full-blown intercourse... I didn't even know what it was, just that part of me liked how it felt, part of me hated the feeling afterwards, and that at all costs no one could ever find out. This went on intermittently for about three years until I didn't need a sitter anymore. Then when I turned eleven, old enough to understand what sex was and how much I'd already had, I became sick to my stomach and buried it. *What the fuck was wrong with her that she could do that to me?* I thought. *And keep doing it even when she was fifteen? Didn't she know better? Should I have known better?* I despised her.

I wasn't drunk enough yet to face the rest. I hit the bottle hard and made a beeline back to Cholula.

The Cholula exit blew by an hour later, unbeknownst to my blurred vision in the now black night. With empty bottle in hand I found myself in Puebla without a clue as to which way my pyramid lay. Dead-end after dead-end, my heart began to race. Drunk and confused, the horrible realization that I was fiercely lost sunk in, so I began to drive faster and more recklessly up every road that might lead back to the highway. Things only got worse. My lips quivered frantically in prayer, and then I saw the red and blue lights flashing behind me. Panic gripped my entire body as I pulled over. The patrolman said something over his intercom but I couldn't understand. He yelled even louder, so I quickly rolled the window down, stuck my hands out and shouted, "No habla Español!"

He climbed out of the patrol car with gun in hand and made his way cautiously up to my window.

"No habla Español, lo soreiento," I repeated, my voice cracking.

"License?" he asked in English. My hand shook as I handed it to him. He continued, "Where are you from?"

"Canada, sir. I'm lost."

"Dis your car?"

The hair on my neck stood up. "No sir, it's my friend's."

"Where is your friend?"

"He's in Cholula; we're here on vacation visiting a friend but I can't find my way back."

He shifted his weight from his left leg to his right and leaned down to give me my license back. "Give me de registration."

I fished nervously through the glove compartment and handed it to him.

"What is your friend's name?"

"Graham," I croaked.

He handed it back and pointed over the windshield, "You're going de wrong way, Cholula is dat way. Slow down or I give ticket!"

My blood pressure plummeted so that I thought I was going to faint, but heard myself say, "Yes sir, thank you officer, gracias!"

"You very lucky Canada. Have good vacation. Slow down, okay?" he said sternly as he holstered his gun then turned back to the patrol car.

"Thank you sweet Jesus!" I gasped for air. That cop must have had a bad sense of smell because I reeked of alcohol. Plus, if he hadn't pulled me over and pointed to Cholula, I would have carried on in the wrong direction! He was an angel in cop's clothing.

It was still hard going even on the right path. The old streets were impossible to make sense of, with pointless turns and random dead-ends so that it was evident there were no civil engineers involved in their layout. Over an hour later I still had no real bearing and the frustration drove me to tears. As I sobbed out one last prayer in tired desperation a familiar building passed by my left. I pulled over, jumped up on the hood, and did a three-sixty. There was the big pyramid! Not in the direction I expected, but there it was! "How did I get so lost?!" I said out loud. And still it was hard to wind my way through these ant-farm-like alleys, until I was finally speeding down the main stretch towards our plaza. "Thank you God," I chanted over and over.

Half-expecting the Hotel Reforma to no longer exist I now found it with ease and parked our beloved Tercel in its usual spot. I was painfully lonely now and hoped Graham, hell, even Adele was on the little pyramid next to our tent like the night before, but they were no where to be seen. A walk around the coffee shops, the bars, and the rest of the neighborhood proved fruitless as well. With no one around and nothing to do I longed even more than usual for my precious marijuana, so I resigned myself to the next best thing: whiskey and junk food. My wallet was empty so I stopped at the bank for some cash and made the idiot mistake of using the same machine as before. It swallowed my card, to which I responded with a loud curse and a swift kick to what I imagined was its ass. At least it spat out my money. I bought my liquor and chips next door then wandered out into the vacant plaza under the cool starry sky to drink alone and face a few demons.

In the center of the gardens where the gazebo stood I settled myself down on one of the park benches nestled amongst the dark green bushes and caught myself in one of those moments, that kind of silent reflection so bitter-sweet you can almost taste it fermenting under your tongue. I remembered how romantic I thought the setting was when we first arrived in Cholula, and now here I was. Everything seemed so beautiful and the loneliness was unbearable. I put on my headphones in search of a piece of home and played an old mix-tape Jordan had given me back in high school. It was of some comfort, and it reminded me of nights just like this one, when I was younger and still new to the feeling of being drunk or stoned with what I thought at the time were glorious memories and revelations. And better yet, the nights before I started using, when the thoughts were pure and inspired simply by music, by girls, and best of all just by the mysterious complexities of the late night sky itself which God spread before me as the rest of the world slept. What freedom, and I had marred it.

David Bowie's *Heart's Filthy Lesson* came on as a couple walked passed me holding each other. I imagined it was Lori and me. *Whoa!* There was the taboo subject of Lori that I had managed to pretty much avoid all trip. Now, after trying to prepare myself to bone some strange girl, a thought crossed my mind. I recalled Lori sitting reluctantly at a distance from me the first time we hung out outside of our gigs. Here I was, this older guy full of testosterone, and it couldn't have eluded her to think that all I wanted to do was get in her pants, when in reality there was nothing further from the truth! I loved her and yet never once expressed my honorable intentions; it hadn't even occurred to me whilst lost in my fear of women— and there it was. I never understood what the abuse in my past had done to me. I was scared to death of women, so much so that part of my unconscious had begun to hate them. Was that why I had been a monster to Wanda and a pig to Adele?

And all the while I couldn't turn the other side off, the boiling, uninvited lust that had haunted me since I was small. But it was never directed at Lori, in fact I barely thought of her in that way out of sheer fear and respect. Instead, I looked at porn without relating the two at all. My lust was a being unto itself, completely disconnected from my real emotions and my true desires! I was born an innocent! Without these external struggles I had a heart unlike generic men. I was made to be pure and whole-heartedly wanted nothing more! What if when I was at my weakest there had been no Internet in the house? What if the older boys had never shown me those magazines in my pre-teens? WHAT IF I NEVER HAD THAT HORNY BABYSITTER?

But wait. There was something more, something even before her. I remembered that when I was four or five years old I began to imagine bizarre things: vile sexual fantasies about naked women deep underground stroking me until I had an erection and then breaking it off...

Um, yeah... First, let me assure you that there was absolutely nothing in my upbringing to have inspired any of this. Now some readers may consider themselves intelligent and well-educated, some proficient at interpretation, and some even experts in the field who could psycho-analysis these self imposed waking-dreams and say things like, "Well, there must have been some trauma during early-development which he in turn related to an image he saw in a book or on television after his father died blah-de-bloom-blah—" but this is not that sort of nonsense. An innocent, untainted mind concocted this perverted swill of its own volition? I'll tell you exactly where that came from: Hell. All the filth that had followed me from my childhood up to this moment was the work of dark-forces hell-bent on distancing me from the great plans God had for my life—and it was working.

So there, on my last night in the plaza of Cholula, drowning my shame in whiskey, listening to Marilyn Manson and some other wholesome tunes from Jordan's tape, I came to know these spirits by name. Wait until you see what they had in store for me the next day...

CHAPTER 35
The Climax

Wednesday, September 29, 1999

Graham woke me in the tent with coffee and a bag of sweet breads.

"Mornin' hose-head; you're all alone I see. You hung-over again?"

"Surprisingly no," I said rubbing my eyes and taking the coffee gratefully. "Where'd you two go last night? I thought guys weren't allowed to stay in the girls' building after dark."

"We got a room at the hotel," he spoke casually. "Did you hook up with Rosalita last night?"

"No. She wasn't there."

"Did you knock at her door?"

"I chickened out."

"Oh well, it's probably for the best. So what'd you do with yourself?"

I went on to explain how I got horribly lost and

narrowly escaped getting arrested and he laughed amusingly at yet another "Marky-Mark-story" while we took down the tent and packed our stuff in anticipation of hitting the road once more. It felt really good to see the now all too familiar buildings of Cholula pass by for the last time.

"You know, this is one town I'm actually going to miss," Graham remarked.

"'Cause of Adele?"

"Na, I've had my fill of her."

I was scared of the truth but had to ask sooner or later: "Did you bone her?"

He paused then gave a little smirk, "Almost. She wanted to. We laid there all night cuddling and she kept staring at me with those puppy dog eyes, then I realized I find her too annoying to go that far."

"Thank God," I actually sighed out loud. "We did good man. That's it, I'm seriously waiting for marriage."

"I wouldn't go that far, but yeah, somehow I'm glad we both got through that unscathed."

I laughed, "Yeah, something tells me sex with Adele *would* get you scathed!"

"You really didn't like her, did you?" he asked.

I caught myself, took a couple deep breaths then said, "I'm really sorry about all that man."

"No you're not!" he laughed almost angrily. "You made it perfectly clear what you think of her right to her face, and she still let us stay!"

"I know, I know; I was a total ass and I had no right."

"Whatever dude!" he continued. "Don't say

you're sorry just to make it better when you're really not!"

"Graham! Jeez man! You know me better than that! Yes, she bugged me—hell, even you just called her annoying, but I'm not apologizing to her, I'm apologizing to you! You're my best friend, I love you, and I'm honestly sorry I was so rude. I wouldn't say it if I didn't bloody well mean it."

Lucky for me Graham was such a sharp kid. He didn't hold on to the drama begrudgingly like a lot of people would. He immediately replied, "Alright dude, I believe you. Thanks. Sorry I dragged us there; it *is* more fun out here with you, but it's good to get a break—we were turning into an old married couple."

"Ha! Yeah. Tensions tend to mount with folk like us," I agreed.

"Yeah dude."

"Yeah dude."

"Yeah dude."

"You know what? I really like saying yeah dude."

"Yeah dude. We just need to smoke more weed," Graham joked.

"Dag yo! I know. That was the one crappy thing about Cholula."

"Hey Mark? Sorry I was such a paranoid dick about smokin' up back in Ixtlán."

I was stunned. What a strange and wonderful thing to admit at that point. There was always something about the guy where at times you'd feel increasingly disconnected from him, almost to the point where you feared he possessed a hard and indifferent spirit, then you'd share a conversation like that and you'd realize he was keeping all the rich treasures of his beautiful soul from the light of the world so he could relish in them on his own terms. He was a born traveler.

Did you notice I never got my bankcard back? Well I didn't until about ninety minutes southbound and Graham was pissed at me again.

"You stuck it in the same bank machine?"

"I thought I had flattened it out enough," I explained.

"Damn man, can't you just forget it? I don't want to drive all the way back; we finally got out of there! You can get a new one back home."

"But who knows how long that'll be! I need money dude," I argued.

"You can borrow mine until we get home."

"I already owe you for gas. I'll drive back okay? It's only an hour and a half."

"Exactly!" he exclaimed. "Three hours to get back to where we were! I want to get to Oaxaca before dark!"

"Don't worry," I coaxed him looking at the map, "it's not that far; we'll make it. I'll buy you a beer, okay?"

Agitated but convinced it was better to have more money between us, he gave up the wheel and I headed back to Cholula remembering what he'd said after the last time I lost my card: "Next time you do it yourself."

I did my best to explain to the teller but her

Sinning Man's Heaven

English was as bad as my Spanish and Graham ended up helping me anyways, partially because he was in such a rush to leave town again before Adele saw us. Mission accomplished.

In the next small town we ate *tortas* and stopped at a shop for road beers. Graham discovered rum-and-coke in a can, which he thought was a real novelty.

I drank and drove us all the way to the city of Oaxaca (Wa-ha-ka). Adele told us it had plenty of pyramids and art galleries to check out, so that was our plan for the following day.

The traffic in Oaxaca was like the hyper-speed level on *Tetris* when we arrived in the early evening, and it didn't help that it was pouring down rain and I was buzzing off four beers. I struggled to focus amongst the mayhem of crazy cab drivers, big trucks and tiny cars whizzing around the sketchy traffic patterns. Graham held his breath and I flexed anxiously as we found ourselves caught in the frenzied merry-go-round of a giant three-lane circus. Vehicles spun around us like bees as I tried to find an opening where I could take the exit we wanted. A bus changed lanes and braked so that I saw my chance. I threw the stick into fourth and gunned past it, narrowly missing a yellow Volkswagen that honked as it tried to merge. With enormous relief, we escaped the beehive and sped up a one-way street where I found a tiny parking spot on the left side. I banked hard into it before it was taken.

"Whew!" Graham released the tight air in his lungs joyously and praised me: "All props dude! You

243

really are the ninja drunk-driver!" And as I stepped out of the driver side Graham opened his door into oncoming traffic and the Tercel was slammed forward half a foot, causing me to fall forward and catch myself on the door! Graham was unharmed apart from a little whiplash, but the passenger side door was smashed in real good. And worse, the front end of this lady's brand new Ford Sedan was toast! Graham jumped out to make sure the lady was all right. She was obviously annoyed, but really quite forgiving once we were sure no one was hurt. Without local numbers to exchange, the lady thought it best if Graham went with her to her insurance office immediately, and before I knew it, I was sitting alone in our poor little car baffled at the sudden change of circumstances, which were nothing yet.

    I drank the last beer and found a garbage can up the street for the empties, bought some smokes in the adjacent corner store then returned to our sad little car where I struggled to close our now mangled door. I thanked God the window had been broken back in Guadalajara otherwise Graham would have been turned into *Captain Glassface*.

    It was almost dark an hour later when Graham showed up with the lady's family and their insurance guy who snapped some photos of our door before they all left again. Another hour passed with some *King Crimson* in my headphones until Graham returned again in the rain with his long wet hair drooping sadly over his disheveled expression. Resting his head on the roof of the car he moaned, "One thousand

American dollars. I owe them one thousand American dollars tomorrow morning at 9:00 a.m."

"You're kidding me?" I gasped.

"Nope. I wouldn't kid you Mark. Actually, that sounds about right. Yup, I think that's all the money I have left in my account; enough to buy that nice family a brand new bumper with just enough left over to get us the biggest bottle of tequila in the city."

We moped our way to the corner store and my defeated little buddy purchased the mother of all tequila bottles; not the two-six, not the forty ounce, but the eighty ounce family pack: over two liters of hard alcohol to drown our sorrows and knock us out so we could sleep in the car. Graham wasn't exaggerating. His account would be literally empty in the morning and mine was sinking under the three hundred dollar mark. There would be no more hotel rooms, no more reckless living, and the pitiful realization that we were going to have to turn back sunk in as we drank, drank, and drank some more.

We got drunk. Now I've said that a lot up until now, but listen: we got D-R-U-N-K. We worked that bottle so fast on empty stomachs that I am positive there has never been that much alcohol in my blood stream in all my life. Graham watched as I gulped it like water and said, "Nice work. You've turned into a regular lead belly."

The wet streets of the now dark and quiet city glowed faintly under the faded yellow moon as a hazy, drunken sleep began to creep over us...

And now I'm afraid our story really begins.

A silhouetted figure crept out of the shadows and scurried up to the driver's side window where I was just passing out and knocked. I startled and looked up to see a stocky, head-shaven thirty-something Mexican peering into the car. He said something in Spanish and Graham whispered, "He's asking for a light." I rolled down the window and lit the guy's smoke. He took a deep drag then said, "Gracias amigo! Hey, you guys American?"

"No, Canadian," I answered woozily.

"I love Canada!"

Graham perked up and asked, "You ever been?"

"No amigo, but I was in de Middle East for a year and I met some Canadian soldiers. Dey were good guys like you! I'm Paco; wanna' come party?"

Graham chuckled and said, "Hell yeah we wanna' party," and before I could say anything he jumped out of the car, pushed his seat forward and let our new friend into the back. Paco patted me on the shoulder from behind and exclaimed, "Alright amigo, drive up de street den turn left at de lights."

"Hold on a second you guys," I protested. "I'm in no condition to drive right now."

Graham argued back, "C'mon man. You're the ninja remember! We're gonna' live it up with this guy."

"I already lived it up with that giant bottle of tequila and I drank way more than you! Besides, I'm so freakin' tired now."

Graham implored me, "Dude I've had the worst day and all I wanna' do is get wrecked! This could be

Sinning Man's Heaven

our last chance to really get our kicks before it's all over. C'mon, please? I'd drive but I trust you more."

There was nothing I could do. I fired up our little wreck and sped dangerously up and down the semi-vacant streets ready to dig in to the blur...

We stopped at some dungy bar (where everyone seemed elated to see us) to chug down a beer and meet a drunken acquaintance of Paco's who gave Graham and I each a great big hug, then we had to drive to Paco's "mother's" house to steal her marijuana (at least he said she was his mother), the old white haired hag who came running to the window screaming furiously as he leapt from the second floor and landed right in front of our getaway car and half yelled half laughed at me, "Go go go!" which I did while Graham rolled a joint with the stolen weed that Paco accidentally spilled all over the floor as we hot-boxed our ride on the way to "Javier's" house who was in the middle of shagging his girl when Paco pulled him off her right in front of us and told him to get dressed so we could go score some cocaine which we did up the block before dropping Javier back at his place on the way to the Mayor of Oaxaca's house to which I asked, "Why the hell would we go to the Mayor's house?" and Paco replied, "To party with the Mayor!" as he pointed down an extremely narrow driveway between two close set walls which I scratched up badly with the beaten side of our car in my droned attempt to park outside the front door that was locked, so Paco climbed the wall like a monkey, reached inside the window, pulled up the leaver, dropped inside

247

the vacant house and opened the door for me and Graham who asked hesitantly, "What if somebody comes home?" and Paco laughed, "It's okay, I'm a policeman and the Mayor is my amigo!" as he closed the door behind us and proceeded to cut the coke on the table where we took turns snorting and puffing on another fatty-ala-Graham until Paco coughed, "We forgot beer," and he made us walk up the street to a tiny grocery where we bought cigarettes and two six-packs which we brought back to the house again to drink, smoke, toke, and do more lines off the Mayor's coffee table with this officer of the law.

Fuzz. Stinging, biting, electro-magnetic fuzz tingled and danced all around and all inside me. It was the first time I could actually feel my liver. As Paco's thin, chapped lips flapped relentlessly about his time in the Gulf War my knees vibrated fiercely in rhythm like two jackhammers on autopilot. Graham sat wide-eyed squeezing his nose and sniffing repeatedly while Paco rolled up his sleeves to show us the multitude of scars he had on his wrists and forearms from knife fights he'd been in with black American soldiers saying, "De blacks hated us."

We arm-wrestled and Paco destroyed me. We had a mercy fight (locked at the fingers to see who bends first) and I managed to beat him with my strong drummer hands. To prove his superior strength he told me to sit on his back and he started doing push-ups with ease! The night melted into utter chaos and my body hurt amidst the pulsing feelings of pleasure, power, and semi-awareness. We got our kicks at the plateau.

I don't remember driving Paco home that night, just Graham exclaiming afterwards, "It's five in the morning! I have to be at the Ford Center Building in four hours!" He spotted five teenagers on the side of the road painting graffiti over a bus stop billboard and told me to pull over for directions. Their directions were scant at best, so in the end three of them drove there in their little Volkswagen and we followed with the other two in our back seat. They led us to the outskirts of town where the Ford Center Building sat between a strip mall parking lot and an open field that stretched out into the hills and woodlands surrounding the city. We thanked them profusely for their trouble and gave them what little pesos we had left. Barely able now to keep my chemically saturated head up, I somehow managed to pull the car around to the side of the enormous building where we could rest unseen until Graham's inevitable appointment. I slipped into the nightmare...

CHAPTER 36
Hell

Thursday, September 30, 1999

"Shit! It's almost nine thirty!" Graham woke me to the pain, the mother of all hangover-comedowns: eyeball spinning, head melting, body wrenching anguish.

"I've *gotta'* meet these people— owe, my bleeding skull! This sucks."

"Ugh... I don't think I can get up," I moaned.

"You look bleak dude, stay here and rest. I should be back in an hour then we can get the hell outta' here."

I could barely see. The gray, drizzly morning appeared overcast like my brain, which swirled in torment. It hurt so bad I couldn't stop wriggling uncomfortably in my seat, trying in vain to find a position I could stomach. This went on and on, each infinite second bringing with it new dizzy forms of tortuous nausea. The cocaine was evil; I had no idea how much I'd done, not like my meager experiments in Guadalajara. My mind slipped in and out of consciousness like this until, all of a sudden, my entire body began shaking violently! *Oh dear God! I'm having a seizure!* A sharp spasm threw my head back so that I could see the Ford Center Building (which was three stories high and half the size of a football field) splitting up the middle, with huge chunks of concrete breaking off the top and crashing down right beside me! I wasn't having a seizure! A 7.4 earthquake was leveling Oaxaca!

It finally registered in my swollen head that I was about to get squashed by the falling debris, so I dove out the opposite side of the car where the quake knocked me to the ground. The muddy puddles splashed high into the air and fell on me as the car was pelted with debris from the building.

In my dreadful state the severity of the situation didn't fully sink in. Struggling to my feet, I crawled back into the car and fell into the driver's seat. Time oozed by agonizingly. The quake had added whiplash to my suffering. I thought I heard a scream in the distance, but from my limited vantage point on the outskirts of the city there was nobody to be seen. I saw smoke in the sky, and then on an adjacent hill I could actually see fire. The outlines of distant buildings and homes on the horizon now appeared altered or gone. How much damage had ensued? How long had I been lying there before or after the quake? My head throbbed and my tongue stuck to the roof of my mouth like sandpaper. The thought of standing up and hunting for water was insurmountable. I dug my watch out of my shorts: 12noon. Where was Graham? He'd bring water... 12:30 p.m. Gone three hours? He said he'd be back in one. I couldn't survive any longer without hydration, so I dragged myself with great difficulty across the street to an empty McDonald's. The door was locked so I peered through the window. A man inside shook his bandaged head and waved me away. The mall was my only hope, although the empty parking lot was a bad sign. To my great relief the doors were unlocked and I stepped in over the fallen racks, broken glass and other debris. No one was inside except for a couple of clerks rummaging through the damage. A beverage cart lay on its side with bottles and cans strewn about, so I snagged a Pepsi and a water bottle then made my way back to the car hoping Graham would be ready to leave. No sign of him. That's when I started to worry. It was 1:15 p.m., almost four hours since he'd left, and the looming notion of what could have happened began to linger with the pain of my hangover. Moms always talk about how teenagers think they're immortal. Cliché or not, I still felt that way. I promised myself Graham was fine. He had to be. He must have had some trouble with the bank and needed to get in touch with his own back home. Convinced that that was it, I waited uncomfortably in the car with my drinks staring up at the giant crack in the Ford Center Building.

Two businessmen came out a little later to assess the damaged wall. One of them knocked on my door and said something. I asked if he spoke English. He said, "You go now please! Dis car can't be here!"

"Por favor mi amigo. I have to wait here. My friend... mi amigo is meeting me here. I can't move."

His associate stepped in and said something that I assumed convinced him to let me stay. He gave a hesitant smile and said, "Okay, little longer."

2:00 p.m. He had to be all right. I knew he was all right; it was Graham.

2:15 p.m.... Five hours. The worry grew into fear. I staggered inside the building to use the bathroom. Car dealers and secretaries were busy cleaning up the quake's mess. The lady at the front desk hesitated to let me go but couldn't refuse when she saw how desperate I was. My fever went down a hair after I threw up and wet my sweaty forehead, then when I returned to the car at 3:00 p.m. it was far outweighed by the horror that Graham was still missing. Five and a half hours.

Where is he? There has to be a good explanation. I can't be alone; he'll show.

Six hours.

Dear God help me. Please Jesus, bring him back! I can't do this! What do I do? Where do I go? I don't have enough money to make it home! Even if I could speak this language, who would I go to for help?

4:00 p.m. Six and a half hours. My head finally cleared enough to comprehend the reality of the situation: An earthquake had just hit Oaxaca. I was outside of it surrounded by solid concrete and trees; I had no idea how much damage was inflicted. The city

253

was a relic, made of brick and mortar, thatched roofs and crude stonework. It must have been devastated! Nobody cares about me! There must me thousands of people wounded, hundreds dead...

    4:30 p.m. The headache, the confusion, the fear was more real then anything I had ever known. I flashed on my mother telling me once, "It's a scary thing to reach adulthood and come out from underneath your parent's roof."

    My spirit began to give. The tears pressed hard against the inside of my eyelids but I held them back, still clinging to my last shred of hope. He couldn't be dead; it was impossible. Why did we come to this God-forsaken country?

    Dear Jesus, don't forsake me now! I'm sorry! I'm so sorry for this life I've lived! You are my only savior! You are my only hope! Please God save me from this mess! Please bring me back my friend! I need him! Forgive us! I will change God! I will live the life you want me to lead! Please show me what to do!

    Nothing. I was lost. Sin had finally broken me, there in sinning man's heaven. The brutal revelations I'd had over the journey rose like flooding waters and broke the levee, that stubborn will I'd kept holding up for so long. The lust, the drugs, the booze, the selfish dreams fueled by demons I'd invited into my life and grown too lazy to rebuke after recognizing their hideous faces. Now I was drowning in them. Now I would suffer for my evil ways.

    5:00 p.m.
    5:30 p.m.

6:00 p.m.

6:30 p.m.

Nine hours passed, the worst hours of my life. Graham was dead, and I knew it then. I trembled under God's wrath and groped desperately into the nothingness for even the most remote sense of guidance as the dreary sun sank amongst the foggy hills. Terror and loneliness so pure and disturbing came with the evening, finally crushing my spirit completely, and I gave in wholly to the abyss.

As my head flopped over like a rag doll my eyes fell on the rear view mirror to see a dark figure approaching the car. It was Graham.

I leapt out of the car in whitewashing joy and almost screamed, "Where were you, you asshole?!"

He dragged himself up to me like a beaten dog and gently spoke, "Mark, can I cry on you?" And my best friend fell into my arms and wept.

CHAPTER 37

Get The Hell Out Of Dodge!

"Thank God you're alive! Oh thank God," I sang, squeezing him tight and stroking his hair as he sobbed into my chest. "This is it man, this is really it! I'm changing my life; Jesus led us out here so this could happen!"

"No he didn't," Graham whispered standing up straight and taking off his glasses to wipe his eyes.

"Are you kidding me? "

"Dude, I just lost everything I worked for this summer, dragged a guy out from underneath a building, and saw a bunch of dead people. Does that sound like Jesus' doing?"

It wasn't worth getting into now. I just hugged him again and said, "Whatever man, all I know is I just spent the entire day convinced you were dead and now you're here, you big jerk! What the hell happened to you?"

"Long story. Did you eat yet?"

"Everything's been closed, besides, I was way too sick—but I'm dying for some grease now. You wanna' hit up that McDonald's even though it's not Mexican food?"

"I'd love a piece of home," he said with a deep breath.

"Graham?"

"Yeah dude?"

"I love you man."

"Yeah dude. I love you too. I'm glad you're all right. Now let's eat then get the hell out of Dodge!"

My joy overcame the hangover at least for the first half hour together again, and McDonald's never tasted so good. As darkness overtook the city we passed through it on our way northwest following a route Paco had helped us outline on our map as the fastest way home. I saw some of the carnage Graham had witnessed and in some places entire buildings had fallen over and crumbled onto the streets where ambulances, fire trucks, and police cars were still whizzing about. Graham asked from behind the wheel, "So now that you're changing your life does that mean you won't roll one up and smoke it with me?"

It would be ridiculous to think I could just quit everything right then and there, even with my new, hard-earned convictions. I reconciled the fact that some treats would be unavoidable until I got home where my real work would begin. Plus, my head was still killing me and there's truthfully no better cure for a hangover then a good toke. So when we were out on the highway, climbing the mountains into the depths of the jungle, I rolled three *doobs* with Paco's left over weed and we huffed one back. The pain subsided and Graham launched into his side of the story:

"I was half an hour late and hurting bad from last night—what a trip hey? I can't believe we're still breathing. But the lady's husband, Jon, was really cool and I'm pretty sure he understood why I was late and hung-over. I almost feel bad for him; you could tell he felt guilty taking a poor sap's money. But after we filled out the paper work I had to go with him to his bank downtown to make the transaction. After it cleared we went across the street to a little café where he bought me breakfast. Then right after the waiter put my coffee down the quake hit and everything came crashing down around us. I don't think anybody in the café got *really* hurt, but the buildings on either side of us *both* fell to the ground..."

"REALLY! Holy cow Graham! That's a miracle! See, God was watching out for you!"

"I don't know; he sure wasn't watching out for those other people."

"Oh man..."

"Yeah dude... It was really scary. The first thing I noticed was that my *full* cup of coffee was now completely empty, but then we started hearing all this crashing and screaming, so we ran outside and there were people bleeding and crying and trapped under junk. Jon helped me pull the bricks off a guy next door then disappeared to make sure his family was all right. Everything just turned into this blurry nightmare. My head was pounding with sirens blaring and people running all over the place. I sat on the sidewalk for a while to collect myself and saw some messed up stuff dude, kids bawling, trying to find their parents amongst the fallen buildings with limbs sticking out. Then I wandered around for a while trying to figure out what to do next while paramedics and looters scrambled around...

"Oh man," I gasped, "you saw way more than me... But why did it take so long for you to come back? I was going insane!"

"Sorry man, I know. I was trying to get through to my mom to put money in my account. I doubt we'd make it home on your three hundred dollars dude."

"I was too wrecked to think that far ahead," I admitted.

"Yeah, but because of the quake the payphone line-ups were stupid-long. I waited in line, called her at work, and it was busy! The people behind me got impatient so I had to get back in line, wait, and try her again. After three or four tries I called my grandparents and gave them the message to pass on, but by the time I called them back they hadn't had any luck either, so I ended up waiting 'til she got home where I finally reached her. Then I had to walk all the way back to the car."

"Holy crap Graham, this is the worst road-trip ever."

"Yeah dude, I wanna' go home. My plan is to

make the world-record driving-time between Mexico and Canada."

"Amen," I agreed whole-heartedly. Easier said than done. At one in the morning we got a flat tire in the heart of the jungle.

"You've got to be kidding me!" Graham laughed psychotically. We climbed out into the pitch-black surrounded by mammoth trees and scary animal noises. I pulled our gear out of the trunk and stacked it on the side of the road and Graham lifted the flap up to get the spare tire. Dig this: the jack was stolen.

"Fucking Gilbert!" Graham swore into the night. "Everywhere I turn that prick comes back to haunt me!" Usually I was the angry one while Graham kept his cool; but now, in this terrible predicament, I felt a strange calm. I prayed aloud, "Dear Jesus, please send someone to help us." Within seconds we heard a car coming up the road and I waved it down. A short Mexican hopped out of his taxi and without a word pulled a jack from his trunk and threw on our spare in a matter of moments. With a quick smile he disappeared into the night. I didn't bother to mention the timing.

The Lonely Planet warned us that people like to play with the road signs. We should have turned right not left at the fork in the road. At 2 a.m. we ended up in an eerie little village bordering the jungle and a vast stretch of farmlands, and after an exhaustive search we discovered that the only way out of town was the road we'd come in on. Graham was now very tired and frustrated. He insisted we pull over and rest but something told me we didn't want to hang

Sinning Man's Heaven

around. I forced myself to catch my second wind and took the wheel with surprising alertness. Graham passed out at as I drove up the cobblestone street and past the ancient architecture where creepy, toothless men waved charms at me and hollered drunken, angry things from behind their burning barrels. I smelled witchcraft. A chill stole over my bones as I escaped the ghostly neighborhood and sped back up the nauseatingly windy road at a dangerous speed to make up the lost time. We'd gone 70 kilometers the wrong way, which meant 140 kilometers of useless travel. I didn't dare let myself get discouraged. The jungle towered over us cold and dark and I wished Graham were awake. Still, I couldn't help but feel a certain pride in my endurance; still pressing on after the great trauma we'd been through. My soul yearned anxiously to devour the difficult miles ahead of us as if I could get Graham home before he awoke. There was still so much to conquer.

Finally back where we turned astray I checked the old hand-painted road sign against our map and saw that indeed someone had switched the directions. I shudder to think what might have happened had we stayed the night in that foreboding village. The feeling traveled with me as I climbed higher and higher up the steep mountains through dense fog and thick vegetation. The view from the top was otherworldly, with sheer lush cliffs spiraling down into the misty blues and purples of a bottomless pit bordered by infinite crags and floating mountains. Their beauty was immeasurable, vast and mysterious, marrying my nerves to the notion that we were now quite literally in the middle of nowhere. This was the top of the world, that mystic place between heaven and earth, and as the road wound around the summit and plunged back down into the heart of the jungle the exhaustion began to take hold. It took every ounce of concentration to keep my blurred eyes open and focused on the dizzying road spiraling unpredictably down at dangerous angles, my body tense and sore from flexing constantly to control the car. My legs ached terribly from braking and shifting and I was certain that at any moment the spare would blow or the engine would die. Besides fear, the only thing that kept me going was the fact that I had no other option. Even if I wanted to, the road was too narrow and dark to pull over for a rest. It was hell on wheels.

At 4:00 a.m. I crushed an opossum. I wasn't the only one; there were dead animals all over the road. At 5:00 a.m., still lost in the jungle, I could make out figures passing through the trees. As the sun rose, its faint rays seeped down into the undergrowth and revealed barebacked natives wielding machetes. They glared solemnly at our intrusion as Graham awoke from (or into) his nightmare. A wiry, muscular native emerged from the jungle right in front of the car with fiery red eyes staring hard through our windshield. Graham whispered, "I sure hope we don't run out of gas dude 'cause I don't feel like being breakfast."

Without exaggeration, at 6:00 a.m. the engine sputtered out as we rolled dry into the first gas station we'd seen in ten hours.

CHAPTER 38

What Sunday School Teachers Say

Friday, October 1, 1999

The torment went on as Graham took the wheel. The humid weather grew more unbearable with the sun approaching its zenith and both our heads were swollen with ache and fatigue. It was too hot to sleep so I lied there in my wretched state fantasizing about my bed. A nasty buzzing sound brought me back to reality and Graham swerved to the side of the road yelling, "What the hell is that!?" An evil looking dark-red insect the size of a quarter lunged at me and I swatted it against the dashboard. Graham leapt out of the car, threw back his seat and tossed me the Lonely Planet. The bug buzzed between the windshield and the dash in that awkward spot you can't reach and both of us got a good look at its massive stinger.

"It a freakin' demon-bug!" I panicked.

"DO NOT let that thing sting you dude! I'm not going to any hospitals today!"

Cracking the book open to make it flat enough to reach inside the crevice I scooped it out of the window. It tried to fly back in and I swatted it out again. Graham jumped back inside and peeled out of there—I could swear it was still following us.

"That was the freakiest looking bug I've ever seen!" I exclaimed. "What is up with this country?"

"What's up with this trip?" he added. Then, just a few minutes down the road, we ran into a drug check. Our remaining two joints were tucked under my crotch and Graham said, "Lose them!" I tossed them out the window into the ditch and nobody noticed. Then I remembered the pipe I bought in Cholula and ditched it two cars behind the check unnoticed. I was sure we were home free, but these *"Federales"* knew exactly what they were looking for. A big Mexican in civilian clothes asked us to step out under the guard of two uniformed men with machine guns. A fourth guard came out from the hut behind us and began to inspect the floor of our car. He was on his knees less than a minute before he placed something in a little plastic bag, held it up to my face and said, *"Sesamia!"* Suddenly both guards cocked their guns and held them right up to our heads! The big guy snickered at Graham, "Why is dere marijuana seeds in your car?"

Graham spoke earnestly, "Because some drunk idiot dumped it there last night by *'accident'*."

Big-guy fought back a smile then resumed searching the car with his partner. They found my shaving kit where I forgot I had stashed 100 American dollars then handed it to me. *Weird.* They found some extra cash Graham had hidden and did the same. In fact, every valuable article they found, trinkets we bought, my watch, and some other odds and ends, they pulled out and told us to pocket. Then Big-guy returned to the hut and the guards pushed us to follow. As we entered Graham whispered, "We're fucked dude."

"Take off your clothes," Big-guy commanded. We stripped down to our sweaty underwear and he went through our pants and wallets and took everything. My blood began to boil. As we put our clothes back on he noticed my gold ring with the family emblem on it and said, "Das a nice ring!"

Now I was pissed. I was so sick of being afraid that I stepped back and said angrily, "Forget about it man!"

Graham hissed under his breath, "Stay cool Mark!"

Big-guy reached out his hand, "Relax amigo, is okay!"

"No it's not fucking okay!" I raised my voice as the guards raised their guns. "This is my dead grandfather's ring and it's been in my family for four generations! If you want it, go ahead and shoot me 'cause I've had it with this fuckin' place!"

Big-guy stared at me for a moment perplexed as Graham hurriedly translated the part about my grandpa, then he smiled and patted me on the shoulder saying, "Is okay gringo, you keep de ring. Is okay now?"

"Oh sure, it's okay," I muttered contemptuously. He led us back to our ransacked car and sent us on our way. The four of them smiled nonchalantly as I called from my seat, "Say hi to Paco for us."

Half disgruntled half impressed Graham exclaimed, "You're crazy dude! I don't know how you get away with that shit; don't think they don't know what you're saying when you curse them out like that."

"I don't care man, I've had it with this country."

"Yeah, me too, but watch that temper or you're gonna' get us both killed, alright?"

"Whatever," I grumbled.

"Don't *'whatever'*. I'm serious man. You say you're going to change your life then do it. Are Christians supposed to blow up and cuss like that?" Graham challenged.

"No, you're right," I said checking myself. "I'm just sick and tired of getting ripped off; they just stole like 130 U.S.!"

"I know; I lost about 50, but at this point it's so ridiculous who cares?"

"Yeah, I know its just money. Sorry man, I drove all night through the freaky-ass jungle after everything else and that was the last straw; again…"

Graham was silent for a little while, and then he asked, "So if you're going to change your life now, does that me you weren't a Christian before?"

"I've always considered myself a Christian, I just haven't been a very good one."

Then he argued, "But isn't that an oxymoron? Isn't the point of being a Christian to be good?"

"I wouldn't say it's the *point*. I think being 'good'

is one of the fruits of leading the proper Christian life."

"Then what's the proper life? Following every single rule in the Bible?"

I answered, "God wants us to be perfect but that doesn't mean he expects us to be able to pull it off; that's why he sent us Jesus, to bare our sins and be the final judge."

"So then what if you died in the earthquake before you had this conviction that you needed to change? Would Jesus have sent you to hell?"

I had to reflect on that a moment then rejoined, "I don't know man… I've been a huge hypocrite, but there hasn't been a moment in my life I didn't believe in him. Maybe that was enough before."

"And now it isn't?" he asked.

"I guess not. I've learned my lesson out here dude."

Graham lit a smoke and from the expression on his face I could tell he'd been building up to something. He said, "When I was a kid my Sunday-school teacher taught us an analogy comparing sin to buildings. She said that people look at each sin from the side where we judge which ones are bigger or smaller, but God looks at them from above so it doesn't matter which ones are taller because they all appear the same to him. Would you agree with that?"

"Yeah, I like that." I answered.

"But aren't they two conflicting points? You were just telling me Jesus would have had mercy on your habits before, but now that *you* deem them sinful he wouldn't. If sin is sin to God doesn't that nullify the fact that it's all relative to us?"

"It's just an analogy dude! In life you can judge a person's character, like it's obviously worse to kill somebody then to steal a candy bar, but both are sin. The point is that God judges you by your heart in the end, not your tally of sins. The murderer can repent and be forgiven whereas the shoplifter could care less and be condemned."

Graham responded, "So you've repented now and you won't be smoking or drinking with me the rest of the trip? What about the *doob* we shared last night?"

"Well I'm kinda' stuck man. It's not like I can just drop the bag right here and now with my partner in crime! There's going to be a whole slew of issues for me to work out if we ever get home."

He rebuked me, "That's unbelievable Mark! You always have some excuse don't you? You're still being the hypocrite after all your preaching!"

"What do you want me to do Graham? Are you going stay sober the rest of the trip?"

"No," he said plainly.

"So you expect me to be able to resist the temptation while I watch? Listen man! I know I've been the worst possible example of what a real Christian should be to all you guys. Yeah, I'm the big hypocrite and now I have to deal with the shame. But ever since you turned your back on God I've had nobody to be accountable with and it's gone from bad to worse for me. You have no idea how deep this crap lies and all the garbage I've had to struggle with 'til now! But dude! You're going to see me change, I promise you!"

We drove in silent tension for a few miles then ran into another drug check, this time by the army. They were much more civil and let us go after a quick inspection. An hour later we passed through yet another check and the truck in front of us was torn apart. Somebody yelled something and the driver tried to make a run for it! He was tackled and cuffed while two *Federales* removed the straw in the back to reveal four crates of guns! Yipping and hollering they let us pass.

"What are the odds of seeing that?" Graham mused.

We arrived in the famous city of Acapulco under a scorching afternoon sun. Our poor spare tire had somehow survived the long road and after much searching we managed to find an auto parts shop and got the mechanic to replace it.

When the car was ready we drove up and down the coast in hope of finding a beach we could sleep on, but Acapulco was no longer the tropical paradise we had imagined. Every square inch was owned or blocked by resorts and restaurants. The frustration called for beer, so we ordered a couple bottles at one of the outdoor bars with tables right on the beach. The harbor was colorful and loud, jammed full of boats and water-skiers and every kind of partygoer. As we sipped our drinks and dug on the ole' boys yipping in falsetto at the passing bathing beauties, a handsome twenty-something Mexican with curly black hair and a moustache approached us.

"Hey amigos!" he said with a deep and husky voice. "You looking for some good times?"

Graham small-talked with him while I sipped my beer disinterestedly; all I could think about was sleep. "Chindo the water-ski instructor," as he called himself wanted us to go out on his friend's boat. Graham declined politely then asked where we could get some weed. Chindo sprinted back to his amigos at the other table and returned in an instant with a bag full of bud.

"How much?" Graham asked in surprised delight.

"Don't worry about dis one!" Chindo smiled wide and proceeded to roll a fatty right there in plain sight. He assured us there was no risk, as his buddy owned the property, so we got high. This was how I had always envisioned a trip to Mexico and now I wished we'd spent our time on the coast. It was a nice break from the turmoil of our travels, even if it only lasted a few seconds. Chindo got that look in his eye; I knew it. He said the word "coca" and Graham was sold.

"No more Graham," I pleaded. "I'm so tired dude…"

"You don't have to do anything," he blurted, "but I'm still gonna' get my kicks while we're stuck here."

There was nowhere else for me to go. They dragged me across town to another bar where we had a drink and struck out, so Chindo took the wheel (he knew the busy streets better) and drove us to the next place he thought we could score. Inside, drinking another beer against my will, I realized we were in a whorehouse. The owner called down the girls even though Graham and I both declined. He asked if we were gay then made us check out his selection anyways. Chindo pressed us saying, "Whas de matter? Dey give you good love!" The skanky girls were offended after we declined a third time and gave us dirty looks. I didn't give a rat's ass. I was so tired I almost fell asleep with my head on the bar while Chindo made the connection. Then it was off to his place to watch him and Graham snort.

Chindo actually seemed like a great guy. Like I said, I wished we'd come sooner. Under different circumstances we probably would've stayed a week and *pal'd* around with him. He lived in a tiny one-room shack he'd built in his aunt's back yard, and when we entered, a little boy ran in and jumped on his lap. Chindo introduced him as his favorite cousin Jesus (Hey-zeus). He pulled a half bottle of Pepsi out from the little fridge, smelled it to make sure it was okay, and let the kid swallow it all up before his mom came to put him to bed. Graham commented on this later saying, "I love how he deliberately smelled the bottle for his cousin in front of us to prove he's a good guy, as if pop could go bad."

After auntie gave us a suspicious look-over and took Jesus to bed, Chindo and Graham got their kicks. I just smoked a little weed to numb the pain and leaned wearily against the wall trying to stay conscious until we got back to the beach where Chindo had worked it out that we could crash in front of his amigo's restaurant if we promised to go fishing in the morning and pay for the trip.

Graham related some of the highlights from our

journey and Chindo said wide-eyed, "De angels were watching you hey?"

"Are you a Christian Chindo?" I asked. He looked towards the crucifix above his bed, crossed his chest and replied, "Si amigo! You?"

"Yeah man, I'm all about Jesus."

"Das good man; is de most important ding."

Graham ignored us and cut his last line while I asked Chindo what he thought about believers and drugs. He answered, "Si, de Lord made de marijuana and de coca for us too enjoy."

Late that night Chindo drove us back to the beach, introduced us to his amigo who was locking up the bar, and showed us where we could crash. Before returning home he made us promise we'd still be there in the morning for our trip. As he walked away Graham whispered, "You don't want to go fishing do you?"

"Dude, I just wanna' go home."

"Good, me too!"

"Thank God," I said relieved. "I was sure you were gonna' make me go."

"No way man, I can't get out of this country soon enough! I hate to ditch Chindo, but based on our track record here, if we don't screw him now he'll screw us later." He set his watch for 6 a.m.

The beach was all ours, dark and tranquil with the gentle lull of the waves rolling to shore and the distant laughter of party-people on sailboats and yachts resounding over the harbor. We situated ourselves on towels in the sand under a giant beach-umbrella and tried to sleep. Graham was obviously too high so he penciled furiously in his sketchpad. I was so exhausted and uncomfortable in my grimy, sunburned skin that I had to strip down naked and make my way out into the cool and inviting Pacific waters. The ocean revived me as I swam through the darkness and up to the tiny village of warm-lit boats huddled closely together, forming a glowing maze for me to explore. A few party people waved hello and invited me up, then giggled when I confessed I was naked. My starlit swim was luxuriant and serene, a perfect moment to myself amidst our trials.

Back on the beach I conked out like a baby, but at 4 a.m. I awoke in itchy torment. My towel had bunched up underneath me so my legs were eaten raw by sand bugs. Graham was awake when he heard me moan and moaned back, "This sucks. Let's go."

Chindo's amigo returned while we were throwing our stuff in the car and looked very disconcerted. I lied and said that we'd be back for our trip after breakfast; who knows if he bought it, but Graham fired up the engine and tore out of there. We gassed up down the road then hit the highway. Sorry Chindo. Thanks for the grass.

CHAPTER 39

Music, Memories And Nicotine

Saturday, October 2, 1999

During the last forty-eight hours I'd had the equivalent of four hours of sleep, so as Graham sped north that morning I slipped to and from consciousness. An army drug check woke me before noon. You're going to think we were retarded, and you'd be right, but both Graham and I knew after the checks we'd survived that nobody was going to be looking under my scrotum, so that's where I stashed Chindo's weed. We passed two or three checks like this without even having to step out of the car. When I took the wheel Graham rolled it up into three *doobs* and we smoked two; the last I stuck back in my crotch. At the next check though, two army dudes with M-16s made us get out and I panicked. As one searched the car the other stood just two feet away from me with his head turned, so I reached between my legs and flicked the last joint behind me! It didn't get very far and I was sure they'd see it lying under their noses before we could escape. An angel must have stepped on it because we made a clean getaway.

Every turn we took was dangerous. The road was terribly windy and unpredictable on the coast and we both drove like maniacs, possessed with the anxious impulsion to eat every mile as fast as humanly possible. It was torturous. The heat was atrocious and every inch of my legs itched and stung from the bug bites. This only added to my fatigue and blurred vision and in the late afternoon my discomfort became unbearable. I pulled over next to a small river emptying into the Pacific; it worked itself down from the secluded hills and ran between rocky knolls with green patches and little white bell-shaped flowers. Graham made some joke about my constant need for baptism as I took off my clothes and lay down in the refreshing water.

With my spirit somewhat restored and my resolution to stop scratching in tact, I gave the wheel back to Graham with my stomach growling.

"I wish we had some food," I whined. Graham reached into his bag in the backseat and triumphantly presented a grocery bag saying, "Adele gave me the junk we bought in Mexico City! I've been saving it for just such an occasion!"

"You beautiful man you!" I sang. There were smoked oysters, nuts, some crackers, and most importantly, Smarties! It was enough that we didn't have to stop until we reached the city of Manzanillo late that night. We didn't stay long. After a quick dinner of tacos and Pepsi (I had two for the caffeine) and a stop for gas and smokes, we were speeding north again.

Graham passed out around midnight. When I started to climb up the mountains and back into the jungle something felt off. Thirty miles up I came to a steep bend in the road and pulled over to think. Contemplating whether to continue forward I looked up and saw six glowing red zombie eyes staring down at me and I jumped! It was only a family of opossums but they were sinister looking and gave me a good fright! That was it; screw the jungle! And upon further study of the map I realized sleep deprivation had thrown off my bearings, and to my great dismay I had to drive back to Manzanillo cursing at myself for losing another hour to the jungle. Getting home was proving to be obscenely difficult and I wrestled with paranoia and frustration as I drove through the agonizing night chain smoking and listening to one of my mix-tapes to stay awake. *The Foo Fighters* kept me company, and *The Verve*, and *HUM*, and *aMiniature*, and *hHEad* (it's a total coincidence that I liked bands with weird spellings). Music, memories and nicotine kept my eyes ever fixed on that yellow line for six straight hours.

In Puerto Vallarta Graham woke to the rising sun and exclaimed, "Holy crap! Have you been driving all night? Nice work hose-head!"

CHAPTER 40

Ground Hog's Day

Sunday, October 3, 1999

I'd had roughly five to six equivalent hours of broken sleep in the last three days, and that's after the four hours of hangover sleep before the earthquake. Needless to say I wasn't looking too good, nor was Graham. So after I finally caught a couple *Z's* we hit a huge Federal drug and gun check outside Las Varas, looking like a couple of heroine addicts, and they tore our car to pieces. Much to our amusement, a lady from the *UN* approached and asked how we thought we were being treated as two officials dumped out our bags and inspected every article of clothing, checked the engine, rummaged under the trunk, peeled the molding off the doors, and even pulled the back seats out! Graham chuckled his chuckle then said coolly, "Everything here is fine."

She started in on a short survey she had attached

277

to a clipboard and Graham cut her short repeating, "No, everything here is *fine*. Tranquilo."

I nodded my head gritting my teeth. She stayed to make sure the officials put our car back together and we stepped in to hurry things along. There was no time to tell her what we thought of her country; we just wanted to get out of it.

At noon I took my shift and Graham fell asleep again. Déjà vu. It literally felt like I was living the same day over with one maddening exception: the engine suddenly died.

"NO! Please not now!" I cried waking Graham.

"How long has it been since we gassed up?" he asked drearily.

"I don't know, it doesn't seem that long ago… Time's all melting together!"

Graham swore, "That fucking fuel gauge! Dude, you should fill up every time you see a station!"

"Don't get pissed at me! I was sure we had enough to get to the next town and I didn't want to stop! I don't know man, I think we've finally killed it!"

"I bloody well hope not or we're royally screwed!"

The tension was thick. Graham stuck his thumb out begrudgingly from the side of the road and it was half an hour before a young guy in a red truck picked him up.

The sun beat down hard on me as I drank the last of the water and stretched my sore body out under a tree for shade. I tried to do the math in my head. *Are we really just out of gas?* Time stood still. It grew hotter and hotter. It was infinitely worse sitting still than riding in the car where at least the wind blew through the windows. A grueling ninety minutes crept by when finally a family in a big old station wagon dropped Graham off. He hopped out with a jerry can and waved goodbye. As they disappeared over the hill he poured the gas into the tank and said gravely, "Time for you to say another prayer Mark."

I said it out loud, "Dear Jesus, please let this all be my stupid fault for not getting gas. Bless this little Toyota and bring us home safely. Please make it start!"

I turned the key and she turned over.

"Hallelujah!" Graham exclaimed.

Ground Hog's Day continued. Once again we had to backtrack to return the jerry can and gas up. Graham forgave me and said he'd drive a while.

As we passed the spot where I'd run out of gas he said, "You'll love this: that guy who picked me up in the red truck said he was on his way home from church, and when he saw me, God told him to pick me up and share the message he'd received that morning..." Graham trailed off and wouldn't say anymore.

We forgot to buy water and neither of us had eaten a thing all day, so a while later we stopped in front of a little grocery and Graham grumbled, "I'm tired of doing everything. You go in, you're running out of time to practice your Spanish."

"Screw you dude," I defended myself. "Just 'cause you're better with languages than me! I've spent plenty of time alone on this trip and handled my business."

"Fine, I'll go in and get some bread and water."

"Oh no you don't," I said irately, "*I'll* get it."

I marched inside and said to the clerk, "Agua por favor?" She reached for a small bottle but I wanted a big one and said, "No, lo soriento. Mas grande por favor." She looked around but I spotted the 2-liters in another cooler first. I pulled one out and said, "Aqui esta," but she shook her head. I said in English, "Yes, this is what I want." It read AGUA on the side so I didn't know what her problem was. She shrugged and ran it through along with some chocolate bars, pita bread, and smokes.

Back on the road Graham cracked the bottle open, dying of thirst, and took a huge gulp. He paused, grunted a, "Hmm," and then drank some more. He passed it to me casually and I slugged it back for a bubbly surprise: it was soda water. I hung my head for a moment, a lesson in humility learned yet again, and Graham said, "It's all good dude, close enough." Then we both started laughing hysterically.

I wanted so badly to sleep but it was too hot. It cooled down after dark so we pulled over to rest. Graham passed out in the passenger seat and I struggled to get comfortable in the back. Too tired, too sore, and too scared, sleep refused to come. The noises in the fields were freaking me out and I had to drive out of there. Unbeknownst to my now snoring companion I drove dangerously all night long, yet again! And it was even worse than the night before!

I gassed up at 1:00 a.m., bought smokes and a 2-liter of Pepsi, then steadily consumed caffeine and nicotine whilst listening once again to my headphones.

Sinning Man's Heaven

Everything from *The Tea Party*, *Mystery Machine*, *Autechre*, *Autour De Lucie*, *Shostakovich*, *Danny Elfman*, *Terje Rypdal*, *Ketil Bjørnstad*, *Beck*, and the *Beastie Boys* kept me focused on that fuzzy yellow line. My one advantage was there were now no bends or hills in the road, just a vast stretch of highway that I sailed down at 130 kilometers an hour for five hours straight with my poor brain throbbing rhythmically through wave after wave of dizzy-spells and uncertainty. It was unquestionably the most tired I've ever been in my life and somehow I managed to cover more ground than any previous shifts. By the time Graham came to in Santa Ana, well before dawn, I had driven myself completely insane. Back in the passenger's seat I erupted into an uncontrollable laughing fit and cackled maniacally in delirium. I haven't the faintest notion now of what I said but I remember Graham saying, "Mark? Dude? Are you all there? You're freaking me out man..."

CHAPTER 41
Hot And Cold

Monday, October 4, 1999

Graham was totally in love with me when I woke to the bright morning sun.

"Dude! You're an animal! We're going to be at the border in like an hour thanks to you! Sorry for being so edgy lately, you've completely redeemed yourself in my books. Thanks for driving all night again."

He was beaming. I couldn't believe we were almost there and I smacked his knee gleefully and exclaimed, "It's all good Graham, anything for a bro. Thanks for getting me outta' Victoria and taking care of business."

He smiled, "Yeah, I'm kinda' realizing you didn't exactly come for the cultural experience. We haven't talked about it at all; how's your head with the whole Lori thing?"

I laughed, "Ha! You know, once I was talking about

B.B. King and she said, 'I don't like the blues,' and I gasped, 'WHAT? How can you not like the blues?!' And she said 'It's just a bunch of old black men complaining about their women.' So I figure it's all-good: how can I love someone who hates the blues?"

Graham laughed out loud and exclaimed, "Oh that's rich! What's cooler than old black men complaining about their women anyways?"

Good ole' Graham.

We had vowed never to return to San Luis or Yuma Arizona, but now that Graham had lost so much money he couldn't afford to sacrifice the $750 deposit. It was the same bureaucratic nightmare all over again. They didn't have the money in the office by the gate, and the guy authorized to withdraw it from the bank wasn't working, so we both lost our temper this time and forced the stupid cow behind the desk to call him up and get us our freakin' cash so we could bolt. She told us it would be an hour and we were forced to kill time.

Graham wasn't taking any chances going through the border this time, and even though I'd done a meticulous job cleaning the floor and seats of the car by hand (after we got busted for the remnants of Paco's mess) he insisted we get it vacuumed. We found a gas station where the manager insisted we pay him to do it. Afterwards, we found a small grocery store to hide from the growing heat and took our last opportunity to buy a carton of cheap smokes. Finally, after hanging out next to the freezer too long, the suspicious clerk asked us to leave. Outside, a psychotic looking Mexican screamed at us in a blood-curdling voice, "I'm gonna' kill you fucking gringos!" No joke. We bolted down the street without looking back, burst into the office and snatched our money from the cow without a word, then flew out of there like a bat out of hell. I just love that that was the last thing anybody said to us in Mexico; it's very appropriate don't you think?

At long last on American soil, the border guard raised his brow at the look of us. He inspected Graham's license and said, "British Columbia, Canada, hey? I got a brother-in-law says marijuana's pretty much legal up there."

Graham chuckled that chuckle and said, "No sir, it's not legal. The laws aren't as strict as down here, but it's definitely not legal."

"You boys smoke marijuana?"

"No."

"Have you got any illegal substances in your car today?"

"No."

"Alright, have a good day."

To our great surprise he let us go without even searching the car and we were homeward bound! And as soon as we arrived in Yuma, Graham was pulled over for speeding! (On and on it goes.) A tough looking black cop on a motorcycle asked him to get out and step behind the vehicle so that I couldn't hear them. I prayed anxiously as the officer explained that in Arizona, when you're caught going that much over the limit, they take your license away for a few months, then to get it back you have to go back to driver's-school and take the test over again! Graham begged and explained our situation saying that he didn't even realize he was going so fast because we'd been tearing down the Mexican highway for days in desperation to get home. I saw the cop write up a ticket. Then he approached my window and asked all the same questions to which I gave all the same answers. He paused a moment for effect then said, "You guys have no idea what a huge favor I'm doing for you here. Take this warning ticket, and never come back to Arizona again."

The heat was devastating. It was by far hotter then anything we'd experienced yet and we stopped at the old familiar Burger King for the one-dollar *whoppers* and air-conditioning. When we left, the heat struck like we were Thanksgiving turkeys going in the oven. Even sticking your hand out the window with the car in motion was unbearable; it was like volcanic fumes rushing against your skin. We stopped at a gas station for gas and ice. They were sold out of ice. I cannot express the sheer agony we endured for those next five scorching hours screaming through the desert with nothing to drink but boiling hot water. At the very least, it kept our weary souls awake.

It cooled down at twilight and we stopped to refuel. When I stood up the skin on my legs felt like sackcloth with the still itchy bug bites and my new sunburn. We hadn't had any alcohol or weed for a couple of days and all I wanted to do was get drunk to numb the pain. Graham bought a small bottle of tequila to help him sleep, but it was my shift and I wasn't taking any more risks, so I bought a bottle of milk. In my condition it was ecstasy; you can't find cow milk in Mexico and I'd been fantasizing about it for days. Besides, after our romp with Paco the thought of tequila made me ill, and to this day I haven't touched another drop.

    I drove us into California. Then, at 1 a.m., in the middle of Highway 10, the tire blew—the same freaking tire. I just couldn't believe it. Graham woke up and said, "Okay, now it's not even funny! Whatever. I got this one; you rest up," and he left to find a phone to call *Triple A*.

    Around 2 a.m. I woke to a flashing yellow light and clunking sound. The tow-truck driver threw on our poor spare and told us it would be stupid to try to push it any further; we'd have to wait around until morning for the nearest tire store to open. I would have preferred to drive all night but I welcomed the chance to rest, so Graham took the wheel and drove to a giant parking lot he had seen where we parked and passed out.

    Weird dreams unfolded, the kind that disturb and clutch to your emotions as if they're real. They morphed into the eerie sensations we'd had on Devil's Pass. The same black withered phantoms leered in my peripherals when suddenly a booming voice said, "Open the doors and keep your hands up!"

    I lunged out of the dream state and into reality, disoriented by a blinding light. As my eyes adjusted I realized that three police cars had us surrounded with spotlights and an officer was yelling over an intercom. We raised our hands and stepped out of the car slowly, only to be rushed by four *LAPD* pointing shotguns and pistols!

"What the hell are you boys doing here in the middle of the night?"

"Sleeping!" Graham winced. As they patted us down one explained, "You guys shouldn't be out here! We thought you were picking up or dropping off!"

"What, drugs?" I asked.

"Or guns. That's what goes down around these parts at night! You don't have any sort of contraband in there do ya'? "

"No sir!" Graham exclaimed. "Our tire blew so we're waiting for morning."

"Well, I wouldn't suggest waiting here, but then I wouldn't suggest waiting anywhere else either. You can stay if you want but don't be surprised if another patrol wakes you. Sorry for the scare boys."

When they were gone it was Graham who said, "Okay, I'm officially freaked out right now. Were you having crazy dreams like on Devil's Pass?"

"YES!" I exclaimed.

He continued, "That's messed! I knew you were having them too, and I could feel people running around the car like before... I think you're right dude, there must be evil spirits following us 'cause this trip is fucked!"

I added, "And the only reason we're still alive is 'cause there's angels with us too."

"I can't argue that... Man, it's freezing cold! You'd

think the ground would still be smokin' hot after that day, but I'm shivering!"

It *was* absurdly cold. Something happened out there and we were both too cold and spooked to go back to sleep, so we went for a drive and found a tire shop to stare at until morning.

CHAPTER 42

Radiohead (Not The Band)

Tuesday, October 5, 1999

After everything we'd been through, it was a young Hispanic dude getting his tire changed who made us fully realize just what a stupid idea the trip was from the beginning. He laughed in awe, "What? You guys are loco! I don't know anybody who would *drive* through there! Maybe a few years ago, but it's way too dangerous now. You're lucky to be alive!"

Graham's face bled revelation. "We should have listened to that crazy hick with the gun-rack!"

The marathon lingered on. I drove past L.A. to switch from Highway 10 to 5 and the traffic was mind-numbingly slow. We inched our way through the morning rush hour for what seemed like hours and Graham praised my lane changing intuitions: "This is ridiculous! I gotta' say it again dude, you're a helluva' driver."

Once we cleared the major cities it was full-speed ahead to Sacramento where we stopped for gas and one-dollar *whoppers* (thank God Burger King had that special on then or we would have starved to death), then on until dark where we stopped just before the state line to gas up again.

Some little punk was cussing out the old lady behind the counter because she wouldn't sell him cigarettes without I.D. Outside he convinced Graham to boot for him, and I guess the lady's math skills were as bad as the waitress back in Arizona because she checked his I.D. and thought he was 21 as well. Then the punk was pig-headed enough to march back in while I was getting a *slurpee* and yell at her, "Ha ha! You dumb bitch! I still got my smokes!"

When I returned to the car he was talking with Graham and I was about to tell him off when he said, "Sure, I know where you can score some weed."

Him and his buddy jumped in the back and we drove into the little town to some drug dealer's house. Pig-head ran inside and came back with a gram of really nice looking bud. It tasted so sweet after four stressful days of painful sobriety, and as Graham drove us into Oregon under a cool night sky I embraced the comfort and felt once again why I was so addicted, so in love with marijuana. Convictions suspended, I couldn't wait to get home and smoke some good ole' B.C. weed from *The Doctor* with Joey and Dave and Craig and Spidey.

The never-ending hum of the engine started to play tricks on my stoned brain. Have you ever come home from an all-night rave with your ears still audibly pulsing to the constant beat of the bass drum, even though there's no more music? Well this was like that multiplied by a thousand. Five and a half days of straight engine noise was now morphing in my mind into this bizarre rock motif in 6/4-time, complete with complex orchestration and choral arrangements. And it was hauntingly real! It was literally as if I was wearing my headphones listening to this brilliant but dizzying composition and it went on and on so that I thought my head was going to split! I cringed and covered my ears, strained the blood vessels in my lobes to make that white-noise sound, but nothing would stop it! Graham's eyes darted from the road to me in deep concern as I cried, "Oh my gosh! It won't stop! There's a freakin' radio implanted in my head and it won't stop playing this song! It's so beautiful, but it's driving me insane!"

"You're really buggin' aren't you?" he asked in concern.

"Yes! It's SO loud! It's like *you* should be able to hear it!"

"That's weird dude."

I went on, "I'm serious! I've had music stuck in my head before but this is plain messed! Like there's an antenna from my brain to heaven and they won't cut the signal!"

" I believe you man; you're freakin' me out again!"

"I'm freakin' me out too!"

It went on until I fell asleep; then I dreamed it. It continued when I woke in the middle of the night

Roy Milner

and took my shift at the wheel. I reached Washington in the morning and it was still there, ever-progressing complexities of melody and rhythm spewing out of the engine in that same 6/4-time all the way to Seattle...

CHAPTER 43

Oh Canada!

Wednesday, October 6, 1999

In Seattle we switched at a gas station. To my surprise Graham pulled fifty dollars out of the engine to pay and joked, "I can't believe those pigs didn't find this! Now we know where to hide the drugs next time."

We smoked a *doob* before crossing into Canada then had a little argument. He wanted me to toss the rest and I said, "Why throw away perfectly good weed?"

"Dude, we're almost home and I'm not taking any more risks!"

"What risk?" I said. "It's not like they're going to strip search us going into our own country!"

"How the hell would you know? Besides, I thought you were gonna' go straight when we got home?" he argued.

"Yeah, but not this second! I have to settle back into life and get a good home-coming session in with the boys first."

Graham shook his head. "Wow. You weren't kidding, eh? You really are addicted... But I'm not crossing any more borders until you ditch that."

I tossed it begrudgingly. We drove to the border where the guard simply looked in the trunk and sent us on our way.

Sweet, sweet British Columbia! It could not have been more beautiful. Two days ago we were burning to death in the desert, now we were sloshing through cold west coast rain under an overcast, dark-gray autumn sky: my favorite place during my favorite time of year! Suddenly I was wide-awake and tingling with joy, my spirit restored by the heavenly smell of damp air and fallen leaves. Thank God Almighty for the little Tercel that could!

On the ferry my heart began to weigh heavy as I drew nearer to my old life on the island. There was serious work to do and it was going to be hard. Sobriety. Finding a new job. I tried to forget it momentarily and my thoughts turned to Lori once more, blues jokes aside. I was angry. Before the boat docked I wrote her a letter; you know, the kind where you try to convince the person and yourself that you didn't really love them by being mean-spirited with your honesty? My mom told me once that I had always been drawn to the mysterious and that was why I fell for Lori, who was so quiet and enigmatic. But I flipped that and wrote that she was only quiet because she was young and had nothing worthwhile to say, that I realized I was only in love with the idea of her. I did apologize for acting so strange and even admitted it was mostly because I'd been secretly struggling with substance abuse for so long. But then I foolishly blamed it partly on her and I actually wrote something like, "What does it take to get you to talk? Do you have to insert a quarter?" Regret gnawed at me after mailing it, not that it even mattered anymore.

As we rolled off the boat and onto our beloved island Graham said, "Yeah dude," and I actually laughed out loud at the thought of still being alive. My parent's house was fifteen minutes from the terminal and I buzzed with anticipation to hug my mommy and call Joey up to plan the night.

Graham said, "I'm getting so high tonight!"

"Yeah dude, me too! Oh man does this place feel good!"

"What about tomorrow?"

"What about tomorrow?" I repeated his question.

"Are you going to stop?"

"...I don't know...maybe...really soon though. What about you?"

"What about me?" he repeated *my* question.

I replied, "Are you going to be a stoner for the rest of your life? What about everything we've been through? I mean this goes way beyond coincidence!"

"No it doesn't," he said plainly. "It was just a messed up road-trip."

"Graham, can't you see God's hand in anything?

Two nights ago you agreed there must have been angels watching us."

"No I didn't, I just said I couldn't argue that."

I rubbed my eyes and said, "Dude, why are you always on the teeter-totter with this stuff? Did your dad's letter mess you up that much?"

It was the first time I'd brought it up since it'd happened seven months earlier and we were just moments from the end of our journey. He answered by telling me a story:

"When I was eleven I was playing street hockey alone in my driveway and I prayed, 'Lord give me a sign that I'll make it to the NHL when I grow up: if I score this goal YES and if I miss NO.' I shot, and missed, then ran upstairs crying to tell my mom what God said. And I remember her being so happy that she had me brainwashed enough to believe so strongly. Well, I'm not going to let my dad do the same thing from beyond the grave."

As he pulled into my driveway I said, "Graham, I believe, and *not* just because my parents do. You *don't* believe *because* your parents do."

He didn't say anything as he jumped out and helped me with my stuff. As I pulled the last bag out he turned to leave and said, "It's been educational."

"Hold on," I stopped him, "you can't just take off like that after everything! Give me a hug hose-head; I love you man!"

He turned around, embraced me out of duty, then drove away, and I realized that he was entirely sick of me. My heart felt as empty as my parents' house:

nobody was home. I was itching to tell my story and called up Joey. He answered and said, "You're back already?"

CHAPTER 44
Home

Like a city whose walls are broken down is a man who lacks self-control.
                                                              Proverbs 25:28

It was hard to learn my lesson. The first week I was back I blew my last $100 getting high at Craig's and Spidey's, which was no longer as fulfilling as I remembered it being. Tripping on all the other drugs I'd missed, I found it very frustrating trying to explain my travels. There was no way I could make anyone comprehend just how gonzo the whole trip had been, or how it had affected me, especially since the effects were proving fruitless.

With my uncle's bakery gone my folks spared me the cost of rent for a little while and I moped around the rest of that fall getting secretly droned with what little I made teaching. I tried to start up another band with some of the boys, and even though I had their good company like always, something was different. By December I felt terribly lonely and fell back into the same old trap of wandering the peninsula listlessly. Graham was nowhere to be seen.

Two months later I was out on one of my treks when I stumbled upon the docks and heard jazz music. I crept up to see but it wasn't Lori. Still, the misery sunk in for a moment then turned to that same bitter anger. I hated jazz, I hated girls, and I was beginning to hate myself.

Late that night I had a terrifying nightmare that I was tied up in a dark, pulsing jungle with hideous black creatures forcing my head down to bow before a massive idol of glowing stone. I awoke in a sweaty panic and my bedroom walls were shaking! I'd never felt a quake this big on the island before, and though it wasn't huge, it was violent enough to scare some sense back into me. I didn't touch a drug for days in an effort to get my act together, then for two weeks I pounded the pavement with resumes bearing the shame of the unemployed, only to come home feeling lowly and obsolete before my disappointed step-dad. So I drank.

One night my mom, my brother, and Seth were chilling upstairs, and it was apparent to all of them that I was miserable. Mom said, "Don't worry honey, something'll open up soon. Heather and I prayed you'd find work this morning."

Seth said, "There's nothing better you can do than that. We should pray right now."

So we did.

The very next morning Heather called my mom from her job at the grocery store bubbling with excitement and sang, "This is amazing! God answered our prayer overnight! Tell Mark that if he wants a job here at Thrifty's he's got it!"

Mom ran through the house screaming the good news. The seafood manager had unexpectedly lost a guy and needed an immediate replacement! This never happened at Thrifty's; it had an amazing reputation and people would sign in at customer service for months without ever getting an interview. It was such a long shot I hadn't even applied! As an added bonus, Spidey worked there too! My friends would call it coincidence, but this was more than a job, it was a great job; with an awesome boss, benefits, and ultimately the chain of events that make this story so good.

Being a fishmonger kept me relatively busy the next few months. I read my Bible daily and made damn sure to keep away from heavy drugs and porn, but my romance with weed and beer was in a constant state of flux. I'd do okay for short periods, hiding alone in the studio working on my music, but then I'd finally get too lonely and attempt to hang with the boys sober. It never worked—temptation owned me.

One night that spring I was walking out of a club with Jocelyn after watching her band, and there stood Graham talking with the drummer. It was as if our half-year of silence was sacred: we barely gave each other a glimpse of acknowledgement and walked on. I didn't want to talk yet.

Summer came, and with it the sweet memories of summers past, memories you yearn to relive but cannot replicate. My schedule between Thrifty's, teaching, and building yet another band with my studio partner Jesse kept me too busy to spend time partying with the boys like I wanted, and even though I knew this growing distance was probably for the best, it drove me to great sorrow. Sorrow drove me to weed, weed drove me to shame, and shame back to sorrow: the cycle of my strongest addiction, the one that started it all.

Tuesdays were cheap beer nights at our local pub. My fellow employees would meet after work, and since Spidey and I always went, it was usually when I got to see all the boys. Graham started coming around again, and one night we staggered outside together to smoke a *jay* and break our holy silence. We walked around the peninsula until morning relishing in each other's conversation like old times. He told me he'd sold the poor Tercel to some kid for a $100 and then laughed, "And *I* had to throw in a pack of smokes!" It felt so good to be with him again.

The next night we met at the pub again and huddled in a quiet corner to check out my journal from the road. When we were finished reading through he looked at me awe-stricken like we were lucky to be alive and exclaimed, "Oh man! I forgot just how messed up that trip was!"

"It hasn't even been a year dude!"

"I know, but it seems so long ago now."

"Yeah," I agreed then added, "Lest we forget."

As the anniversary of our departure approached I started to feel it again: that need for escape—for change.

Meanwhile, things in the studio weren't going so hot. Jesse and I had had it with this weird dude playing bass and I kicked him out of the band just two weeks before our first gig. We needed a replacement fast, so I begged my go-to-man Seth to come learn the songs. He replied, "I'll help you out again, but this time you have to do it sober."

I thought for a moment then rejoined, "I've been wanting to get sober for months dude, and if promising you helps me do it then I'm down. But I can't try to get clean under the stress of putting this show together and performing it in such little time. You know how my nerves get."

"Okay," he said, "then what if I draw up a contract that says you go straight for two solid weeks *after* the gig; will you sign it?"

I didn't have any Christian friends left aside from Seth, my younger brother's best bud, so I sprang at the chance for some real accountability and said, "Write it up."

During that short time before the show I worked hard and partied hard, practicing every day with Seth and Jesse, then getting in as much Graham and marijuana time as I could before the contract took effect. It went by really fast.

We rocked the gig and Seth was worth my imminent torture. There was a little *hotty* from Thrifty's at the show named Lisa who came to see if I could actually play. She'd heard I was a good drummer and was looking for someone to play on her upcoming project. I promised to invite her to the studio, but then avoided her calls and made excuses when I saw her at work so I could go get high. Besides, my sketchy past with hot girls who played music left me cynical.

After the show though, she was stoked that I could drum and sing, so we made some vague plans to jam then I took off with the boys for my last visit to *The Doctor*. Weed never tasted so bittersweet.

Three days into sobriety I was terribly sore and shaky. I called in sick at work and lay in bed watching movies, drinking orange juice, and pouring over my Bible. A week in, the immediate suffering was gone. Now emerging from my self-medicated haze, the hardest part was coming home from work everyday bored out of my skull. To keep myself busy one night I decided to clean out the studio and found an old notebook in which I used to write quotes from friends. One from Graham when he first started *toking* read, "The thing that's so attractive about marijuana is that it makes even being bored interesting."

Eleven days in I felt all right, but I was beginning to have a hard time understanding what the point was. Sure I was abiding by "God's rules", sure I was proud of myself for still honoring Seth's contract, but all I really felt was empty.

Shawbuck was working the gas station the next night so I stopped in to grab a Pepsi and say, "Was'up." He knew all about the contract and asked if I was going to make it. I took my usual seat on the ice-cream freezer (as was my custom when we shared these conversations during the late-night lull) and spilled my guts:

"Oh, I'll make the last three days no problem, I mean, I feel fine, it's just— I know I'll probably start right back up again when it's over."

"Just don't start," he said plainly. "You've come this far, why go back?"

"Easy for you to say, you just up and quit one day like that! But I'm addicted man, I mean, who gets this addicted to weed? All this time I've said one thing and acted another; why is it so freakin' hard for me to live what I believe?"

He paused from taking cigarette inventory, put his pen down and asked, "Your parents still go to church right?"

"Yeah, so?"

Then he said something I'll never forget: "You know what you need to do? Go with them on Sunday, find some *babely* Christian chick and marry her; then she'll keep you sober."

I laughed, "That's the stupidest thing I've ever heard! I can't get married until I'm like, thirty-five; after I've become a rock-star!"

"Yeah, good luck with that— so you're going to wait until you're thirty-five to get laid?"

I checked myself and sighed, "I'm starting to think waiting for marriage is going to be impossible."

He shrugged and went back to counting cigarettes.

Driving home in mom's van under the cool starry night, I felt such the fool; frustrated, alone, and without purpose. After all I'd been through, it's so strange that that was the moment it really hit me. Maybe it was because I was the soberest I'd been in years, or maybe because I'd just laid it all down and humbled myself before my most skeptical of friends. Whatever it was, I finally gave it up: the *me*, the *self*, the stubbornness of human nature. Even as a believer I'd been trying to live by my own strength, and I finally realized how weak I really am. Trembling and scared of what was to come if I didn't give myself up wholly and entirely to God's will, I tore down the highway and prayed aloud, "God I'm so confused! I know I'm going to backslide when this contract is up. Why do I have to be sober? What's the point? I tried so many times to get straight before Mexico, and I've fought twice as hard ever since you kicked me in the head on that damned trip, but I can't do it! I desperately want to follow you but I'm too weak, so I'm giving it all up to you. Give me a sign Lord! Show me a reason to stay clean!"

Before bed I found a verse in the book of James where he starts by quoting Proverbs 3:

God opposes the proud but gives grace to the humble.

I'd read this before and yet, like most hypocrites, had never counted myself among the proud. Now, with my delusional pride exposed, I was ready to listen to what James had to say:

Submit your selves, then, to God. Resist the devil, and he will flee from you. Come near to God and he will come near to you. Wash your hands you sinners and purify your hearts, you double-minded.

You double-minded. There it was.

CHAPTER 45

My Next Trip

Flee the evil desires of youth, and pursue righteousness, faith, love and peace along with those who call on the Lord out of a pure heart.

2 Timothy 2:22

There were two days left on Seth's contract. The boys called me at work about our regular beach romp and it hurt so much to decline. The lingering summer sun cast long shadows between the trees and across the pavement of my youth as I drove home swallowing the fermenting taste of nostalgia. Alone and bored again in my parent's house, I resigned to following through with my promise to hear that girl Lisa's music. She had forgotten our tentative plans since I'd been so elusive, so when I called she was already busy. But she was determined to get her project moving and decided she'd better grab the chance to come.

Down in the studio she pulled out an old acoustic guitar and began strumming her chords. I sat at the drums with my brush sticks and accompanied her

Sinning Man's Heaven

with a light shuffle rhythm; then she began to sing... She could sing. She could really sing! And much to my surprise, her lyrics didn't suck like most female vocalists. In fact, they were really quite good, so much so that we began discussing where they came from, where mine came from, and suddenly where we both were in life. After three songs we stopped playing altogether and ended up having an absolutely incredible heart to heart! With each word we were drawn closer together, almost in shock at how paralleled our current paths were. I can't get into her issues here, but let's just say we were both in the same fix with ourselves and with our faith, and it was utterly mystifying! After I told her a little about my Mexico experience and how the earthquake in Oaxaca had changed the course of my life, she gasped, "That's where I grew up! We were missionaries in Oaxaca until I was eleven!" The conversation went on and on with utterly bizarre coincidences like this.

There was a *Mojave 3* song I had to show her and she was deeply moved. Then another song by *Slowdive* called *Miranda*, and she put my hand on her chest and said, "Feel how hard my heart is pumping!" It was so strange, so fast, and completely unexpected. I studied her countenance as she was overcome by my favorite music, baffled at how familiar it seemed. Yes, I'd noticed how tasty her skinny little figure looked at work in those tight black slacks; how her long, raven-black hair fell so exotically over her tanned skin and dark blue eyes, but there were lots of pretty girls around. This was something entirely different, and it caught me off guard. The situation I had half consciously created was becoming more and more romantic, and I hesitated: "Maybe we shouldn't get too involved here seeing as we're about to start working together."

She sat back and sighed with a little pout, the cutest little pout I'd ever seen, and I scratched my head and said, "I should have just kissed you right?"

She nodded with a sly smile and drew close to where I was sitting. We lingered for a few moments and breathed each other in. Then, ever so slowly, she pressed her lips to mine and we kissed; the longest, most tender kiss. It tasted like home. (And I must point out, not just to affirm how extraordinary the whole thing was, but for her reputation's sake, that she hadn't had anything to do with any guy in over two years since her last jerk-off of a boyfriend. And it should be noted that this poor girl did not trust men after some very painful events.)

The next day she had to leave town to visit her sister. Alone once more, and on my last day under contract, the temptation to breathe in that sweet smoke again was too much. I drove downtown, bought a couple joints, and sped back home to stare at the clock. At the stroke of midnight, my contract served, I sparked that *doob* and smoked it straight to my head. As the buzz came upon me I entered my room with my dog and fell on the bed to trip.

Now for those readers who don't know this, when you take a break from a substance your body is used to, something happens when you use again: it hits

Sinning Man's Heaven

you four times as hard as you remember and knocks you on your ass. Well that joint crept up on me like an acid trip and the paranoia swelled incomprehensibly! My room began to ooze and move, and my dog Teddy suddenly leapt to his feet growling furiously with his eyes fixed on that spot where the wall joined the ceiling—and I saw it. There, hovering in the corner of my room was a grotesque, demonic figure, flexing and boiling, then lunging rapidly at my trembling body. The fear was devastating, and all I was doing was lying on my bed tripping out! The room filled with more and more evil spirits riling about the thick melting air, and I *knew* Teddy was really seeing them as his snarling face moved every which way they did. It was far more real than the dark figures around Graham's Tercel and it shook me to my very core. I grabbed my Bible, and the first thing I opened to was in 1 Peter where he starts by quoting Proverbs 3 as well!

> *'God opposes the proud but gives grace to the humble.' Humble yourselves, therefore, under God's mighty hand, that he may lift you up in due time. Cast all your anxiety on him because he cares for you. Be self-controlled and alert. Your enemy the devil prowls around like a roaring lion looking for someone to devour. Resist him, standing firm in the faith, because you know that your brothers throughout the world are undergoing the same kind of sufferings. And the God of all grace, who called you to his eternal glory in Christ, after you have suffered*

a little while, will himself restore you and make you strong, firm and steadfast.

Whoa. I meditated on the words and the activity in my room subsided. Teddy stopped growling and lay back down on the floor. While I flushed the other joint down the toilet I decided to make that girl Lisa my new drug.

Two days later she came home.

Three days after that we were engaged.

Now, dear reader, you're probably thinking, *WHAT! That's crazy!* Well my boys thought so too when I told them. I'll never forget the way Spidey had to steady himself with his arms spread against the kitchen counter as he heaved a huge, worried breath of disbelief. Craig, in his usual passive fashion congratulated me, though I could tell he was pretending not to think it would dissolve like so many of my other rash endeavors. Joey at least seemed prepared to consider the notion and said, "Are you sure man? Really sure?" Dave, bless his soul, was always accepting of all things and gave me the only positive response by inviting Lisa and I over as a couple. But nobody took it worse than Shaw. He called me up and said, "What the hell's going on? Joey says you're getting married? Have you gone mental? Get over here right now!"

When I got to his house he launched into it: "You've only known this girl for a week! How can you possibly know that she's the right one? And even if she is why would you want to get married? You're both 22! Marriage is a prison, don't do it!"

I said, "You're the one that told me to get married in the first place!'"

"Yeah, theoretically; I didn't mean *now*! I'm really worried about you man, explain this to me."

I'm not even going to try and explain how two people can fall so desperately in love that fast. How do you put the measureless convictions of the heart into words? Still, I offered my most honest and sincere explanation to my hard-hearted friend and he deafly replied, "Why don't you try living together first and see if you're really compatible?"

"Because that's the world's way, not God's."

He argued something back, and before it turned into one of our heated theological debates I remembered a verse from 2nd Timothy I'd been digging on:

> *Don't have anything to do with foolish and stupid arguments because you know they produce quarrels. The Lord's servant must not quarrel; instead he must be kind to everyone, able to teach, not resentful.*

I loved Shaw too much to argue anymore. I said, "Words have never done us any good man, and I'm sorry I've been such a terrible example of what a real Christian should be, but now I'm going to try and live by action. I hope you'll come to the wedding." Even as I said it I knew how it must have sounded.

The next night Joey told me that Shaw said I was getting married because I was deluded by my religion and that it was going to ruin my life. That's when the real awakening came. With the unshakeable passion I felt for Lisa and the life I knew God was calling me to live against my friend's disbelief, the veil of lies the devil had been holding in front of me my whole life was lifted. The drugs, the lust, my babysitter, my weird relationship with my step-dad, the kids who teased me, the anger and false pride which flowed through my veins as the result, all came to the surface and I saw everything for what it truly is. It was like Keanu Reeves waking up in *The Matrix*, only for real. I wanted nothing to do with this lost world anymore: it was time to release the guilt and pain. And as I forgave the people in my life I felt God's sweet mercy as he forgave me. I cried, bawled for the first time since I could remember, and called aloud to God all night long in torrents. With pen in hand I scribbled furiously through my tears a plan to get my life in order and my debts paid off so I could marry the girl of my dreams as soon as possible. The next day in her arms I felt like a different man.

CHAPTER 46

Was Shaw Right?

Graham heard about everything last and his response was the best. We went out to lunch where I confirmed the wedding and he said, "Well, you've consistently been the most extreme person I've ever known, so I guess I can't be surprised. Congratulations Markman!"

Before the wedding I paid him back every cent from our trip.

Exactly three months from our first kiss, Lisa and I were married before God and 250 people. Shaw wasn't one of them. But do you know who was? My babysitter. After the ceremony she was one of the first people in line to congratulate me, and I could tell from her swollen eyes that she meant it deep down. I said, "Thanks darlin'," and gave her a hug; a real hug—the kind that says I forgive you.

I made love to my bride for the first time that night—yeah that's right, old school baby! When you wait you find out why God intended it that way, not that three months is that long, but when you're as horny as me that's like three years! Which I shamelessly admit is why we moved the wedding up from my original seven-month plan!

Shaw said marriage was a prison, but he didn't understand that I'd been imprisoned most of my life. Everyone is in one form or another. I know how that may sound to some but I don't give a rip: God set me free! I'm still happily married, and loving raising our two amazing kids. I make music for a living now: composing for film, television, and commercials. And though the life of the artist is one of feasts and famines, I've been fortunate enough to learn how to work through the dry spells and find satisfaction in the successes. I feel myself becoming everyday more like the man God intended me to be, and the trials he's carried me through have transformed my life.

Graham disappeared shortly after I got married, always the mystery. He has yet to meet my son who I named after him. About three years ago a mutual friend told me he was living in Nepal working for the Red Cross as an interpreter to inmates. Good ole' Graham, the enigma, the humanist, the traveler who once told me in Mexico he'd found his home in the third-world. I haven't seen him in nine years.

I tracked down his email address about a year ago to tell him I was writing our story. His message back read:

It's really good to hear from you. There's a line in

the first paragraph you wrote that made me think for a bit: "it didn't feel like the right time to email you. Don't ask me why now is," as in my own strange way I've started praying again recently and have been recalling you and your family daily. Seemed like it was one of those things from a different time in my life that was asking to be dealt with, and now you write out of the blue. Strange and mysterious ways I suppose.

I read his words and wept.

His contract in Nepal ended shortly after that and he emailed again to say he was back in town, but I decided to finish this book and write him as I remembered before seeing him; then he disappeared again.

Jordan comes and visits me sometimes when he's home from teaching out east, and he told me just the other day that Graham and Adele are living together somewhere in the States! I thought that was a riot! And I'm happy for him. Looking back I realize how great she really was, someone who could have such grace while I was being a colossal jerk. It's good knowing Graham is with someone who believes; I don't care if she's "Catholic" or "Protestant"—anyone with *true faith* knows denominations don't mean a hill of beans.

I guess now the time has come to end the silence with my old friend. I can't wait to share his company again, regardless of whether he's been praying to Buddha, Vishnu, or Jesus Christ. Either way, my days of trying to sway anyone with words are over.

Dear children, let us not love with words or tongue but with actions and in truth. This then is how we know we belong to the truth, and how we set our heart at rest in his presence whenever our hearts condemn us. For God is greater than our hearts, and he knows everything.

1 John 3:18-20